FOREWOR

There is a Medium in all of us. We .... psychic powers, the ability to see and communicate with other worlds and dimensions that exist around us. This is the greatest gift of all. A natural tool given to each and everyone of us the moment we arrive here on earth. To see it, just watch a new born child. Once they can focus watch as they look with glee and smile to a world around them, which we do not appear to see - we can only surmise. For the majority of us, as we grow and begin to develop our own minds, so our intuitive side begins to fade into the background. It never dies, just merely becomes hidden behind wants, desires, every day issues and different sets of priorities. Yet it can at any age during your adult life be re-discovered, polished and developed and brought back into action. How well you can use it will depend upon many things. What is clear is there is a psychic hidden within all of us and I think this book will hopefully help you to discover your own psychic side, as well as doing many, many other things.

It is designed to take you on a journey, through my life as a Medium and through all the people and experiences this role has presented to me. All the examples from the readings are based on fact. I have merely changed the names to ensure they cannot be recognised. Thus you as the reader may be helped, or learn from their experiences, without eroding their privacy and dignity.

Sandrea Mosses

To Barbara,

Enjoy

Love & Light

Sandrea

Spheres
of an
Unseen World

A Medium's Notebook

By

Sandrea Mosses

Black Leaf Publishing
www. blackleafpublishing.com

ISBN: 978-0-9561590-3-8

Black Leaf Publishing

83 Clipstone Rd West
Forest Town, Mansfield
NG19 0ED
Nottinghamshire
England

www.backleafpublishing.com

DEDICATION

To Val Smith a wonderfully gifted Medium, for her help, guidance and inspiration.

To my father Albert for making me who I am today; to David my motivator, my partner and soul-mate, who has always helped and supported me, and enabled me to get where I am today. Who without his support, this book would not have been possible.

ACKNOWLEDGEMENTS

To my wonderful children, Beverley, Carl and Ben. My brother Malcolm for all his help; to my friends both socially and at work, especially Ann and to Karen, who have been there for me through thick and thin. Martin for his spiritual support and guidance. My circle at Wolverhampton Spiritualist church for their help in my development. Last but not least, Stella, who developed with me and inspired me along the way.

Thank you to the Old Rectory on the lake in Tal-y-Llyn for providing me with spectacular views of the mountains and the lake. Which in turn gave me peace, strength, inspiration and internal power to keep writing.

Introduction

'Spheres of an Unseen World' is a spiritual journey of my own development and personal and spiritual experiences. It is designed to show the reader there is more to this world than we at first believe. There is another universe that exists around us, that is easily in our grasp. It's inclusion into our own world is only a thought away.

The book journey's though my own experiences and life and heartache of others, which I live through my spiritual work, as a Medium.

The book is designed to show the wonderful gifts that are available to us all. Gifts we were born with but have simply forgotten that we ever owned them, let alone know how to use.

It is a journey which will show that life is not a 'bed a roses' for anyone and was never designed to be. Fact. We will all, at some time, encounter extremely painful periods in ours lives. We will also experience many happy times. And sometimes what appears to be the worst thing that could happen to us, opens doors we never thought possible.

This book explores the painful experiences people face when coping with the death of someone close to their hearts. It catalogues how we cope and deal with these situations. But more importantly, how we are helped by the unseen hands of the world of spirit.

The book begins by mapping my own personal life and how in a couple of years my life changed beyond words. My journey, as like Alice in Wonderland, after each doorway lay another doorway which opened worlds to me, that I never realised existed until this point. I show how I developed my own physic abilities in order that people may learn they can also access these places and skills, with patience, perseverance and correct guidance.

I journey back into my early childhood memories provoked by the eager questioning of others. Only then do I realise my early life was peppered with unusual occurrences. Events that would have lain forgotten had I not carefully explored my early years. This chapter sits as a reminder to all. We are born with the ability to tap into psychic skills, which we lose as we journey through life. Our early memory serves us to show us we once held and used these ethereal tools.

The book explores our ability to feel emotion and the negative effect some of our emotions can have on us. It is designed to bring emotions to the forefront and for us to recognise the effect our fear and anger can have on us and those around us.

Each part of the book has a story in it to emphasise and hit home the different points the book tries to get across. The stories of pain and heartache are not designed to evoke tears and sympathy. But merely to show there are people, every day, walking amongst us, who are masking pain and heartache. But they have survived the journey and will live on to survive other painful journeys, before they finally return home.

We are not alone in pain and heartache. It is an everyday occurrence. Unfortunately society is not built or designed to allow us to openly share our pain, without people feeling the need to feel sorry for us or pity us. Pain is a norm of life. When we accept this and accept it will happen to us at sometime during our lives, life becomes easier. For we will know everyone goes through it at some time, but more importantly they come out the other side.

Chapter one - Divine Intervention?

My life changed very rapidly in the early to mid nineties, although I had no idea what was around the corner. On a regular basis I would wake up during the night, gasping for breath, as if I had been under water for a significant period of time. I would have to get out of bed and it would take several minutes to stop the gulping and gasping for breath, I discovered that only by gently sipping water, could I regulate my breathing. This carried on for several of years, before I was able to understand what the dream was trying to show me.

Around the same time I had an appointment with Mystic Ed, a local Medium who has had success as a writer and appeared on local radio and television. Several of the staff at work had visited him and thought him to be wonderful. As I listened to the conversations in the office, over several lunch breaks, I could not resist the temptation, to see him and within two weeks I was nestled down in his front room fascinated and in awe of how this man could know so much about me.

During the sitting he brought lots of evidence through, past and present, enough for me to know he was very good at what he did, in fact I was amazed at what he was able to tell me. My life in several areas was a mess and I needed help and guidance. He addressed every one of those issues, giving me re-assurance that the pathways I had chosen were the correct ones. This reading brought lots of comfort to me, that some of my dilemmas would end soon - not soon enough for me I can tell you - and direction for those issues of which I was unsure.

The session did me a power of good, until towards the end. You know a Medium don't you? He added. Me? I don't think so, I replied. Was this man even hinting I could do what he was doing? Although I always had a keen interest, I had never seen a pack of tarot or received information like he did. "Yes you are", he stated again. He was adamant. I had the same gift as he did and one day I would be as well known as he was. I was truly gifted, I just hadn't learned how to use it. This man who had truly amazed me, was now suggesting I could do what he did? I felt very confused, I rather liked the idea that maybe, just maybe, I could do what he did, but I never believed I would be as good as he was. He went on to tell me he could see scenes around me. He told me he could see a little dog and in detail described my own dog, Toby a black Scottie dog. He then described a beautiful oriental woman with black hair, piled up and held in place with two sticks. She was dressed in a lovely white kimono. Her name was Quan Yin. Being quite well read, I knew we all had a guide who stayed with us all our lives. "Is this my guide?" I enquired. He nodded in agreement; he felt she was a Guide I would be working with. When I look back he never said she was my main guide, he merely said she was someone who had been sent to help and guide me at that moment in time, which is different from your life long guide, as I would discover in time.

As I drove home, I couldn't help feeling mixed emotions. He had been so accurate in working out what was bothering me and brought me wonderful evidence through, of things he could not have known about, some of which I had almost forgotten myself till he reminded me.   I was completely bowled over by his ability.   I has seen a handful of Mediums/Psychics before, but no-one with his skill.   In fact the only aspect clouding this wonderful experience was the information that one day, not too far in the future, I would have the same gift as he did. This really confused me.   I repeated what he had said in parrot fashion to several people, hoping for some reaction either way, which would help me to work out how to view this information.   He was accurate, but me a Medium?   While I couldn't dismiss it completely out of hand I was rather excited at the prospect.   I could not for the life of me, contemplate how I could get from where I was now to where he was. This truly was beyond me.

Mystic Ed's words did not change my life. What he did do or what the spirit world did, through him, was to get me to re-evaluate my life and open myself to the possibility that I just may have some talent; in which case it was worthwhile investing some time into it, and this is exactly what I did. When I look back it is hard to understand how I got from where I was then to where I am now, but somehow I did, as it all seemed to happen rather quickly. What I do know is his words gave me courage to explore courses and pathways I may not have otherwise done.

At around the same time as this reading, a further twist had taken place. I had casually asked a friend at work about a cottage her sister's mother in law rented out in a little fishing village called Mousehole in Cornwall. The, normally, very laid back Stella had within two days booked the cottage for me. I did not want to go, but felt in a quandary. My gentle enquiry had turned into a firm booking and I was due to go within six weeks. In the end, I decided it was easier to go along with the plan. I was in desperate need of a holiday, still not fully recovered from my mothers death, so I went along with the plans. On the morning I was due to leave I sat crying in the lounge, unable to contemplate the journey ahead. With a heavy heart I loaded the car and made the 6 hour journey to Cornwall. From the early part of the journey I had a tingling sensation on the back of my hands, as if a pair of spiritual hands where encasing my own. As I drove, I felt safe.

The cottage was wonderful. It was the former post office, located on the corner overlooking the harbour. I felt at peace as soon as I arrived. I had brought my 5 year old grandson along for the holiday and as we stood outside the cottage looking across the bay, I knew the holiday would be wonderful. As we began to bring in the luggage I noticed a note on the kitchen table from Stella's sister, Cherry.   It was a short update on my astrological chart. She had all my details, as I had ordered a chart from her in the past. I couldn't believe that some-one would be so kind as to take the trouble to do this for me, for nothing. I felt quite comforted by it.

Early evening that day, a very tearful Cherry called to see me, and check how I was. Her wonderful dog Hammer was critically ill. His timing was awful. He had chosen the very week her sister and mom were both abroad on holiday, to depart this planet. Tim her husband was at the time quite ill, leaving Cherry feeling totally alone. Her openness and frankness brought out the best in me. I moved from the position of grieving daughter to responsible adult as I tried to be as supportive as possible, in her hour of need. Cherry on the other hand, despite her own grief, made a point of calling in, to check on me. This created a bond between Cherry and I which lasted several years and resulted in many, many trips to Cornwall. Together we began developing our skills and communicating and exploring worlds, other than the one we currently occupy, through the art of meditation.

Later that summer I returned to Mousehole several times as we began meditating together. Cherry was a gifted Astrologist, with infinite knowledge of the planets, having studied this subject for nearly thirty years. In fact her knowledge all matters, esoteric, was vast. I was in awe of her. Her chart interpretations were all hand written and she clearly had the wonderful gift to be able to interpret transits and aspects astonishingly accurately and could use this knowledge to explain to people what was happening to them at that moment in time or what was around the corner. She would go on to offer ideas how best to use this knowledge and how to get the most out of the situation. We would walk and talk for hours as we discussed all matters relating to the planets. In the summer months she worked in a small wooden kiosk, with an external seated area, with stunning views across the Lizard. In quiet moments we explored every aspect of the esoteric, from life on other planets, to life in other dimensions, the different levels in the spirit world and life before life. We constantly swopped books and ideas with each other. This was one of the most wonderful experiences of my life and I only have to relax and place myself back in that small kiosk and all the wonderful experiences come flooding back to me.

Cherry at the time lived on one of the oldest houses in Mousehole. A large house, nearly four hundred years old, with four bedrooms and a large annex attached to the side. The house had been derelict for several years when they purchased it. They had, over several years, completely modernised it. We had begun meditating in the main part of the house, feeling the energies to ensure we found the room which would create the ideal atmosphere for meditation. Over time this involved using six of the eight rooms, excluding the bathrooms and kitchen. As more people began to join us we had to change rooms, finally settling on the annex. On our first meditation together, we were both quite nervous and not quite sure what to do. Cherry didn't see, but was clairsentient, whereas I on the other hand could see, hear and sense. We decided after saying our protection (yes she was as brave as I), which we had adapted from a Dawn Hall book, we would, once we had reached a meditative state, talk to each other and share what we were feeling or seeing, as it came to us. This we duly did. I remember we both saw or sensed a large wooden door and were given a key, which we used to open a doorway and we wandered through what appeared to be an old church, but the building inside appeared a little odd. We finished our meditation after a short while and were quite pleased with our experience. We estimated our little event had lasted around 20 minutes. As we had spoken all the way through, it was quite easy to keep an eye on

3

the time. When we arrived downstairs we found we had in fact been gone 90 minutes! We couldn't believe it. To this day I still cannot understand how we could have mis-judged the amount of time spent in meditation, to the extent that we did. But this wasn't the last time this happened to us. Each time we were amazed by what we experienced, each being better than the last.

On our second meditation we sat on the settee in the living room and had the most wonderful experience of taking-off, as if the settee had physically somehow turned into a magic carriage. We could feel it rising and turning and our stomachs churned and lurched, as we appeared to shoot off into the ether, ducking and diving as we journeyed through the galaxy. We explored the concept of E.Ts, and felt as if we were meeting wondrous beings from other dimensions, who communicated pure love. I can honestly say I had the time of my life and the most exhilarating experiences working with Cherry. When we parted company. and went our own separate ways, I felt as if a huge part of me had been left behind. I continued to reach these heights, going higher and further, but still missed our experiences.

Following my message from Mystic Ed I duly began to talk to Quan Yin and over time had got to know her quite well. As far as Cherry and I were concerned we had someone from the other side to help us on these magical mystery tours. Whenever I felt her draw near to me the only way I can describe it is of a feeling of pure unadulterated love and compassion which swept over me in waves. At times it could be almost overwhelming. It was as if it was difficult to breathe in her presence, so deep and pure was the energy that surrounded her. In fact once I discovered her through Mystic Ed, both Cherry and I got to know her really quite well.

This overwhelming feeling did not deter me. Several times a week I meditated, sometimes by myself though more often with a group of friends, and each time asked her to draw near. She was always there. As I was the only one lucky enough to know my guide, when a group of us got together, everyone knew her name. I often wonder if I would have reached the heights I did in those meditations had I never been introduced to her? I can honestly say I don't think so. To have a link with someone of this pure vibration made it easier to reach up to the realms she occupied, and by doing so it was easy to reach other people of such realms. When I look back I see life as a jigsaw puzzle, with the pieces slowly joining together. How differently we would respond if we could see the final picture before we embarked on any single journey.

Two years after I met, or realised Quan Yin was around me, I was told who she was, three times in three days. My daughter had begun a psychic development class with another well known and extremely good Medium/Clairvoyant, John Starkey. After her Thursday evening class she informed me they had covered some ascended masters and Quan Yin was one of then. The ascended masters are very wise souls who have finished their journeys on earth and can be reached by all of us, for advice, knowledge and guidance. Buddha and Jesus are two of the many masters.

On the Friday evening Cherry also rang, full of excitement. She had discovered who Quan Yin was. That very day she had been looking through a book and come across her. She was full of excitement. She is an ascended master, "what is one of those?", came my reply. On the Saturday my daughter handed me a book on the Masters and there was Quan Yin. I sat and read the passage over and over again. She was the Eastern Goddess of compassion, highly revered in eastern society. It is believed she hesitated before entering the Kingdom of Heaven to hear the cries and pleas of the world. In the East they believe one heartfelt cry from you will bring her to your side. In the Philippines they believe she used her gown to catch the unexploded bombs and place them gently onto the ground. She is described as either everything beauty represents in a woman or as a matriarchal figure. As I read this passage I felt her standing alongside me, watching me.

Now I really was in a quandary. Had I known I was working with an ascending master would I have made contact with her? I don't think so, it was only my ignorance which allowed me to work with her. How could I continue to call upon her knowing she was this great figure? Was it the same one? The sense of her standing there watching confirmed she was the Quan Yin referred to in the book. How could I call her now? That night I mediated, I immediately felt her draw close to me, re-assuring me, comforting me. Within I knew she had joined me at a time I needed her and she would remain with me for as long as I needed her to join accompany me. When the time was right she would move one, as would I. I also knew at the same time, like many of these great spirits, she was working with many others. She was not exclusive to me. That was the hardest bit for me to understand. These great guides can work with many, many, beings at one time.

In time I began to work more closely with my own Guide, although on a regular basis I still feel her presence around me.

I am not sure when I met my own Guide. I guess I had always known he was around me, for as long as I have a memory he has been there. However it was around the same time I began acquainted with Quan Yin, that I began to see what he looked like and I finally got a name for this being of wisdom, who offered me the right words to say when someone needed guidance. I began to see a very tall man with long flowing silver hair, encased in a robe made of small white feathers. I had worked it out for myself that his name was White Feather, although this was confirmed and repeated to me by several Medium friends, during meditation. While he does not appear to dress how we perceive Native Americans should dress, I have always felt a very strong connection with indigenous Native Americans, yet I feel he goes back to a time frame beyond our own knowledge of history.

In 2006 we went to Canada on holiday, nowhere more so have I felt his presence as I did when we travelled around the parks of Alberta and British Columbia. I have come home resonated through my body. As we sat in the complete silence, surrounded by tall pines as bald eagles glided silently above our heads, not a sound could be heard. I knew this resembled something like the environment he had occupied all those thousands of years ago. I had seen it many times when he had taken me on those spiritual journeys high in the mountains, to a camp fire, by a turquoise lake, where the air was fresh and cool. As we travelled round I saw facets of those visions, scattered across Canada.

The feather has always been his calling card to me - a large feather - which is reassurance that he is with me, before I go onto the platform; and small feather, usually when he trying to communicate something to me. Over the years these have appeared in the strangest of places, as you will see later in the book.

Over the years I have only ever seen them, Quan Yin and White Feather, together once standing side by side. This happened when I attended an assessment at Stansted College. I was sitting at a desk completing a paper and finding the whole experience quite negative. I was trying to decide if I was going to stay, or at that very point lay my pen down and go home, without completing the course. Very clearly I saw a vision in my mind of both White Feather and Quan Yin sitting together, quite solemnly at two old fashioned desks, with quills in their hands, posed waiting to start writing. The whole scene was quite bizarre. There sat White Feather and Quan Yin, in all their regalia, at Victorian style desks they barely appeared to fit behind. I began to smile and it was if the sun had come out, that very moment. I pondered briefly, if they can do it, so could I. This picture in my head gave me the strength to complete the assessment and then to complete the course. The platform experience the exponents course gave me, and the invaluable assistance of Val, were instrumental in catapulting me to where I am today.

All the time the drowning dream kept reoccurring, as I developed my psychic ability, so I began to see more in the dream. I saw myself underwater, in very deep, very cold water. I am panicking and full of regret. I have a very heavy chocolate brown lined dress on. It is made of the most exquisite lace and is etched with sequins. It is extremely long in length as I can feel it wrapped around my ankles and legs. I am disorientated, turning frantically and rapidly running out of breath. But it is too dark, I cannot see where the surface is, it's too dark. I suddenly become aware that it is above me. I turn over, but have no strength to make the final push to the top. The one thing I am not, is afraid. I wake up gasping for breath and it takes me several minutes to regulate my breathing. This dream would continue and it took me several years to unravel it.

Developing my Skills

Throughout our lives people come and go. We have the friends that last a life time, then we have the friends who are of equal importance to us who come into our lives, sometimes for very short periods of time, but the effect they have on us is catalytic. They help us to move forward, to face and overcome change. We may not believe this, but if we look back to different periods in our lives look at the point when a new friend has entered your life and it is usually associated with some pattern of change in our lives.

This has happened to me time and time again. After Stella and I completed our psychic development course I heard by chance of a workshop in Kidderminster. The workshop was arranged by Olwyn Griffiths, who used to work quite closely with Eamonn Downey, who is a brilliant Teacher. I attended two of these workshops, both provided me with invaluable insight. During the second workshop I got talking to Sebra, Cheryl and Mary, who clearly knew each other quite well. From following their discussion it would appear they were all studying another course through the spiritualist movement, the SNU (Spiritualists National Union). As I listened to them discussing the pro's and con's of the course, I began to enquire about it. All three enthusiastically talked about the course and what it involved, and as I listened, I was sold. Within four months I was enrolled on the course.

Part of the requirements of the course was you had to sit in a closed circle at your own church which at the time, before I moved house, was Stourbridge. After a while of patiently sitting in the open circle which was lead by Heather Hatton, a woman who dedicated her whole life to spiritualism, she arranged for me to join the closed circle. As I moved from one circle to another in a way I was sad to lose the teaching skills of Heather who had a wealth of knowledge and experience which she gladly shared with the group. Between Heather and her husband Eric, I am sure they must have been responsible for the development of hundreds of platform Mediums, who in turn would continue to serve spiritualist churches, ensuring the continual existence of the spiritualist movement.

The closed circle was run by Val Smith. Val was a very down to earth character - a brilliant Medium, who had been on the circuit for nearly twenty years. To this day I still place her as one of the best Mediums I have ever seen; watching her work giving name after name, while 'holding up to five links (where the Medium is talking to five people from spirit at the same time), held me in awe. I always found it hard to understand why Val had not found national or international fame. Why? She didn't want it. Arthur (her husband) would never have agreed to it, she used to tell me, "he likes his tea on the table and he doesn't like me out at tea time". She once casually told me how she was offered the opportunity to work in Germany for a week, but refused, stating Arthur wouldn't like it. She had battled with him to be allowed to go out and take services and had seen this as a triumph. I often wondered if Arthur would have objected. Val was very much a home-bird and as long as she had her home family and could serve her churches, was as happy as Larry.

Val had a heart of gold and a wonderful kind nature. During her long battle with cancer I, would sometimes call in to see her. On one such day I was in the garden with her as she fed the fish in the pond. "Mabel come on", she called as a very ugly Koi Carp gently rose out of the water to take food from Val's hand. Her gentleness and love of animals was apparent and I was fascinated as she called this fish, as if it was a dog or a cat, and it responded to her. She was a vegetarian before it was trendy to be one and was much loved around the Churches and renowned for her lovely character

To me that all changed when I sat in circle with her; she was merciless! And for that I thank her from the bottom of my heart. "Questions Sandrea, do not ask questions", she would intervene every time I attempted to ask a question from the recipient of my message. "Questions Sandrea, questions, you are asking questions. Just give the evidence as they give it to you". "But" I would protest "I need to just know if they have a father in spirit". She would merely look at me and shake her head. "Give off the evidence, don't question it, say it as they are giving it too you". "I can't", I would protest meekly. She was merciless and heartless when it came to asking questions. When it came to teaching me how to deliver a message she was uncompromising, ruthless and relentless. On several occasions we had 'mock' congregations at Stourbridge Spiritualist Church, as one of these people my son has a very different view of Val as he watched her interrupt me and shake a pointed finger at me for daring to ask a question.

I always knew Val was doing it for my own good and she always did it with love and a smile. On reflection I fully understand it was this solid grounding which had made me the Medium I am today. She taught me that by asking questions I interrupted the flow of the energy, which in turn interrupted the flow of the information. Instead of merely relaying what was being given, by asking questions I got in the way and this in turn would break my concentration. As a Medium it is far more difficult to flow the information, without asking questions, especially when the information is slightly confusing, but thanks to Val it is the only way I know how to work.

Halfway through the 18 month period where I sat in circle with her, she began to take me to Churches with her. I don't feel I was any different from the other members of the group - in fact I was very proud to have sat in circle with them all. Connie and Cheryl in particular became very good friends. But Val had a particular role in life with me, which was to get me on the platform. That I feel sure of. From this don't make the mistake of thinking she made me feel special. She didn't, I always felt she was harder on me than the others. She was very quick to put me back where I belonged if she thought I was getting too big for my boots, which thankfully wasn't too often.

My first experience as a working Medium with Val was at a Supper with Mediums at Bromsgrove Church. This is probably one of the hardest events a Medium can do, as you are expected to give message after message in a short period of time, then move onto the next table. When Val told me I was booked to do this, I was a little unsure "I'm not sure I can do it Val", I faltered. She was having none of it. "You'll be fine", she added changing the subject. I shook for two hours beforehand and changed my outfit three times. I walked to the bottom of the road, where they were picking me up, like a lamb to slaughter. I cannot remember ever feeling so afraid, and only half listened to the banter in the car as we made the 30 minute journey to the Church. As we walked up to the door Val turned to me and said "Come on, don't be nervous, you can do it". She promptly changed the subject. Her unmoving faith in my ability helped me endlessly that night. I felt if Val thinks I can do it and she is a Medium, she must know I can, so I must be able to do it -as simple as that. It proved to be the best approach because when it mattered I kept my composure throughout the night. As I sat down, very nervously, at the first table I desperately tried to blot out Val on the next table rattling message after message, before the event had even started. Prayers ended and I began describing a gentleman, the woman with the kind gentle face could accept everything I said, including names and dates.

After this first message I was away and for the remainder of the evening the information flowed, fast and furiously. I could do it, yes I could. Afterwards as we sat in the back she insisted I charge ten pounds and buy myself something with the money. What did Val charge? Nothing! Not only didn't she charge she purchased raffle tickets and helped with washing up. While I sat there thinking what must they think of me? I later found out Val had rung this church and several others telling them she had a cracking little Medium and could they please give her some bookings! Bless her.

This was the first of many events Val took me too. It is sometimes quite hard to get onto the 'circuit'. By far the easiest is personal recommendation. As Val had such an excellent reputation and as her recommendations were few and far between the Churches accepted Val's word and the bookings began to trickle in. There were several psychic suppers and days of sittings, but none bothered me as much as that first one. As time went on they got easier and easier. Val and I only worked the platform together a few times, one of those was Walsall. "Are you ready to work?" she asked. "Yes" I replied. "Do you want to go first or last?" she enquired. "I have to go first" I said, "Why?" came the reply. "Do you really think I am going to get up after you Val?" "Don't be daft" she answered "I am not daft, I'm a realist" came my reply. Her Mediumship was second to none. While at the time I wasn't a bad Medium, against her it would have been professional suicide to get up after her. No I would be the warm-up act and she could follow me. I don't think, regardless of how I progressed, that my views on this subject would have changed - Val first, me second.

Unfortunately my time with Val was very short-lived, although she had crammed an awful lot of learning into a very short period of time for me, she wasn't to be around much longer. Val fought a tough battle against cancer and if someone could have survived through healing power, she would have done. She was in every healing book going, in all the Churches she served. She had hands-on healing, absent healing and when she was too ill to attend, healing at home.

When she passed I always hoped I would be able to fully communicate with her how grateful I was and how much she meant to me. My life was certainly a better, richer place, thanks to her assistance. I left her funeral directly after the service not wishing to intrude on the family or close friends. As I drove back to work I asked her how I could be more like her, because if anyone lived their life in spirituality she did. As I silently talked to her, I immediately heard the words in my head, 'take the best that's in you, give the rest away'. I pulled the car over and sobbed for 20 minutes, knowing that part of my life was over and knowing how much I would miss this wonderful woman. As I cried I said out loud, "You're supposed to make me feel better, not worse!" I could feel her smiling and that message has stayed with me ever since. If I try to model myself on anyone it has to be this very special lady.

I was hugely mistaken that her influence was to leave me. I only have to struggle slightly on the platform or feel nervous and even today I can still feel her with me, I pronounce my words in an exaggerated fashion as she would, I move my arms in the way she did and move across the platform as she would. Sometimes before I start I can feel her standing there waiting to help me, should I need any assistance. In fact to this day people still come up to me and say

'you know I have only ever seen one other Medium work the way you do and you probably wouldn't know her". "Val Smith?" I reply. God bless you Val Smith.

I continued with the Exponents Course right through to the end of the three years. Complaining, kicking and screaming, but it gave me some wonderful experiences and excellent opportunities, which I could never have achieved without this course.

Eight years on from the very first supper, I found myself still doing some of the suppers at Bromsgrove. On one particular evening I settled down on my second table and began to give one of the people a message when suddenly I realised that I had sat at exactly the same table and given a message to Mel as my first link, all those years ago. I hadn't seen Mel at a table at a supper, for years, but here we both were. I knew a circle had completed in my life and I had returned from the point I began.

Psychic Ability

What do we mean by the term psychic? For years I had heard this term and was never quite sure what it actually meant, to 'be psychic'. Over time I have formulated my own views which are:

'Psychic ability' is a very broad idiom, which relates to any gift or ability not pertaining to one of five senses. In other words it is an additional sense, sometimes called the sixth sense.

Many writers have attempted to explain this ability and will probably have achieved it much better than I will. Therefore I shall only address this very briefly.

When I first began to read about third eyes and seeing people and hearing voices which did not belong to people of this world, I was fascinated, and the more I read the greater my interest became on the subject. As I read my mind would conjure up visions of 'third eyes', as massive lenses, that could see along time lines and visualise the strangest of worlds.

In time I began to realise the one facet we need to nurture and utilise, as we begin to tap into our psychic gifts, is our imagination. A good imagination is vital if we are to begin to explore concepts, which to date have been alien to our existence.

As a child I had the wildest imagination, in fact I still have it now, but it has over the years got me into no end of trouble. If you had asked me when I was in my twenties or thirties, I would have denied this. It is only as time has progressed have I realised not everyone can see in colour as clearly as I have always been able to see. Describe something to me and I see it, as clearly as if it was present in the room. Which is why I cannot read about animal cruelty. As soon as I read the article I can see the scene, I can picture the event and begin to feel and see how the animals felt. Because of this there are certain subjects that are definitely taboo when I am around.

As a child I loved the plays that were put on in the sports hall-cum-dining room at my small primary school. I sat enthralled as the actors told the stories of wicked witches who lived in woods. I looked deep into the stage and could see the forest, the animals, flora and fauna and the witch's house in the distance. I saw the thousands of rats following the Pied Piper and the wonderful candy covering the house in Hansel and Gretel. I came home from school full of the tales and gabbled for ages about what I had seen. It was only in later in life that I realised, without today's modern technology the theatre company could not have created the things my child eyes had seen. It was the same when I read a book. I had the ability to be able to become part of that story to picture the events as they unfold, feel the emotions and could almost re-live the scene moment to moment.

I remember my Mom buying me two record singles as a child of about ten from Brierley Hill market. I was thrilled to bits and felt so grown-up and important to own my own records. The one told the story of Cinderella, but with, of all things, a female talking pigeon was advising the prince, throughout the story. I can still recall most of the story today, of the ugly sister and the shoe she cooed

"Rookety co, rookety co, there is blood on the shoe, the foot is too wide, she is not your real bride".

I can still remember it today. In fact it feels as if it only happened yesterday. I can recall the words, but more importantly the scenes I saw in my head as I listened to the song. I can still see the pretty female pigeon, with a thin bright pink ribbon draped around her neck, which was held together by a tiny bell. I can see her eyes sparkling as she nestled on the Prince's shoulder, whispering into his ear as she knowledgably advised of the deceit by the ugly step-sisters. I listened to that record until I knew it as well as the pigeon did, and could say the words before she did.

Unfortunately for me the second record was Old Shep, by Elvis. I cried buckets as I saw that black and white border collie looking at his master with its head cocked on one side as Elvis sang

" ...with hands that were trembling I picked up my gun and aimed at Shep's faithful head, I just couldn't do it, I wanted to run, I wish they would shoot me instead".

As I saw him hang his head in total despair, I cried and cried. My mother used to get extremely frustrated with me, "for goodness sake Sandrea, it is only a song" she would say, or if it was a sad book I was reading, "it's only a book", it didn't really happen". It made no difference to me; I saw the scenes with the greatest of detail, as if I was watching it unfold in front of my eyes.

It is difficult to try and explain to a child something is not real when you cannot see what they can see. I know if my mother had realised the clarity with which I saw these scenes, she would have been more understanding. Try to imagine watching something in your head and then try believing it is not real.

So, to all you moms and dads out there with children with vivid imaginations, put yourself in their shoes and try to feel what it is like to see with such clarity. As I have developed my skills over the years I have begun to see a real connection between the term 'a sensitive' and someone who is very sensitive and feel these people need handling with care.

As I began to develop and explore my psychic abilities I realised I could see people and hear voices, but not externally. Everything I saw was in my head. All I had to do was relax, begin to meditate and the images flowed fast and furious. The more I journeyed the easier it became, to the point I can now see these scenes with my eyes open. During these times I went on journeys with both Quan Yin and White Feather back to the different worlds of spirit. I saw beautiful colours, beyond belief, which were outside of the colour spectrum of this world. I felt beauty that words could not describe. I saw colossal buildings that shimmered and glowed and appeared to be alive with energy. Beings of great beauty and others, which I can only describe as visually challenging. But above all I felt peace like I have never felt during my time on this planet and saw and felt love, unadulterated love that appeared to shimmer from these beings, but always, always in my head, not visually in the room. Displayed on a screen which appeared huge, which I now realise is my third eye.

As time progressed I realised that for me, the majority of what I was to see was going to be inside my head, not external to me. This is very difficult to explain, but I will try. Whether I am giving readings or on the platform I will often say to the sitter "I have someone with me" and I will go on to describe the way they look, then interpret their personality and mannerisms, if appropriate. Now I am not seeing this person as I see the person I am giving the message to, I see it differently. I see the communicator within my mind, with the same clarity as I see the person I am giving the message to, but it appears, somehow as an image in my mind. The names they give me are mostly written down and depending where they appear on the screen, indicating whether they are family or friends, what side of the family they belong to, high to show they are in spirit and low to show they are on earth.

In my earlier days of development, if someone had been able to explain to me that to be clairvoyant, is not necessarily to see with your physical eyes, but merely to see, my life would have been much easier and my pathway of progression would have been less arduous. So for anyone else out there who is beginning to develop and like me, sees clearly in their head, but not in the physical, perhaps you will understand what is happening to you. As life has progressed I do sometimes see spirit external to me, but for most of the time it is inside my head, so to speak.

As I have stated before, each and every one of us is born with psychic gifts and they are there for the reclaiming again. Several years ago a main road was shut for six weeks while a bridge was replaced. On the morning of the re-opening I was travelling along the road very early in the morning. As I drove I couldn't help but notice the amount of debris on the road, twigs, leaves etc., were scattered across the road. The debris had been able to build up because the road had not been accessed for six weeks, except for the occasional workman. I immediately saw this as being similar to our psychic ability. Because we haven't fully utilised it for many years the connection to our psychic senses is blocked by debris of a different kind. It is difficult to harness it due to doubt, beliefs of a different kind and lack of faith, to name but a few. But all is not lost, our sixth sense is our gift from birth and regardless of our age we can re-discover it and begin to use it, and the more we use it the easier it becomes and the better we get at it. We would not expect to get behind the wheel of a car and be able to drive it proficiently the first time we try, so why should using a defunct, until now, sense be any different? Like driving a car the more you utilise it the easier it will become. And like driving a car where you have the help of an instructor, you also have the assistance of guides, angels and loved ones from the world of spirit, waiting to help and guide you in the use of this gift. They don't want to live your lives for you, just make the journey a little easier and your sixth sense is one of the tools that can help you on the journey of life.

Early Memories

I never expected my life to change direction in the manner in which it did. I had always been a keen reader of books, but not just any books, always esoteric books, in fact anything that related to the unknown. If it had a psychic connection in it, I would read it. I still believe books are wonderful means for gaining knowledge and believe me I should know. Over the years I have read thousands.

Despite my keen interest in all aspects of spirituality and ability to know if someone was telling the truth or not - and believe me this has often felt like a burden rather than a gift - as I discovered the hard way, there is no mileage in telling someone you know they are fibbing to you. In hindsight giving someone as open and frank as myself the gift to detect untruths, does not bode well. As a child I remember my father telling me two ghost stories, or at least telling the family, as I keenly listened. One involved the tale of a ship travelling in the fog, when the boy in the look-out basket kept hearing a voice, but couldn't make out what was being said, then through the mist a coffin dropped onto the deck. The Captain said the Angel of Death had come for someone and ill-fate would affect them all, until they handed the person over. The First Mate got in, he was too big. Then the Cook, he was too wide. Then the Second mate. As soon as he got in the lid closed, the coffin disappeared, and he was never seen again. How I don't know, but I knew this was untrue, nothing to do with logic, I just knew. The other story involved a working pit. A young lad was sent onto the pithead during the night-shift to fetch a tool. As he walked past a slag heap he heard footsteps walking across it. "Who goes there" he called, three times, but received no answer. He went back and told the men he worked with. The Foreman went up to the pithead. He also heard the footsteps and called several times for the person to identify themselves, but received no answer. He returned to the coal face and told the workmen "this is an omen". They all laid down their tools there and then. That night a huge shaft of rock fell, blocking off the access to the area where they were working. Had they ignored the warning, they would surely have died. I always knew in my heart this story was correct. I discovered in later life, it was actually my Granddad who, as a young man of 14 years old, had heard the footsteps.

Despite this keen interest in all aspects of spirituality, an ability to detect if someone was telling the truth, (believe me for majority of life this has been a burden rather than a gift) and a strong capacity for giving very good advice, my natural gift did not transpire until I had reached my more mature years.

When I look back I know it was present, I just didn't know how to use it; somewhere along the way I had forgotten how to tune into it. I believe I had chosen to use this in my later, rather than early, years as there were other issues I had chosen to deal with before I moved onto this part of my life. I believe I had my own karmic duties to fulfil, but that is another story and maybe another book! In more simplistic terms I believe I was destined to do my spiritual work in the later years of my life.

Now since I have developed and begun to use my skills, people would often ask me, "did you always know you had the gift?" "No" was the short answer. "Did things used to happen to you when you were a child?" "No" again was the only answer. People would look puzzled at my response and walk off. They had assumed, to have developed my ability to the extent I had, then it must have developed over a significant period of time or I was born with it. I found myself racking my brains trying to discover if there was anything buried deep in the grey matter about which that I had forgotten. Perhaps if I could find something I would not be left with this feeling of 'letting people down' because I was normal, not a psychically gifted child, just normal and very ordinary. Initially nothing out of the ordinary came to mind, but as I searched I began to remember a couple of events. So apart from these questions making me feel inadequate, as if I was letting people down by being 'normal', with a normal childhood, it actually reminded me of events which on reflection were perhaps a little out of the ordinary.

When I was around seven years old my mother got a job at a Country Club, running a small bar. A job of which she was very proud. Apparently this job had some credibility because it was an exclusive club. Unfortunately for me, part of the deal of her going to work three evenings a week, was I had to be in bed by 6.50pm, the time she left for work. Not in the slightest bit tired - ever, as I recall - I would be carted off to bed, where I used to pass the time away amusing myself in any way I could. The curtains were drawn and in the winter months the light was turned off, but above all, winter or summer, I was forbidden to get out of bed or make any noise, as I was supposedly going to sleep. I distinctly remember lying in bed and, in my head, asking lots of questions and somehow I would receive the answers.

You don't realise the significance of events such as these, because they have always been there, since you can remember, so you don't give it a second thought. It is only when you someone says something to you or makes a comment do you look back, search and scrutinize. As I did this I began to realise that maybe, just maybe, my life wasn't as ordinary as I had at first believed. Only by delving into my memories of my early years did I begin to recall and analyse these events. I remember watching scenes like motion pictures on the walls of the bedroom and wondering why people had television sets which could only display scenes in black and white, on a very small screen, when they could see huge scenes in colour, just as I was doing.

When I look back I was extremely grateful for my mother's evening job. Without this time of isolation, I expect my life would have been too full of stimulation to make the wonderful connections I did. Without voids and gaps in time, I doubt I would have been able to recall this information or decipher between what was fact or fiction. These long drawn-out periods of time were in fact a blessing in disguise.

One such question I remember asking was 'where did I come from'? - possibly the one question every curious child is guaranteed to ask. The only thing that is unclear regarding this incident is how I actually received this information. Was I asleep and given the answer in a dream or did I

16

receive information, through scenes in my head (we will come on to this later), I really don't know. What I do know is that I can remember the event, as if it happened only yesterday. I was shown a scene where I am walking around a huge room accompanied by a man (I now know to be White Feather, my guide) and I am looking at models of bodies. These are lying, face up, side by side, on tables, with aisles either side to allow space for people to walk around. I am being shown how I was helped to decide what shape body would suit me. There were thousands of different sizes, tall, short, thin fat, with hundreds of different combinations, down to the skin tone and features on the face. As we walk around White Feather is showing me all the different combinations and guiding me to select a body, which will help me to achieve all the things I would like to achieve in this life time.

When I recall it, I can still see the scene today, as if it only happened yesterday. I felt very satisfied and pleased with myself. Now I knew where I had come from and that I had chosen me. Rather oddly I recall as I grew up I had no interest in knowing the 'facts of life', I already knew them.   But as time passed I became aware of the 'real' facts. Whenever I thought back about my dream I felt embarrassed, that I had believed bodies were made and I had picked the one I wanted.   Ironically it was this acute embarrassment which helped to keep the memory alive.

But as is often the case life goes full circle. During my journeys with my guide, through my meditations, I was shown how we choose our family and partners before we come to earth. We also choose the body which will best serve us to achieve our goals in life. So I wasn't wrong after all. That child who had been shown the scene of selecting a body, with the help of a guide, was in fact correct. So, many years later, I finally reached where I had been when I was seven years old. I re-discovered the true 'facts of life'. And if I ever doubt this knowledge I ask myself: "Would a soft, gentle personality, encased in a tall, stunningly beautiful body have helped me to reach the goals I have achieved. To have overcome the challenges I have met on the way?" The answer is emphatically 'no'. My body and personality has stood me in good stead, so far.

Now as the youngest of three and the only girl, I appeared to get all the bad things in life that go with a family trying to protect the youngest in the family, who happens to be female. Like being sent to bed early; told not to go off on my own; ride home-made trolleys, or climb trees. As a child you do not appreciate why your brothers are allowed to do things which you are not. This was the case one winter's night when, as many people did in those days, the family decided to burn some rubbish after mom had gone to work, which meant after I had been to bed. My brothers of course were allowed to stay up and assist with the fire; everyone was allowed to stay up, except me. My small child mind could not distinguish between a fire and bonfire night, which meant they were all going to have fun, apart from me. No matter how much I howled - something I was quite good at as a child - the decision had been made and I was sent to bed.

Imprisoned in my tiny bedroom I imagined them letting off fire works and eating chestnuts and potatoes roasted in the fire, while I was incarcerated within these four walls. I suddenly had a brilliant idea. I would get out and go downstairs. I would sneak down through the rafters and the cavity below the stairs. I duly remember doing this, loathing the cobwebs I had to negotiate around, trying to avoid the dust, dirt and cables that lay underneath the boards as I made it outside. By the time I had come up with my ingenious plan, dad was now sitting in the living room. As the fire was well under way I made no noise as I sneaked past him, having emerged from the floorboards by the back door, which was behind him and some distance away. As I sneaked outside I saw my two brothers standing alongside the fire. I hid behind the dog kennel, which was close to the back door, in case they saw me and told my father what I had done. I looked and waited for the action, but all they did was stand watching the fire. No fireworks, or food. I was incredibly disappointed and suddenly it didn't feel like such a good idea to be here. Suddenly I began to feel unsafe, I wanted my body back. No sooner had I had thought it than in an instant I was back in my body, in my bed.

When I look back the only thing which felt different, was everything appeared much duller. The lounge appeared incredibly dull, yet the lights were on. On the other hand while I was underneath the floor boards, there was still light, a dull light, but there had definitely been a source of light. I lay in bed having joined back up with my body and decided I didn't like the experience; I didn't feel safe and secure, and as a child I needed to feel safe and secure. I decided I would never leave my body behind again, so I didn't. This was my one and only flirtation with astral or out-of-body travel and I didn't like it, so I didn't do it again.

These are the only two incidents from my memory which made me feel I may be a little different. Or maybe I wasn't that different, but I was one of these people who could actually remember these incidents. Apart from the colours and scenes I used to watch on the walls of the room - but then again I didn't think this was strange, as I felt every-one saw things like this didn't they? I probably noticed them more, for the many hours I lay awake trying to amuse myself. These early to bed experiences lasted a couple of years. In many ways I am glad, as when I look back I can see it gave me some wonderful early experiences that I may not have had, had I been allowed to stay up later at night.

Finally perhaps there was another area where I was a little different from other children, much to my parents despair; my bedroom was full of plants. The windowsill was crowded with a variety of plants, from cactus plants to Bizzy Lizzies. My parents felt they were unhealthy, but the people I chatted to at night, told me otherwise. I knew they were the healthiest thing I could possibility have in my room. I also knew they needed very little assistance from me apart from a regular supply of water. Why? Because they had little fairies looking after them that's why! Did I see them? Yes on several occasions I was aware of a fairy and an elf, who watched over my small plants.

As parents how can we ever expect our children to maintain their psychic abilities, if we do not provide the space and opportunities to explore nature and their own souls. A room free of electrical appliances, early nights and time to explore nature are all the components that are required.

The pain of Physical Death

Nothing in life prepares you for the death of someone you hold close to your heart. All the reading or listening to someone's tales of woe does not prepare you for such an event. It was only after the death of my own mother did I fully comprehend how she must have felt when her own mother died. I was in my early twenties when my mother lost her own mother. When I look back, I remember feeling that I knew exactly how she must be feeling. After all we all felt the pain - her mom was my nan, so I understood, or at least I thought I did. We tried to be sympathic and understanding especially around birthdays, special dates and holidays. It was only after I felt the pain of losing my own mom, did I realise I could only see and feel the loss of my nan through my own eyes. I had never understood how my mother must have truly felt, to lose someone who was as close as she was to her mother, because I hadn't experienced loss at this level. How did she live through the pain of losing someone as quickly as she had lost her own mother? She hadn't been there to say her goodbyes and didn't realise that she was in fact as seriously ill as she had been, with a faulty valve in her heart. In fact the only person who knew this was her younger brother Tony, whom she loved, admired and idolised. Neither did she say one word of hurt or regret when she discovered he had known the seriousness of her condition, but had held it back to protect her. Several times a week mom had visited nan, staying for significant periods of time. How did she fill the gap afterwards? I don't know. But I do know I only truly understood this terrible sense of loss and pain, after I felt it through my mother's own death. There are many words of wisdom encapsulated in the old wives' tales and proverbs. Some of which I will address later, but when I see some-one trying to understand someone else's sense of loss or pain, an old Chinese proverb always springs to mind: 'a wise man learns from the mistakes of others, a fool learns from his own'. Unfortunately many of us are the fool here, as we can often only truly feel the pain of others when we have had a similar experience.

In a strange kind of way I knew my mother was going to die. I had that awful feeling in the pit of my stomach which would not go away. Every time I thought of her, this feeling would rise within me. Her first hospital admission happened in the October. However, it wasn't until two weeks to Christmas day we learnt the truth. She had been diagnosed with cancer. While they couldn't find the primary, they had found secondaries in the cavity surrounding her lungs. The Consultant had, as gently and kindly as possible, advised us that it was a slow-growing cancer and the prognosis was good. My mother never heard these words. She chose not to. Not that she was in denial; she simply decided she didn't wish to hear the diagnosis. She would accept the treatment, to a point when she clearly knew she wouldn't accept any more and she would fight it, her way.

The medical staff implored us to tell her, assuming it was our choice to hold back the knowledge, and in our absence decided to approach my mother. No more amenable person would you find, than my mother, except on this occasion. She was most indignant when we visited her that night. "They have tried to talk to me today about my condition". 'Doctor I don't want to know' and 'I don't want to discuss it' was her plain simple answer and at that point she totally ignored them and returned to her book. For someone who had always regarded doctors as 'they who know best', her actions showed the strength of her feeling. She was not in denial, she knew what was happening, this was her fight, no-one else's and she would be damned if they or we thought she was going to openly talk to anyone about it.

Six weeks before my mother's death and my life was carrying on as normal. After a busy day at work I had stopped at a local supermarket for some essentials. It was the month of February and still dark at 5.00pm. I pulled onto the car park and as I reversed to park, the song 'Danny Boy', my mother's favourite song, blasted out from the radio. I broke my heart. I sat and cried until I could cry no more, and I knew in my heart - how I don't know - but I knew that my mother was dying and wouldn't be with us much longer. That sense of dread was now amplified and the fear of the reality that I was about to lose my mother appeared to resonate through my very soul. I so much did not want to feel what I was feeling or face the reality that my mother was about to leave me. With hindsight I realise that help from the other side was at hand and they were beginning to prepare me for what was to come. For this I will always be eternally grateful, because I was able to spend quality time with her

Shortly afterwards my mother was again admitted unable to breathe and in the short time she was an in-patient, through the sharing of equipment, she became infected with the dreaded MRSA. I'm not sure if she was clear of this when she passed over or if it contributed to her death. But what I did know was how it made her feel as a person and the impact this infection had on her. I arrived to visit one night to find an empty bed where my mother should have been. I quickly approached the desk. "Where is my mother?" "She has been moved to a side room" the Ward Sister replied, giving nothing away in her face. 'Why?" I enquired. "She has tested positive for MRSA" came the reply. "How"? was my immediate response. The Sister was clearly embarrassed and shot the odd glance in my direction, but never made eye contact with me. Continuing to shuffle a pile of notepapers from one spot to the other, she stated they were not sure exactly how my mother had managed to become contaminated by this dreadful bug, but they were looking into it.

I quickly located my mother, who was a young 69 with a modern outlook on life. One glance at her face revealed just how damming she had found this information. She was clearly upset by these findings and what she saw as the stigma of being isolated in a side room with a sign attached to the door telling all and sundry she was infected. "I'm dirty" she said, while fighting back the tears. It wasn't a conversation, it was a statement. This was the way the knowledge that she had MRSA made my mother feel. Yet she countered it with two further statements. "I have always washed and looked after myself" she faltered, as if arguing within herself, trying to fathom how she had become to be, as she saw it, dirty. Any hospital workers take heed. Take the time to explain to the infected person what has happened, what will be happening, how it has occurred and what impact this will have on the person's life. Because no-one did that to my mother, and this event had a major impact on how she felt about herself at a critical period in her life.

Mom had a further episode of being ill and was advised to go back into hospital. mom chose not to. She hated her time in there, she enjoyed her own routine with peace and quiet to read and spend time with the family. After the last event she was, in a gentle way, adamant she didn't want to go back in. The doctor decided to treat her at home. One Saturday morning I set off to see her. As I approached the village where she lived an ambulance overtook me with the blue lights flashing. The sight of that ambulance hit the pit of my stomach and the sensation rose to my heart, which ached as if ready to burst with emotion. I had seen mom the night before and she was extremely well, but I knew that ambulance was going to her. I slammed the car into second gear, hit the accelerator and drove as if my life depended on it. I matched that vehicle pace for pace through the village. As it turned into my mother's street, I felt the tears welling up in my eyes, just as I am doing now, as I type these words.

I ran into the house behind the paramedics. Mom had, on top of everything, suffered a stroke which had taken her speech and her right side. I followed her to the hospital. During the long wait in the local Accident and Emergency Department at Russell's Hall Hospital my mother had another episode of not being able to breathe, the last two had resulted in previous admissions, but no-one had witnessed these before. Had they bothered to come behind the curtain to see my mother they would have seen the event unfold. It was only at my insistence that someone finally came.

The outcome of that day was a blow to us all, so large was the growth in the cavity surrounding my mother's lungs, that she was being suffocated. If the effects of the stroke didn't kill her this would. We were all devastated. My mother stayed in hospital for six days. She didn't want to be there, so we came to her. In a rota between the close family, including her only brother whom she loved dearly, we stayed with her 24 hours a day.

This was made possible by the transferring of her on the Sunday to a side ward. So we began our vigil. On the Sunday afternoon Joan my ex-sister-in-law sat one side, while I sat the other. I suddenly realised my mother was no longer breathing. I sensed her soul had left her body. As stupid as it sounds Joan was in mid-sentence and I didn't like to interrupt, but my face said it all. Joan walked around to my side of the bed, looked at my mother and went to fetch a nurse, all this had taken several minutes and still my mother lay, not breathing. The nurse checked my mother's pulse and gently tried to explain what was happening. Without reason, I suddenly begged her not to leave me crying, begging her to come back. I watched my mother's soul re-join her body, and as if something had landed on her, she began to breathe again with an almighty gasp, as the two joined together. Startled she opened her eyes.

Mom wanted to go home, so as soon as she was stable enough we got her home. I sat with my mother through the Friday and Saturday night and we had a sitter for the Sunday night. On the Sunday afternoon she was quite agitated and hadn't slept since she arrived home. Her bed was downstairs and located opposite the open-plan stairs; she kept asking who was on the stairs and talking of seeing someone, descending down the stairs towards her. I knew the signs, but closed my eyes to the painful reality of what this meant. The next day I got up early to go and be with her. As I was about to leave the house, I quickly popped my head around the living room door. All over the carpet there greeted me lots of patches of diarrhoea, and a little black Scottie sat looking very forlorn and clearly feeling sorry for himself. Still only a baby at six months, he couldn't be blamed. I picked him up and quickly comforted him. I was now in a dilemma - did I stop and clear it up or did I go? I desperately wanted to go, to be with mom, but felt compelled to clear this mess up, as I couldn't leave it for anyone else; so I duly stopped and as quickly as possible cleared it up and very hastily cleaned the carpet. I raced to get out of the door, but just as I was leaving the phone rang. I ran back to answer it. It was dad – mom had just passed. I instinctively knew why I had been delayed. Had I been there I would not have let her go, I would have selfishly have cried and begged her to stay with me. Now for such a bout of diarrhoea from such a young dog, he was only 6 months old, you would have expected him to have more. He was as bright as a button. It was as if he had taken that on, to stop me from being there. Had I chosen to have left it, I would have been there.

Like most people who love someone close to them, a little part of you also dies with them. I felt at times I would never get over it, as I thought of my pending birthday without her; her vacant seat at Christmas; and the loss of the person I only ever seemed to ring when I was in crisis and who always said all the right things. Did this mean I would never see her again? Hear her voice or her laughter. My heart was broken. It is an unfortunate means to access it, but the trauma of death does expand our psychic gifts and I felt my mother with me on many occasions. She was without doubt an excellent driver, who did love to speed. I remember a blow-out on the car while doing 80 miles an hour on the motorway. I felt her hands gripping mine, as I safely negotiated the car onto the hard shoulder, without so much as a skid or tremble.

But above all, I saw her in my dreams. This is possibly one of the easiest ways for people from the other side to reach us, to join us in our dreams. This world is, at times, incredibly harsh. Whether we realise it or not in our sleep state we go back to where we came from, the world of spirit. Majority of the time we have no recollection of this. If we can recall this occurrence or some of it, then we will receive it through our dreams. How many times have you dreamt of a loved one and suddenly woke during the night and because you have woken, you are able to remember it? We are often woken up during these dreams or immediately afterwards. Why? Because it is a sure way of ensuring you remember the dream. So next

23

time you are with someone from the world of spirit and are suddenly woken up in the middle of it, be glad you did wake when you did, because without this interruption there is a good chance you would not have remembered the event the next morning.

I have heard many people over the years tell me they have never felt their loved one around them, but usually they can remember seeing them in a dream. They regale how it felt as if they were really with them. People say how they spoke to them, told them they were okay or gave them messages for other family members. Others have spoken of how the dream was really mixed up and made no sense at all, which has caused them to doubt the event. Often the events recalled in the dream are irrelevant, what counts is the actual seeing, meeting, talking with your loved one, not what they have tried to communicate. It is that sense of comfort, love and joy that event brings to you. That is the meaning of the dream and it is that feeling that counts. Even when people wake crying real tears, it is a sense of release that has been achieved.

The spirit world is real, that is where our home is. Our time on earth is short lived; our time in the spirit world is eternal. Why do those who believe seem to receive more? Is it that they are making it up, gullible, fooling themselves? So is it because they believe the restrictions of doubt have been lifted, therefore it is easier for our loved ones to reach us? I prefer to think it is the latter rather than the former. If you believe, you do not have the restricted boundaries a person has who does not believe in the life after.

Nestled within our grief is always a sense of regret and guilt. That line from "Brother in Arms" really captures this ...' I just wish I had of told him, in his living years'. For those of us who have lost someone dear how many times have we thought, 'I wish I had told them how much I loved them', or 'how much I appreciated all they did for me'. 'How much I loved and valued their company'. 'How precious they were to me'. Does this sound familiar? Why do we have to wait until they have passed over to want to tell them all the positive attributes they have and what joy they have brought into our lives, just by being part of it? My premonition that day on the car park at Lidl's saved me a lot of heartache. It not only gave me time to spend with my mother while she was still well, it also gave me quality time, so I could appreciate her company knowing that very soon this part of my life would be gone forever and would never be recaptured. I will always value the time I spent with her, more importantly the time I spent in this knowledge. This gave me time to look and absorb her smile, feel the comfort you can only feel in the company of your mother. Cherish the drink she made for me. But more importantly to tell her I loved her; to hug her; and thank her for all that she had done for me.

So for all those out there: don't wait for the death or pending death to appreciate your family and friends in your life. Take the time to stop and feel what they mean to you, then tell them, before it is too late. Make some quality time to spend together and enjoy each other's company and do it on a regular basis. It is that phrase, 'being in the moment'. What on earth does that mean? It is to appreciate what is going on around you, now, as it happens. On a regular basis, take the time to reflect and evaluate all aspects of your life. Recognise those facets that are important to you, then look again and acknowledge what qualities it is that that person brings you happiness and joy......now tell them.

Auras are Us

Whether we understand it or not we are energy beings. We are made up of mind body and soul. The soul is eternal and long after we have discharged our human body our soul will survive. Like any living thing on earth there is a detectable energy field around it. In the 1950's a camera was designed which could photograph this energy. It is called Kirlian photography and is often popular at mind, body and spiritual events. I believe through this field we discharge emotions, which other people can detect. For all those doubting people, how many times have you said, I don't know what's wrong with so and so, but...... and have then gone on to describe how they have made you feel? How many times have you walked into a room and stated you could sense an atmosphere between two people. When we look back it is rather an odd thing to say. "Could you sense the atmosphere between those two?" How many times have you made statements like that or heard someone else say it? It is the kind of statement which we take for granted and don't really read a lot into. If someone was to ask you to explain exactly what you meant by it, I doubt if you could put into words exactly what you meant, but you know what you are talking about. For the small minority of you who have read this, and thought, 'no, this doesn't apply to me', let me try another angle. How many of you have been sitting in your car, when you have sensed the person in the next car is looking at you and as you have turned to look, loe and behold they are staring at you. Or stood at a bar or in a queue and have then had the sensation of someone's eyes boring into the back of you. Or maybe you have fancied someone, and suddenly you know they are looking at you? Yes, in one way or another it happens to us all.

Now I had always been one of those people who prided themselves on being to able to read the 'vibes' around people or in rooms, was it good or bad? Thick or tense? From as long as I can remember as soon as I walked in a room I could tell if my parents had argued with each other or if they were displeased with me. I didn't wait for anyone to speak, I just sensed it as I entered the room. I don't believe I am unique in this manner, I believe most people are able to do this.

When I look back I remember returning to work after my mother died. I could feel I lacked my own sense of containment and felt I was reaching out to people for comfort and people behaved in different ways towards me. From giving me a woman with cancer, dying the same as mother, as the first case I was expected to visit, to someone from another Team sending me a bouquet of flowers. Different people respond to this neediness in different ways. When I spoke to Pat, the woman who sent me the flowers sometime afterwards to tell her how much those flowers meant to me, she dismissed my gratitude out of hand. She went on to tell me how, having lost her own mother she understood how I felt and offered her heartfelt sympathies to me. Like John, a work colleague as we shall see later, and his interview, the actions of some others stayed with me a long time, the kindness of Pat and the lack of understanding with some others.

Although I felt no malice or anger, at the time it was more one of bewilderment. But like many of my experiences, in later life it went on to show me how we respond to others.

When we are needy we give off an energy which tries to draw others close to us. Unfortunately we live in a world where we are rarely honest regarding how we are feeling. We are taught to keep a 'stiff upper lip' and not to tell others our troubles and woes and when we do tell them our worries, people assume we are expecting something back in return. In our self-contained little lives we assume everyone is extremely happy and contented in their relationships, lives, work etc., except us. How much easier would life be on this planet if we were taught at a very young age that life will be full of up's and downs and we will all go through similar things at different times during our lives and it is okay to be open and honest and to be able to say 'I have a problem and it is mine to deal with' and for people to be able to hear this without feeling they need to do something or are obligated to feel they should do something, even when they don't want to.

Following my own experience during this time, I then tried to understand what was happening when I felt people were needy of me or I felt like people were drawing off me. I was beginning to get quite good at reading energies around people and understanding them. Then a strange experience taught me to re-think my practice.

There is only one direct route from my home to Telford, no short cuts, literally one road. When this is closed, you are diverted miles. Majority of this journey is across country lanes. In the winter only small stretches of the road will be gritted. I quickly learnt to 'feel' black ice underneath my wheels and merely take my foot off the accelerator and hope traction returned before I needed to turn the wheel. A little frightening, but it worked, as long as you were not going too fast. There are very few places to overtake on this long road. So if you are following a slow car, it is a case of sitting back and waiting for the couple of over taking places to come. There is nothing else you can do. On one icy morning I sat impatiently behind a woman driver as she slowly negotiated the twisting road. Bored with 4 miles before I could overtake I sent my energies to her in the car to feel how she was feeling. Prior to this I was driving with one hand on the wheel, confidently controlling the car, with relative ease. Suddenly I was terrified, my posture changed from one of slouched and relaxed, to sitting bolt upright, with both hands gripping the steering wheel tightly. I was panicking convinced the car was beginning to slide. I began braking inappropriately, making the situation ten times worse. This was turning into the journey from hell - I was conscious of the road surface, searching for ice patches as I struggled to maintain the car in a smooth manner, without sharp turns or braking, which would make the situation worse. This pattern continued for several minutes when suddenly it occurred to me what I had done; I had picked up all the emotions the lady in front of me was feeling. As soon as I recognised this, all the negative feeling began to subside and I returned to the confident driver I normally am.

It made me realise how easy it was to pick up negative vibration and emotion from someone else. I then started to look at it from another perspective and realised how invasive my behaviour was. I had, without permission, been intruding into people's private space. Knowing there is always a consequence for an action, I apologised, in my head, to all those people I had, unintentionally, infringed upon over the past few months and vowed never to do it again - and I didn't. To this day I don't scan or intrude into people's energy fields, unless invited so to do. A promise I made to my family and friends to which I have religiously adhered, only breaking when asking one of them to tell me the truth, in which case, I will tell them what I am going to do. This usually brings the desired result, the truth, before I do it.

I realised I had to modify my approach. I knew and understood it was okay to sense what vibration a person was putting out, whether it was good or bad and whether it was directed at me or someone else. I further understood, to achieve this I should not to enter into their energy space, merely sense what was coming towards me. By doing this I could often sense situations of conflict before that actually transpired. I also learnt how to send out smoothing thoughts to try and quell angry events before they began to transpire. It may or may not have worked. But I did on numerous occasions, receive the sensation of calming a situation which actually hadn't occurred, because of my calming thoughts.

After I pulled by my energies and stopped intruding into people's energy spaces, I began to notice, what for all intents and purposes appeared to be black flies flying around the room. While in discussion with people, or as part of a general conversation involving several people, as they spoke, I would notice these black flies coming off their heads. Sometimes they would go directly towards someone sitting in the room. Sometimes this someone would be me! After a short while I realised these were dark, or negative thoughts the person was having towards another. While their mouth may not have been expressing negative words, their minds certainly were and I would watch them shoot out.

The easy part was seeing them. The difficult part was what to do about it. As always when in a quandary I will ask White Feather for his words of wisdom and advice on the situation. This I duly did. He carefully explained to me that, unfortunately, while on the earth plane we have developed the ability to be able to hide what we are truly feeling, to be able to disguise this, through empty words. Majority of us are unable to control and contain any negative thoughts we have towards other people. Once we think it and let the thought go the thought, which is a living energy and can be physically measured, goes off on its way to the intended victim. In some ways, it is healing in reverse.

Have you ever found yourself in a situation where few words have been exchanged between yourself and another party and you are no longer in contact them, but somehow the animosity between you begins to build up and grow and over time you begin to feel darker thoughts towards them. Before you know it there is distinct hostility between you both. But it's hard to understand as cross words have not been spoken. We may not be able to understand it, but we can, if we stop and think recognise this situation, time and time again.

Whenever people come to me for a reading and I pick up bad feelings between the living, I will often use the example of the fire triangle. For a fire to burn it needs three factors, a source of ignition, combustible materials and oxygen. Remove one and the fire goes out. It is the same with ongoing conflict you need to break the chain. Stop thinking and unintentionally sending out, negative thoughts. When a thought of a person comes into your head, dampen it with love, send in return a wonderful soothing pink energy. The results are often almost immediate and the chain of negative thought is disarmed. As hard as this is to do, it is the only way to quell the flow.

Tools to help on the Journeys of Life

I believe life on earth was not designed to be easy. We are made up from three elements mind, body and soul. The body is quite clearly what it is, the physical vehicle by which we journey through life. The mind is what manages the body, and the soul is that element which is the most difficult to recognize, but expressed in its most basic form, it is you. When well balanced, the soul should control the direction of life and the mind should control the body to facilitate motion and movement down that pathway. Unfortunately what I have described is in an ideal world and as we all know for most of us, we don't live in an ideal world. For most people there is often an imbalance between these three elements. Take for example someone who is body conscious, attending a gym five nights a week, running in between, obsessed by what they eat and subsidising their diets with body building products, sometimes resulting to taking products, such as steroids. If we think of the three elements we can see that someone who is following this type of pathway does not have a complete balance between the three essential components.

On the other hand we can see people trapped in relationships that are making them very unhappy. They are staying together for the sake of the children or financial reasons and while living most days in the dreadful sinking feeling that life is passing them by. Yet at the same time they feel they are unable to move one. The same applies to staying at home to care for relatives, settling for security while the heart is crying out for a work role with adventure. Living in a neighbourhood where we are extremely unhappy, but we are held by fear of moving away, moving somewhere else and being unhappy, not knowing or settling down. Again there is an imbalance between the three elements; the mind is controlling the soul and body through overwhelming fear.

I believe that when God gave us this life he asked few things of us. His only stipulation was that we live our lives true to ourselves and to live each day as if it was our last. This is not a licence to ride rough shod over everyone's feelings around us or to behave in a reckless manner. But rather to live our lives through our own expectations, dreams and ideology, not that of others, or to please others who surround you. To carefully explore every opportunity that is presented to you and when you feel it is right for you, to embrace it with open arms.

This alone will not balance your mind, body and spirit, but will help you to make informed judgements through sound, careful exploration of all aspects of your life.

On our journey through life we need to care for all three components. We need to respect our body. Love it and take good care of it. We need to control our minds and learn to recognise when it is the mind that is generating unfounded fear, and we need to learn to 'tune in' and listen to our soul to ensure we are following our correct pathway and we are not allowing our mind to make us fearful or reckless.

There are several tools for attuning ourselves to the spirit world around us, or listening to our souls. The first is the power of prayer. So many of us are taught to pray from and early age, to say grace at meal times, prayers at night or during assemblies at school. But no-one ever tells us the meaning of prayer and what we can and cannot ask for. I remember trying to use the power of prayer to extend my mother's life on this earth and being given a gentle 'no', my prayers would not be answered, there were too many other factors included. I give prayers all the time, from the platform, but rarely do I ask for myself. The times I have I can remember distinctly.

We all have leaner financial times, at sometimes during our lives, to a bigger or lesser extent and I am no exception to this. At a period where there appeared to be more outcome per month than income, the next door neighbours approached me. It would appear there was water pouring into their property. After extensive searching the plumber had pin-pointed the problem to the floor boards underneath my kitchen floor, close to the adjoining wall. In normal circumstances this may have gone unnoticed. But in this case the kitchen was located on the first floor of our three storey houses. Consequently in its journey to the ground, the lower walls in my neighbour's property were saturated. So it was over to me. Fortunately a friend recommended a plumber who had done extensive work for them, all at a fair price. As soon as I met him and saw his open honest face, I knew he would charge me a fair price. He located the fault to a joint in a water pipe. As it had risen over the joist the builder had merely bent the pipe, which had caused the problem. Looking by the mess underneath the floorboards this had probably been leaking for years before it was detected. To cap it all the good old Insurance wouldn't pick up the costs attributing the problem to wear and tear, so it was all down to me. So with a stiff upper lip I bit the bullet and began to scratch around to try and muster the funds to meet the bill. But just when you think things cannot get any worse they do. The plumber called me at work, to break the bad news. He had found the main stopcock to the house, but there was a fault with it, the thread appeared to have gone and he was unable to turn off the water supply to the house. So off I set back home to see what could be done.

The kindness in his face told me he was sincere and I felt safe in his hands and I trusted him. Looking quite pained he told me we had a serious problem on our hands, if we couldn't turn off the water supply to the house we couldn't fix the problem. We would therefore have to try and find another source. Our only hope was the valve at the bottom of the drive, but this hadn't been opened or closed since the houses were built 35 years ago. He lifted the flap to show me, it was buried in several inches of both loose and compacted dirt, it was obvious this had build up over years. "look, you can see for yourself, there is no way we are going to be able to open this". He went on to explain he had been faced with this problem time and time again and after this length of time, if they haven't been used, they rarely work. "What's the alternative?" I enquired, rather nervously. We will have to ask the Water Board to turn off the water to this section of the street, it will be expensive he added. "How much?" I tentatively asked. "Several hundreds?".

I consciously ensured I stayed composed, but the reality was there was no way I could afford this. "Could we at least try?" he agreed. I don't think for one minute he minded trying, you could see he didn't want to raise my hopes, he was just preparing me for the worst to come. I stood and watched him as be began to dig, as I did I prayed. I prayed from my heart, there is no way I could afford the alternative. I called on every angel in the heavens I could think of, to shower down their love and energy to provide the power to open that valve. As he dug down I decided this job may be a little too big for the Angels, so I called upon God himself. I asked him that I may be spared this unnecessary cost. I prayed from the bottom of my heart, silently and with my eyes wide open. As he began the task I continued to pray and pray. With the dirt removed he attentatively placed this long handled tool onto the valve and still I prayed. You could see from all his years of experience he knew the valve wouldn't open, but was going through the motions, just to please me. He gently applied pressure and before he had applied any real pressure, it began to turn. A look of total amazement came over his face as the rusty old valve, which hadn't been opened in thirty plus years, began to turn. He began to stutter and apologise for the anxiety he had caused me. "I sorry but honestly, they don't normally open after this length of time". I smiled and dismissed his apologies and added a flippant comment there is nothing so powerful, as the power of prayer. He gave me a quizzical look, as I shot a smile over my shoulder and went on my way. I got in the car and thanked all those whom I had asked to help; I vowed to work even harder in return. Over the years this has been one of many times where I felt I asked through the power of prayer and I was helped.

So why was my prayer answered that day? I don't think it was because I am special, in fact I know it isn't. We are all born with the tool and the ability to be able to pray for help, unfortunately most of us have either forgotten to use it or have lost our faith. My prayer was answered that day, because I asked for assistance with something which was easy for the Angels and God to help me with, because;

- It didn't infringe on anyone else. I wasn't asking for something for which affected someone else. This was solely for me. Had I prayed for a loved one to return to me, after the romance failed, I would have been asking the impossible as this would have affected other parties, not just myself.
- It wouldn't change my destiny. I believe we have selected certain situations before we came to earth, because we wanted to live the experience that situation would bring into our lives. Therefore if we are praying for something which could change the course of lives, our prayers may not be granted. What we would need to do in this situation is to pray for guidance.
- Is my prayer reasonable or am I being selfish. A prayer for new shoes, to match an outfit isn't a good use of a prayer. Yet a prayer for shoes, when you have none on your feet is different.

- Never pray for harm to come to another, in any way shape or form. These things have a way of coming back on you.

So before you pray, ask yourself why you are asking for whatever it is your are praying for and remember the three factors listed above and if it falls into any of these categories, the odds are it won't be answered.

The other question I am often asked is, why we need to ask for assistance in the first place. If those above can see what is happening to us why don't they just give us the assistance? It is all down to the question of free will. I often tell people from the platform of Spiritual Churches, we come into this world with more gifts than we realise and one of these gifts is the ability to be able to express our own free will. During our lifetime people may imprison us, enslave us or dominate us, but no matter what, they can never take away our free will. We are born with it and die with it, we may give it away, but it can never be taken from us. We can express our free will in many ways, the one we are interested in today, is the ability to be able to ask for assistance from God, Angels, Guides, loved ones etc.

The downside of free will, is no-one can give assistance from the spirit world, until we expressly ask for help. No matter how desperate we are or how hopeless our lives may appear, or the dangers that may await us around the corner, unless we ask for help no-one can give it to us. Unfortunately we are often so detached from the world of spirit, we forget to ask for help and guidance and then get angry that God lets the terrible things happen. He cannot intervene until we ask and when we do it has to be in line with our goals in life; our request has to be reasonable and must not infringe on the free will of others.

Having been on the failed side of prayer I remember how it feels. I had moved away from
managing residential units, into an advisory role, in the community. My new role heavily infringed on Health and Safety and I enjoyed the clarity of this role. Legislation was exact, there were no grey areas. After the fuzzy areas of social work, I rather enjoyed the clear cut boundaries of Health and Safety. So when a vacancy occurred in the Central Health and Safety Unit, I decided to apply for it. I felt the change was right for me and at the right time in my life. I was further motivated by the fact staff from within the Unit were actively encouraging me to apply, so I did. All the signs seemed in my favour, so I worked extremely hard for the interview, burning the midnight oil researching all aspects of Health and Safety, brushing up on my knowledge. I spent hours working on my presentations and I prayed every night to be given the opportunity to get this job, as I felt it would be a wonderful opportunity and I knew I could do it and do it well. Unfortunately after all my hard work and encouragement from within the Unit, I didn't get the job. I was devastated. I felt extremely let-down by everyone in the spirit world. I had prayed my little heart out asking for help to get that job, all to no avail. I couldn't understand why they hadn't helped me, when I had specifically asked for assistance. I wasted no time in telling anyone in the world of spirit, whom I felt may be listening, exactly how I felt, which was extremely

let down and misguided. All I heard in return was 'not yet'. The meaning of this was to unfold several years later, when my job would become attached to a Health and Safety Unit.

Having failed miserably to get the job of my dreams, I stayed where I was. It wasn't that I was unhappy or didn't like the job I had or that the people I worked with were horrible, to the contrary, I just felt at that moment in time a change in direction was what I wanted and needed. So having failed miserably in my pursuit of my 'ideal job', I continued to stay in my current position, with no desire to seek alternative positions. Not at that moment in time, at least.

Six months on someone in the office returned to work, following Maternity Leave. This someone was Stella, whom I mentioned earlier. I had known Stella from years ago, so we quickly we became quite good office buddies. Stella was the one who had me away on holiday before I had time to blink; the holiday where I met her sister Cherry, who was a big influence in my early development.

As we shared our views and opinions over lunch, it became apparent we had similar interests. One of these was a keen interest in all matters, not of this world, but of the world of esoteric. We had many a happy lunch break crammed into the little office at the front of the building, where Stella and I would explore a variety of subjects. Our pastime quickly spread around the office and we were soon joined by other colleagues, Sarah and Clio, where the four of us would sit and discuss all aspects of spirituality.

How it happened I don't know, but I happened to see an advertisement for a psychic development course, in the locality. In no time Stella and I were booked on and attending on a weekly basis. This course changed my life.

Now, what if I had been granted the wish and have been given what I asked for, which was that post in the Central Health and Safety Unit. The probability is Stella and I would never have met up again or at least spent the quantity of time together that we did. In turn I would not have met Cherry and very much doubt I would have done the development course, which started my spiritual journey, which ultimately led me to where I am now.

I recognised this about two years on, from the 'failed' interview, when in a rare quite moment of hindsight, I reflected how quickly my life had changed and changed for the better. I traced the time-line in my mind of how events had, in recent years unfolded, right back to failing to get the job and the sharp reality hit me. What if my heartfelt prayers had been answered? I shuddered at the thought of the opportunities I would have missed, had my prayer been granted. I gave a silent 'thank you', to the forces, which are greater than I, that could see the 'wider picture' and the wonderful life-changing opportunities which would have passed me by, had I side-stepped across into Health and Safety.

As you can you see, sometimes we pray for something which we think is what we want and believe is in our best interests to get, but if we

34

would have achieved it, we would have missed some wonderful opportunities. So next time you don't get something you truly want, rather than feeling bitter, angry, or discontent, watch as life unfolds and see what you opportunities come your way that you would have otherwise missed out on, had your wish been granted.

Painted on a wall close to some traffic lights, as I drive home from work is a sign which says 'Be careful what you wish for' and underneath is painted, 'it may just come true'. I have looked at that many times and thought 'how bloody right is that?'

But don't let this put you off using prayer. You don't need to be in a church, temple or mosque to pray. Prayers can be heard wherever you are. All you need is to say it from your heart, with love, send out your plea and know it will be heard.

I see prayer as a one way communication stream, where we are making a specific request for help, whether this is assistance, guidance or healing. We are asking for something to be granted to us or for us, in one way or the other. Mediation, on the other hand is the opening of a two way communication, where in the right circumstances we are able to not only transmit, but also able to receive information back.

For me meditation is the creation of a peaceful state, we will hopefully achieve, once we have mastered the art of relaxation and have stilled our minds. As a Medium when I am working I do not allow any thoughts to enter my mind, it is completely still without any conscious thought. When I am in this state it is very easy for spirit to send information, which I am able to receive with little or no interference. This is how I communicate with my guides or people who have passed onto the spirit world. When I allow thoughts to enter my head, the information is either blurred or blocked. It is only when I have again attained the state of complete stillness that I able to effectively work as a Medium. I can still receive, but when the information becomes mixed with my own thoughts, I start to get into terrible trouble. For those of you who think they can never achieve this, read on.

As I said earlier Stella and I completed our eight week development course together. Despite my misgivings in later life regarding the Teacher of this course, I have to say for me it open doorways. It taught me that I had gifts, which before this course, I could only dream about. Each week we were given work to practice outside of the course. One of our homework tasks was to practice the art of meditation. During the course we were shown how to relax by creating our own sanctuary, a sacred space. To achieve this we were told to build a garden in minds, where we could sit and relax. This is where we would go at the beginning of any meditation. This I duly did and 12 years on I can still remember it. So outside of the class, I duly did my homework and practiced the art of mediation. Off I went into my garden. Then I suddenly I remembered I needed to protect myself. Now I have never been the bravest of people at the best of times. I have always treated the unknown with respect and I was well read enough to know when you venture into the unknown, you need to ask for protection. Unfortunately

Paul, our Teacher, had not covered this aspect on the course. I sat and racked my brains trying to remember means and ways of protecting yourself. Then it came to me: in one book it had said you should encase yourself in an egg of white light, it sounded perfect. As I began to work out how to achieve this, I imagined two halves of an egg and I placed this around me, then I filled it with white light. Fully protected I was just about to start, when I began worrying that the egg wasn't sealed. Did this mean the light could escape? If it escaped would this mean I would no longer be protected? If I was aware of the gaps, would the dark forces notice it to? Over and over these thoughts went in my head. It was no good, how could I relax knowing something terrible could befall me, because of the lack of joints to my egg? How safe was I? Not very I decided, so how could I resolve this? I decided to seal it and in my mind's eye, I began sealing the main joint, which happened to be directly in front of me. Mask in place with an arc welding gun in my hand I meretriciously sealed the joint. I put my welder down and took off my mask and sat ready to receive knowledge and information. I was extremely pleased with my work and could see it was air-tight. Airtight I thought that means air cannot get in. Within seconds I had convinced myself I couldn't breathe and had to come out of the meditation. The whole exercise had lasted five minutes.

For all of those of you who think I am an idiot, you are probably right, but I have shared this story to show you, initially, we all find it difficult to still the mind and maintain that tranquillity in order that disturbing thoughts don't keep creeping in. The ability to achieve this, can, for some, be quite a difficult process. From the earliest thoughts we can remember, our mind has prided itself on being alert and observant in order to advise us, protect us and forewarn us of impending danger. Now we are trying to teach it to be totally silent.

All I can say is persevere, in time it will come easier. For those of you who find it near impossible to shut up those niggling little thoughts, try counting your breathing in and out, this will occupy the mind. In time it will get bored and begin to sit in silence. The more you practice, the easier it becomes and the longer the sessions will last. Believe me, because here I am, the woman who could not maintain a meditation longer than 5 minutes, to someone who can meditate for up to 2 hours, when I have the time, and who can reach a meditative state while standing on a platform giving messages to the congregation. So if I can master it, so can you. But remember, practice makes perfect. If you are serious about developing this wondrous tool remember there are these stages to conquering this art.

- Learn to relax. This easiest way is to create your own sacred space, whether this is a garden, cave or beach doesn't matter. Just create some where you feel safe and are therefore able to relax.
- Protect yourself. Ask for guides or angels for protection against dark forces.
- State what it is you want to achieve from this meditation.
- Sit and enjoy the process

Once you have achieved this you now have a wonderful tool to communicate with your guide, angels, loved ones or more importantly your soul. The more I practised the easier I found it, to see and understand the images that flashed across my mind.

It was during one of these meditations that I received the final pieces to my re-occurring dream. I sat down to do my three times a week meditations, nothing any different from normal. As soon as I closed my eyes I saw a tall willowy woman, on a dance floor. I don't know how, but I knew it was on a large ship. There was me, just as I had seen myself over and over again in my dream, wearing exactly the same dress! The area was in a small secluded part of the ship for the rich and privileged. The colour white and highly polished wood featured predominantly in the scene. The small band had finished playing, when the slightly intoxicated woman asked for another tune. The man with whom I am dancing is dressed in military clothes, naval and he is a man in a relatively high position. I can see bands of gold braid. He is extremely cold towards me, I know it is over between us. He has had enough of me, my behaviour and attitude. I am extremely spoilt. The biggest insult is he is leaving me for someone of a much lower social status. I shall be publicly humiliated by his actions. As we dance I sense there is no point in trying to charm, I have finally pushed him too far. The music ends and I go out onto the deck of the boat, totally distraught, I throw myself off from the ship. It seems ages before I hit the water. I am full of regret now, but it's too late.

I was totally shocked by the scene. I sat in a daze, I knew this scene was showing me how I had behaved in a former life. I had taken the easy way, whether I meant to or not. I couldn't do anything about it, I couldn't change it, but at least I understood what the dream had been trying to show me. From that day onwards the dream never re-occurred again. Although I had plenty of other dreams to replace it as you can see later in the book.

New Beginnings

There doesn't need to be a special occasion or event to make changes to our lives. Unfortunately it usually takes some episode before we stop and take stock of our lives. It is as if we need these events to drive us forward and without them we are unable to instigate change. Change is not always for the good, or at least that is usually how we feel when change is forced upon us, by external forces, albeit a partner's decision to move on or someone being cruelly snatched from our lives. We rarely look back and rejoice, thanking the universe for moving us forward to a 'better life'. We usually begrudgingly state that it is 'no thanks to anyone', that life has in fact improved. In doing so we fail to see the lesson behind the event and until we do, we will continue to attract similar episodes to events to our lives, until we truly understand the lesson attached to the event.

Life was never meant to be one of continual enjoyment, where from beginning to end it is full of joy and laughter. We unfortunately need to balance between tears and laughter joy and sorrow. We rarely grow and learn through happiness. A state of contentment is almost like a platform; a resting place before the next event. We may stay on that platform for several years, but eventually you will move forward. It is a fact. We may choose a pathway which leads us back to exactly the same spot, but if it doesn't serve the 'bigger picture' to present us with opportunities to explore and eventually grow, our shelf-life on the platform will be time limited.

Take the diver who is afraid of diving into the water, he loves the concept of being in the water but he is terrified of the process of jumping from the boat and hitting the water. He knows once he has done it, the fright will be worth it, but it is actually finding the courage to do this. He will walk to the edge, then walk away. He will begin to mentally prepare himself for the act of physically jumping from the boat into the water. He may decide to merely rush the event, so he doesn't have time to think about it. Or he may sit on the side of the boat and dangle his feet in the water as he prepares himself for the incident. He knows the longer he delays the act of getting into the water, the less time he will have enjoying himself. So he knows time is running out. Hopefully, eventually he will find the courage to leave the side of the boat and enter the water and the more times he does it the easier he will find it next time, until he reaches the point where he fear has left him. We can all relate to this, when we see people do something they have been afraid of and they overcome it. Not matter what the physical task is, whether it is bungee jumping, flying or going on a fairground ride. The joy is intoxicating.

The circle is complete he has overcome his inert fear and he is able to move forward. But what if he didn't find the courage to jump from the side of the boat into the water? This is no doubt that there are ways of getting around it. He could have walked down the steps into the water. But would the process have given him the same satisfaction? Possibly no, because he didn't tackle his fear, he merely found less satisfactory ways to get around it. Unlike the glory found through actually jumping from the side, avoidance does not share this same level of achievement. So inevitably we will again try and overcome the fear of jumping from the side and usually, whatever the event we will continue to try until we achieve it.

Once we accept life is full of new beginnings whether they are actual events, or emotional states, small changes or life-changing episodes, we change our approach to life. We begin to see change as inevitable. But what happens when we cannot accept change?

Kelly had met Andy when she was a first year student nurse, at the tender age of 18. He was slightly older at 23 attending the University on a day release course in engineering. Despite the diversity of their careers they hit it off immediately. They were married the day after Kelly's finals. Two boys quickly came along and their family was complete and they were both happy and contented; or at least Kelly thought they were.

Without warning, at the end of a family barbecue, Andy announced he was leaving her, for Carol, Claire's best friend. The very friend she had helped when her own relationship collapsed, in very similar circumstances. Claire's husband had left her for his best mates' wife. She had been distraught and inconsolable, but above all extremely angry at the deceit of a so called friend. In Kelly's eyes Claire was doing to her what she found so undeniably cruel when her own marriage broke-up.

By the time Kelly came to see me, four months had passed. As we started the reading I knew nothing of this, all this information came out during the reading.

As soon as Kelly sat down her nan came though. I could feel a very powerful love from this woman to Kelly. So I began. "Kelly I have a woman here with me who is coming through with the love of a mother, although I feel she was a nan, do you understand?". "God bless her", she replied. "I do have a nan in the spirit world". "She is giving me nursing twice" I said. Kelly nodded in agreement. "This lady is around 5ft 9" tall, with a long face, round eyes and doesn't carry much weight?" I quickly glanced at Kelly to see if she could recognise this figure. The smile and the nod confirmed this was her nan. "She is telling me you would spend time staying with her and I don't feel she lived local to here, but not too far away. She is saying the place and area Longbridge and someone in the family would have worked there?" She nodded and still smiling told me her nan and granddad lived in Bromsgrove and granddad had worked at the Rover factory, in Longbridge. Her nan regaled her with childhood memories of lemon curd sandwiches, her favourite vegetable of sprouts, carrots and especially cabbage, which apparently she made in a special way. Long walks on the Lickey hills, but above all, a wonderful, wonderful love. It was quite clear how strong this bond was between these two people.

Kelly sat smiling the whole time, occasionally she would stare down at the floor and you could feel the memories, one after another flooding into her own mind.

Once Kelly was awash with this lady's love, she began to appear quite serious. "You will understand a break-up in a relationship, very close to you?" "Yeah me", came the reply from Kelly. The smile suddenly left her face. She folded her arms across her body and her elbows rested on her knees. Her whole body appeared to tense as she looked at the floor. It was obvious she didn't want to be reminded of this. With the belief she could make a difference, for the better, her nan soldiered on. "I feel this event is quite recent and she is telling me your partner left you in quite cruel circumstances and I believe this break-up involved another woman?" Kelly nodded. "But she is also telling me he won't let you go." She went on, "be careful Kelly, he is playing games. He is keeping you dangling on a string, as first reserve, just in case things don't work out." I continued. "Your nan is shaking her head and wagging her finger at you. She is also saying be careful, don't trust him, because he will only do it again". Kelly for a moment looked shocked. She was amazed that her nan knew so much about her life. "How does my nan know all this? She's been dead two years, this is all happening now". She asked amazed by what I was telling her. I spent a little time explaining to Kelly. That once a person passes into spirit life is very different, they don't intrude into our lives, but they clearly hear our cries of despair and our calls for help. Kelly during her darkest moments had wished her nan was with her, well she was and here was the information to prove it.

"Kelly your nan is telling me there are issues with the house and you may have to move, but you don't want to. Can I say your nan is telling you not to worry and the move will be for the best." "Is she really sure?" came the reply. Realising the importance Kelly hung on these words, I went back to nan and asked her to clarify the situation. It was affirmative. She was adamant that the move would take place and it would be for the best. Kelly pondered on her words and as if she was talking to her she, she said out loud "I don't know how that can be". She then went on to explain, Andy was not cooperating financially and she needed to downsize, but she was worried for the sake of the children, not wanting to take them away from their friends, school etc.,

You could feel the difference the reading had made to Kelly and her grandmother's words would no doubt give her the strength to move forward and cope with the changes that had been forced upon her. As I left she thanked me and gave me a very quick hug.

Two years later in a moment of weakness I agreed to do a private party for a group of women. I had obviously agreed on the spur of the moment as this was something I was desperately trying to cut down on. In total I saw six people, which is the maximum I will see in one evening.

As the last person sat down I knew I recognised her from somewhere else, or at least I recognised her grandmother, who was waiting in the room before the woman arrived. As she sat down and made herself comfortable visions of where she had lived before came rushing back. It was Kelly. The last time I had seen her had been at my house. Now I was doing another party at her new home

As we sat together I apologised for not recognising her as soon as I had arrived. The truth was it would have been impossible to recognise her. Before what sat before was a thin anxious, depressed woman, who for all

40

intents and purposes appeared to have a black cloud hanging over her head, that followed her wherever she went. The woman who sat here today, was vibrant, serene, with an air of confidence and peace about her. No wonder I didn't recognise her and I doubt I would have, had her nan not reminded me.

I broke with the traditional way I work and I leaned forward and said, "Kelly your nan is asking you to think back to two years ago and how you felt at that moment in time and to remind you how you doubted your life would turn around, and she is saying "look at you now!" Kelly's face broke into a huge smile. Then her hand fled to her face as she remembered her own despair.

As the reading began her nan brought evidence through of the change in home, car, job and the arrival of a new man. As before she brought through memory after memory, including places, street names etc., but above all she gave her the memory of the love they had shared together. Part-way through her nan reminded her that Andy was still playing his games, although it had no affect on her. As time had moved on, so had Kelly.

As I look back on this story I wonder how events would have turned out if Kelly had given in to Andy's innuendos and provocative comments. I didn't need a crystal ball to find the answer. Kelly would have been like the diver on the boat. Her life would have been held in abeyance while Andy continued to through the comments and looks and maybe have taken it a little farther, who knows. What would not have changed was his relationship with Claire. Kelly would have gone from wife and mother, to mistress, unable to move forward.

As it was, her courage to see the situation for what it was and to claim her life back had changed her for the better. She now had a new home, job and car. She felt better about herself and life and had met a new man in the process. Andy on the other hand still tried to play games with her and if she had let him, he would have damaged her new relationship, with his inappropriate texts, at very unsuitable times. Instead she had chosen to stop him in his tracks. You couldn't help feeling sorry for Claire who had chosen to teat a very good friend in exactly the same ways she had been treated. I wondered how long it would be before Andy moved on again, not long no doubt. But one thing was certain he would be moving forwards as the doors behind him were firmly shut.

While the diver knew the treats that lay ahead, majority of us do not know what befalls us when we make or accept change. It is the lack of certainty or the fear that the change may not be for the better, which makes the decision even harder to make. But like Kelly sometimes we have no choice, as the ground is shifting around us, giving us no choice but to jump ship. On the other hand we need to think and feel carefully before we jump, because sometimes the grass on the other side looks greener than it really is, as many of us have found to our peril.

Unfortunately it is this uncertainty that makes the decisions harder to make.

The Spiritualist Movement

Books have always opened doorways for me, sometimes doorways that I didn't know existed until I read the book. Every book I have read on spirituality, new age, esoteric etc., has either confirmed what I thought I believed, or taken me down fresh avenues, where new concepts and ideas have been presented, which have opened fresh doorways. Or the book has simply made me look at a situation with fresh eyes. This was the case with Bettie Eadie's book 'Awakening Heart'. In it she talks of her astounding near death experience, where she journeys back to the spirit world and returns with knowledge and gifts she did not have before. She talks of seeing the most wonderful colours, meeting beings who held such love and wisdom, as she had never felt before. A place so divine she didn't want to return to this world. It is only the promise that she will return, when she has successfully completed her task, that persuaded her to return.

One of these points which really jumped out at me and has stayed ever since. It was the viewpoint she presented on religion. She had been told, while back in the world of spirit that the different religions existed because each of them was there to serve a need in the people of this world. In other words these different religions had something to offer to different people, at different times in their lives. For some one religion would meet someone's needs for all of their lives, for others we may stay with one religion, for the period in our lives where that set of views best serves us.

This made perfect sense to me. We can rarely fully embrace the teachings of religions other than our own, or understand why people follow regimes which we feel are harsh or unnecessary, because we do not understand what need that religion is serving for that person. Throughout history we have a habit of decrying anything we don't understand.

From the passage in her book I understood many things. I understood that it is not for us to criticise or condemn the different religions, but to recognise that they exist to help people in different kinds of ways. I read that passage over and over again and as usual, when something grabs me as being true, I feel it in my heart and solar plexus charka's and my arms respond, with a layer of goose bumps. This is exactly what happened as I absorbed these words of wisdom. At that moment and every time I think back over it, it resonates within my soul.

This is certainly true of the Spiritualist movement, which often provides help, assistance and guidance for short periods in people lives.

There are several types of spiritualist churches in the UK. There are those that belong to the Spiritualist Nation Union (SNU), those which are affiliated with the Greater world, Christian Spiritualist movement and the independent spiritualist churches.

The spiritualist movement has been in existence since the 19th Century and churches or centres as they are sometimes called can be found in most areas. Spiritualism is a recognised religion in Britain, although for some it is one of the least known of all the major religions.

Despite the differences between the different organisations there is one common theme running through them all. Which is, 'to provide evidence that life exists beyond death', this is achieved through the demonstration of Mediumship. This is always a major component within the service, whether it is an evening of clairvoyance or a divine service. During this part of the service, a visiting Medium gives out messages to individuals in the congregation that provides evidence that their loved ones have survived death. For the individual receiving the message, the contact brings great comfort.

For the SNU the continuous existence of the human soul is one of seven principles that underpin the religion and the different services and their components are there to support and uphold these principles.

As with any activity we do in life, we do it because it brings something of value into our life. The same applies to people attending a Church Service. One or more of the components must be of value or meaning to us and it therefore meets some need within us. If it didn't people would cease to attend.

This is a very simplistic view, but nevertheless it is true when a task becomes or feels fruitless, we rarely maintain this activity for any length of time, as we can see no point in it, therefore why bother doing it? So we cease doing it. This is probably why some people come into spiritualism then move on. In their hour of need it has given comfort and strength. Once this need is satisfied, some people will move or others will stay.

Messages to individuals is one form of Mediumship, inspired talking is another. During this part of a service the Medium will receive inspiration from the world of spirit and share these words of comfort with the congregation. It is another means of communicating advice, help, or support that can be shared with many.

Before I fully developed my Mediumship skills I had always prided myself on being able to give people good advice. It was only when I began to develop my Mediumship did I realise those pearls of wisdom had not come from me, in fact without realising it, I had been inspired. I can tell you this was a big let down.

Now as I had allegedly been using this skill for a significant period of time, you would have thought I would have found this the easiest part of the Service. I have to say this was not the case.

As a Medium I had found messages to be the easiest part of my work, I could grasp the thread of evidence, hold it and communicate from it. On the other hand inspired talking or philosophy did not come easy and it took me an awful long time to fully grasp how to work with it.

During my period of development when I attended the Exponents Course at Oldbury Spiritualist Centre, they had to drag me kicking and screaming to give off inspired talking. Now I would argue, what was the issue? For all those budding Mediums out there all I can say is stay with it, inspiration does eventually come to us all.

As a Medium I always take my initiative for inspired talking from the reading. No matter what the subject is, or how short it is. I focus on the words and let the energy flow into me and hopefully the words of wisdom will flow out. In most Churches or Centres this is usually followed by a hymn, again giving a little more time to allow that connection to grow stronger. This was not the case at Matchborough Spiritualist Church. I sat alongside the Chairman as he lifted his reading and began to share it with the congregation. It was four short little lines that consisted of around 12 words. I had just begun to settle down to absorb the words, when it was over as quickly as it began. Still a little stunned from the shortness of this reading and struggling to grasp a thread from, he suddenly turned to me and smiled and handed the Service over to me. Where was the hymn? No there was definitely not going to be a hymn before I stood and gave my address.

Very uninspired I stood up with two smalls words that made no sense at all, they were, 'a smile'. As usual I was not let down and began a talk which lasted around 10 minutes, on the value of smile. As with a lot of Mediumship I don't always retain what I say.

But this evening, for some reason was an exception and I do remember my inspired talk. I remember telling the congregation that

"We rarely remember what someone looks like, we often cannot remember what someone says to us, but we never forget how a person makes us feel"

In order to underpin the value of these words I shared a story John a work colleague had shared with me. He had told me how, at sixteen he had applied for his first job at Leyland Daf, a job he didn't get. His parents had gone to a significant amount of trouble to kit him out for his first interview and had brought him a dark blue suit, of which he was extremely proud. As the interview terminated, unsure how he had actually done, he stood up and thanked the people for giving him the opportunity to attend the interview. He turned to leave the room, when one of the interview panel made a comment about his new blue suit.

In a laughing manner he asked why he was wearing a suit for an interview. Stunned John walked away, not knowing what to say. John had felt humiliated by his comments and that incident had stayed with him to this day, in his forties. He couldn't remember anything about the interview, or subsequent interviews he attended, but this one had stayed with him all this time, emphasised by the crushing way this man had made him feel.

I then went on to say at times we all do this to each other, at sometimes during our lives, whether we mean to or not. We are all capable of making people feel good, but unfortunately we are capable of making them feel not so good. The error is sometimes not what we have done, but what we haven't done. It is very easy to look back and reflect on a situation and realise how badly we have behaved. This is compounded when we fail do something to rectify the situation. What most of us do when we realise the effect our actions may have caused, is to internalise it. To view it from our perspective, how this has affected us, how terrible we feel. We don't view it from the other person's perspective, possibly because that is too

44

painful and we don't try and undo it. So we bury it, with all the other episodes in our lives when we haven't behaved as well as we could have.

What we need to teach ourselves is recognise the consequences of our actions. Determine if we can do something to put it right. If we can, then do so, don't wait. If we cannot, unpick it. Why did we do it? Learn from it, so we stop repeating history. Then after we have reviewed it, forgive ourselves and throw the situation away. In other words let it go, don't bury it. If we don't we will bury it with all the other hurt and pain.

As humans we are very good at holding onto situations or incidents because we have not forgiven ourselves. Over time we look back at these situations, usually one at a time, or unless we really want to punish ourselves, then look at several at once. We re-live the shame and pain associated with that incident. We become slaves to our 'shameful moments', unable to move on. Focusing on our negative points, instead of our positive ones. Now over time when we look at our lives we will see, we find ourselves in similar situations time and time again. Why? If we don't deal with any given situation, life will give us another and another opportunity until we do. The more we re-live old scenarios and beat ourselves up emotionally over the way we did or didn't handle it, the more it will keep coming back to us. So the vicious circle lives on. We re-live, we punish and we attract more of these likewise situations to us. Consequently we find ourselves living our lives looking back with regret and a thousand 'if only's'.

So you can see inspired talking is hopefully addressing a subject or topic that is of general meaning to everyone and hopefully each and everyone in the congregation will get something out of it.

Majority of people who are drawn to a spiritualist church are brought in by the desire to know their loved ones are okay. They have survived death and are able to send words of comfort back through the Medium. For many the clairvoyance can bring joy, comfort and hope.

At a service at Studley Community Centre a very happy, charming sincere woman approached me and thanked me for her message. "You don't remember me do you?" she asked. Before I could respond with some lame excuse she spared me the blushes by launching into her story. "I first saw you two years ago" she said. It was the first time I had come to the church. You asked to speak to me afterwards and you told me how I tried to come once before and not made it and how I had sat outside trying to find the courage to come in. She then went on to tell me how the evidence I had given her had changed her life and how much better she felt. Because of this she had returned time and time again and had found great comfort through the church. Looking at her warm smile, it was hard to believe she had been anything other than the way she was presenting here. She held my hand and thanked me for turning her life around. I accepted the thanks with gratitude, although I hadn't really done anything, but as far as she was concerned, my evidence had turned her world around and that was all that mattered. Whereas in fact it wasn't me, but the clever way in which her father had given the information.

This has happened to me on numerous occasions. Another time a woman came up to me after the service and asked for a hug, she held me tight as tears streamed down her face, this time though they were tinged with a smile. In a 12 month period she had lost her husband, daughter and mother. She had walked into the church not expecting to receive anything; her life in bits and completely worn down by grief. The tears cascaded down her face as all three members of the family came in to say hello. The next time I saw her she was busy in the back of the church making the teas and washing up. She had found a purpose in life, a niche where she could give something back for what she had received. Which is often how people find and stay in spiritualism.

Working the Platform

Now anyone out there who thinks working a platform, which means to stand on a platform at a Spiritualist Church, is easy, think again. As a Medium you are required to be multi-skilled, in a variety of tasks. In fact I cannot think of any other role where you need as many skills as you do when you to serve a church. Firstly, you need to be good at devising prayers, which are meaningful to everyone in the congregation. Although I have to say this is my weakest skill. You must be able to project your voice, to those sitting at the back of the church, who happen to be hard of hearing. A sense of humour is a must, for the times when things do not go according to plan - such as the organist not turning up or deciding to play the wrong tune. Or when the Chairperson forgets your name, smile sweetly! Or merely the spirit people decide to have a little fun.

You must be good at philosophy or inspired talking as it is often referred to and last but not least a good Medium. You must have broad shoulders and be able to leave your ego outside the door. For every time someone says to you how much they enjoyed the service and how grateful they are, there is always the put-me-down. Just stay around and listen as they judge and rate you over coffee, comparing you to their favourite Medium or the one who was on last week. Congregations can be merciless. Forget you have travelled a round trip of 100 miles, for £10.00. Over the years I have heard conversations go something like, "She was alright, but not a patch on our Linda". "What do you think of her?" "Well I couldn't concentrate because of that ghastly blouse she had on. Did you notice it?" And so it goes on. Never mind my skills, my sense of dress is the next thing that is under attack.

People love to tell you how good everyone else is. You wouldn't dream of going into a restaurant and asking to see the Chef to tell how much you had enjoyed the food then advising him that as a matter of fact your favourite restaurant was the one next door. "Have you tried their food?" "You must, their prawn dish is to die for". No I don't suppose you would ever dream of doing this, unless of course you wanted to wear their meal. Most people would never dream of being so rude. That is unless it is to comment on Mediumship abilities. Unfortunately as it is your skills that are on show, it is part of the territory.

On one occasion a mother and daughter approached me after a service to thank me for their message they had received from her husband and dad and how grateful they were to hear from him. Then went on to say it had been extra special today as it was the anniversary of his passing. They then went on to tell me how impressed they were with my Mediumship and the accuracy of the evidence. Mom then leaned on the wooden surround of the platform and with a very serious air about her and a knowing look, asked me if I had ever seen such and such a Medium (her name eludes me, but not the incident)! "No" I replied. "Well do", mom said with an edge of certainty in her voice, as she straightened herself up, as if to add weight to her words "she is our firm favourite and she is wonderful. Isn't she?" she said to turning to her daughter for support. Her daughter nodded in agreement. She is over in America at the moment and is coming back soon. A wonderful Medium, she added. "Anyway, must be off now and thanks again for the message", at that they walked away. I just stood and smiled.

On another occasion a President of a church asked if I was coming to a 'Special', to see another Medium perform and did I want to buy a ticket?

Now I rarely go to church when I am not working. Why? With a full time job, a family to care for, churches to serve three times a week, a development group at Wolverhampton once a fortnight and my book writing, I rarely have time for me. So when I am not working I stay at home and have 'me' and family time. "No" I replied I wouldn't be buying a ticket, as I was a little too busy. "Oh you should come" she raved "he is marvellous, wonderful Medium. Do you know he is the best I have ever seen" "Is he staying for the Sunday service?" I enquired. "Oh no, he's much to busy to do that. Sorry you're not coming and don't forget if anyone asks you, tell them how good he is". I promised I would. I put the phone done and smiled to myself, only in spiritualism would you say that and not think it was an insult to the other person, but that's spirituality. People don't mean to offend, it just happens.

Each Medium works differently. I believe it would be extremely boring if everyone worked exactly the same way. There is some truth to the saying, variety is the spice of life, and Mediumship is no exception. I have always worked the same, I am given either a relationship, i.e. mom, dad, brother, sister, husband or wife - or a name. It is really odd how this works, but it seems to. It also keeps people interested as once their link has been established, they know they will get a message and I will return to them later. I have spend many a moment panicking that I wouldn't receive this information and sometimes I am actually standing explaining how I work before I am given the information. But I have learnt over the years to trust and stand up with the faith that they will come through, as they always do. But this was not the case in the early days.

My first experience of working a platform was through the Exponents Course. The first year was all based at Oldbury Spiritualist Centre. A tiny church set in the town of Oldbury. The course was made up of guest speakers offering their experience and advice on a multitude of subjects, which usually revolved around the core topics, which were prayer, philosophy or
Mediumship. These would be laid on interchangeably, between mini services, where we would take turns to stand on a 'real platform' and practice our skills.

In the second year we were let loose in the churches and the same again in year three. At the end of the three years we passed or failed. Fortunately I passed, but without anything to show for this, no recognised qualification or certificate, just the knowledge you had passed and your name being forwarded to other churches advising them you were a newly qualified Medium. Still in hindsight I wouldn't exchange this experience for anything, not even a certificate, as it taught me an awful lot. I didn't think that at the time, and like many people who completed the course, before and since, we had a fair share of moans and groans. But on reflection it was and is a wonderful opportunity for any aspiring Mediums.

When I took to the platform during the course, it was nerve-racking, but we were students. Wherever we appeared it would be advertised as second or third year students, so the churches didn't expect much as such off us, as they did the 'qualified' Mediums. In fact one title bestowed upon us was 'fledglings'.

Congregations can be quite merciless, but we were often met with a sea of smiles and an air of benevolence as if they were doing us a favour by coming to the church that night.

The first time I stepped onto the platform in my own right was a different story. I cannot describe the angst I felt and the thousand thoughts that went through my mind the night I made my debut at Walsall. Thanks to all the exposure my 'publicist' Val had given me, I was asked by Walsall Church to cover a cancellation. With several weeks notice, my name was duly added to the calendar of forthcoming Mediums. This felt very onerous. I felt as if my future as a Medium hung in abeyance, my pride most certainly did. After I put the phone down from the booking secretary, having accepted without a second thought, the reality hit me. What if nobody turned up? What if no-one came through? My goodness what if no-one came through, because there was no-one sitting in the congregation! Or I dried up after a few minutes, what would I do, as the service was due to last over an hour! Or what if only one or two turned up? These negative thoughts flowed with amazing ease, as I tried to rationalise the whole situation. Believe me the lack of people, is a real possibility. Congregations can be quite fickle and factions with stay away on an evening if they think the Medium will be no good. I was beside myself. After ringing everyone I could think of, several times, to share my fears, the closer the event came the worse I felt.

After barely sleeping the night before, I prepared to meet my fate. The Grim Reaper himself might just as well have been walking behind me that day, because no amount of cajoling could alleviate my fears.

Several changes in my outfit later, we set off, with lots of time to spare, David very cannily removing one obstacle, before it could arise, which was the possibility of being late. So with David driving and I sitting alongside him feigning everything from an attack of the vapours to a chronic illness. We arrived with plenty of time to spare. Once inside I paced the floor like a caged animal. "Would you like a cup of tea", the Chairperson kindly asked. Cup of tea - it might as well be sand; I couldn't swallow properly, let alone drink. "No, I'm fine", I said with all the composure I could muster. "Are you sure you don't want to go and sit in the Mediums' room", enquired the booking secretary? I was like a caged animal, as I kept walking aimlessly around the back room. "No, thanks" I replied. To this day I still don't go into the quiet rooms, laid aside for the Mediums. I have to move around. As soon as I prepare myself I feel the energy surge through me.   Until I start to work I find it difficult to contain or control it and need to keep moving around in order to manage the feelings. I often feel like a great sports person who has charged themselves for the psychical performance of their life. Bend over the starting block, waiting for the power surge to take them first over the finishing line.

"Ready when you are" called the President. I walked onto that platform like a condemned woman. Edward introduced me to the congregation. I nervously looked around there were around thirty people present. My first potential crises had passed my fears unfounded. There were certainly enough people to whom to give messages. This was an evening of clairvoyance, with less content than a Divine Service, so there is an expectation you will give more messages. As I sat composing myself, I tried not to think about the service.

My next great feat was to make the connections. While the introductions were being made I sat in complete stillness, and in my mind said. 'You have got me into this mess, now you get me out of it'.   A lovely sense of calm came over me, the surging energy was still present within me, but I felt centred, controlled and calm enough to be able to work. I was off. I stood up from the chair, walked to the front of the platform and worked my little heart out.

In total I gave 12 good quality messages.   Several no's were challenged with further information from the spirit world. When presented in this different form the person could take it. The first person I went to was, unbeknown to me, a member of the Committee. "You can take a woman in spirit?" "I can take several" came the reply. Focused and unfazed I continued. "You have both mom and dad in spirit?", "Correct" came the reply. "Dad passed before mom", "correct" "you are one of five and sit fourth in the line, with one sister younger than you", "yes" the recipient responded, with a smile spreading across his face. As with all first time Mediums to a church I was being assessed. If I was good I would be booked again. If not, they would discretely lose my number. The smile said it all.   "You can take the name Andrew", I said. "No", came the reply, undeterred I sent the 'no' flowing back to my guides, in a flash further evidence was received.   "You would have worked on building sites when you were in your early twenties" I added, "yes I did", came the reply; you could see the uncertainty of where this was going.   "Andrew would have been a friend of yours from this time?" "Yes he was", came the rather shocked reply. After this there was no stopping me. I finished the link, with a series of other names, dates and towns.

Clearing his throat loudly to gain my attention, Edward called me to time. What appeared 10 minutes, was in fact one hour and ten minutes. In that time I had given 12 good messages, with very few no's. Not bad for my premiere performance. I walked off the platform on cushions of air. I was elated. I knew now, once I had done it on my own, I could do it again. I also knew no other service would make me feel the way I did that for night.

It is difficult to understand the driving forces that keep a Medium going back for more. You certainly don't do it for the money or the thanks;

while people are grateful, it is not the kind of task you do for gratitude. It is much too like hard work to do it for this reason alone. But something does drive you on, otherwise you would fall at the first hurdle. The satisfaction comes from within. There is nothing more gratifying than to see the tears of joy the messages can bring to people. None more so than one night at a spiritual church in Ward End.

I had given off several messages when I came to the left side of the church, within ten minutes I had three people in tears, these were tears of joy, not tears of pain. I went to the first person and gave them a child in spirit. "This is your daughter I have here", I said. "That's correct" answered the young mom. "She has come because today is a special day" Mom could not contain herself, her face crumpled and the tears cascaded down her face. "She is telling me you placed a small teddy in the coffin", mom nodded, through her tears. Throughout the message mom held my gaze, her eyes never left mine. "She has three brothers", more nods and she is giving me the names, Ben, Paul and Claire, "her brothers and sister", came the reply. The message continued for a little while longer. I then thanked her and moved onto the next link. As I glanced back at this young mom, she sat silently drying her eyes, with a lovely smile spread across her face, despite her tears you could feel her joy.

I went to the woman sitting directly behind her, a young woman in her early thirties. "I have your father here with you", I said. I then went on to describe a man of medium build, who would have lost a lot of weight before he passed over, from cancer, which had spread into his liver. Sometimes it is a small comment that does not appear to be of any significance, but to the receiver it hits a cord. This is exactly what happened here. "He tells me you have his nose", she smiled and nodded and the tears began to flow down her cheeks. "You were exceptionally close and still miss him, even though he has been over a while", I said. At this point she was unable to speak, just nod in agreement. As I continued someone kindly handed her a tissue and she sat dabbing her eyes. "He's giving me the name Emma", "My daughter" came the reply, as she continued to wipe the flowing tears "And Carol", "That's me" she said. He then went on tell her he knew about her recent relationship break up and he was trying to support her, at this difficult time. "God Bless", she thanked me as I moved away from her. I then moved farther back towards the rear of the church and the most peculiar thing happened. I saw this gentleman in my head as plain as anything. I recognised him instantly, not long ago he had chaired for me at this very church. I leaned across and asked the Chairperson if this was correct. He nodded. Les came through with all the vigour he had shown in life. A man who, through his healing, had helped hundreds of people in the church, he had fought a brave fight against the cancer he was determined to beat. He had too much left to do in life, he once told me philosophically. Now here he was chatting away to me through my third eye.

He had come to speak to both his wife and daughter, who were sitting at the back in the congregation. Both cried tears of joy as he gave message after message, names, streets, birthdays, conditions etc., he finished by apologising to his wife for leaving her. They had only been married a short a time, but the strength of the love he had for her and his daughter was amazing. I was sad when it was time for me to let this link go. But I did in the comfort this man would continue to come through. He would continue in death as he had in life, helping others.

Now when you are working from the platform you are juggling so many different things. You are trying to receive the information and pass it on accurately without corrupting or distorting it. When the recipient cannot accept this, you are trying to receive more information and clarification. Sort out the messages, ignore or separate double links, while all the time trying to looking amenable to the audience, is not an easy feat at the best of times. Sometimes you don't always pick up other family members, especially if they are not sitting together. Unfortunately you are far too busy to be able to even think other members of the family may be near by.

On one occasion I had made several links, including a husband for a very young woman sitting at the back of the church and an older woman sitting at the front. I began talking to the woman at the front of the church and gave quite an unusual medical condition as being a contributory factor to this gentleman's death, which was listed on his death certificate. You could see this woman, who was in her mid-sixties, searching her memory, trying to remember exactly what had appeared on the death certificate. Suddenly from the back of the church, I heard two voices in unison, with raised tones telling me that was correct. For a moment I was a little puzzled, which must have shown in my face, as they quickly told me they were both his daughters. One of whom was the younger woman who I had just given a husband to, and had promised to return shortly.

I jokingly asked if they had fallen out, all these laughed and explained they all sat with their own friends. I then switched communicator, briefly and began to bring her own husband through. I told her they had argued quite badly before he died. If fact they had said many cross words. He had then passed in an accident and she was left living with the guilt. "That's correct" she said. I also told her he used to smoke and when he passed he still had 14 cigarettes in his packet, she confirmed this was also correct. In fact I told her she still had his lighter. This man then spent several minutes trying to ease her guilt, with words of comfort and explaining he was as much to blame as she was and he was very sorry he went over before they could sort out their differences. You could physically see the difference this made to her. It would take a long time for this guilt to fade, but at least he was trying to ease it for her. He finished by saying he was over there with her dad. He was telling me they didn't get on while they were on the earth plane together, but they are getting on fine now. In fact they passed very closely together and are looking after each other. Her whole face light up,

The world of spirit is in many ways, all seeing and all knowing. They often know what is required. Time and time again I have been proved to be wrong.

On one occasion I had been communicating to a man who was both father and husband to two ladies who always used to sit at the back of the church together. His evidence was astounding and delivered at breakneck speed. It really was a pleasure talking to him. Every time I went to the church, he was sure to come through and as much as I tried to ignore him, I couldn't. If I did try he would just go and stand behind the person I was linking with, not saying anything, just standing still, waiting for me to notice him. His messages always brought lots of laughter. I think sometimes out of embarrassment, because he would hog the limelight. I had chatted with him for several minutes thanked him for coming through and tried to move on. Apart from the initial link, everything I gave the woman to the side of these two women, she couldn't take, but Tina and her mother could. "I have your mother here", 'that's correct" she replied. " She would be quite pushy and would say it, as it was", "no" she replied. Tina and her mom put their hands back up, "that sounds like my mother in law", said Tina's mom. "God bless and thank you", I bowed slightly to them and smiled. I returned back to the other lady, and the same happened again. "This lady loved pigs' trotters", "no" the lady said, shaking her head in disgust at the thought of this kind of food. Back came the reply from Tina and her mom, "I think you are still with us", they both chorused again. I apologised to the woman, "I will try once more, then if not I will have to come back to you later" I said, quite apologetically, she smiled and nodded. She knew me well enough to know I would come back. The same happened again, I was just about to move away, but this gentle lady had other thoughts. She may have been quiet, but she had a will of iron. I was just about to move onto my next connection, when in a flash I had a budgie. "You can understand a budgie?" "Yes", came the reply. "This budgie was yellow", she nodded. "It once laid an egg, but nothing came of it, because it hadn't been fertilised"? "Yes, that's right", she said, nodding her head, as if recalling this herself for the first time, in a long time. I stopped and placed my hands on my hips and said "I cannot believe I am giving a message from a budgie", laughter rippled through the church. Still I kept being given information about the budgie. The woman receiving the message was also laughing. "He liked trill and cuttle fish to sharpen and clean his beak". She nodded, smiling from ear to ear "and he had a little blue mirror". A woman at the back, very dryly said, "He has all the mod cons this budgie doesn't he?" The church was in uproar everyone was laughing. Me? I laughed along with them. Why I don't know, I was convinced I was killing my own career. I have to say as everyone was enjoying themselves so much that night, it didn't matter.

The rest of the service was full of laughter and several people came up and thanked me for a wonderful evening. Several months later, even at other churches people were still coming up to me saying how they had laughed all the way home and it was the best night they had had for as long as they could remember. But one person in particular really stood out. Nearly twelve months after the event, she told me it was her first night in the church that night. She had taken the death of her brother, two months before that night, very badly and was at one of the lowest ebb's in her life.

By the time she arrived at the church she was desperate. I had not only brought her brother through and given her evidence I could not have possibly known, including where he died and how he died, his age and the names of nearly all the close family. I had made her laugh. For the first in months she had actually laughed. For her this was the turning point, in her recovery from her brother's death. Each time I see her she reminds me of this night and what it did for her. So do other people, who still look back, several years on, with fondness of this event. Laughter is a wonderful tool, how true are the words;

'Smile and the world smiles with you
Cry and you cry alone.'

Laughter certainly lifted a lot of people's moods that night, as it did many other times.

As a Medium I work quite quickly which can be a little disconcerting for the recipient who very quickly, have to try and work out whether these barrage of names have any real meaning to them, especially if I am firing one after the other in quick succession. Most of the time I do try to take this into consideration, although I don't always notice the impact the words are having on an individual.

Medway is a lively church in Derbyshire, which is always well attended, with a wide variety of events laid on for the congregation, several times a week. The evening of Mediumship had gone extremely well and the evidence had been strong and varied, with very few no's. At one point I heard Pirelli calendar, so I just gave it off, to a woman in her late forties, sitting at the back if the church. "Yes", came the reply, "I used to model for them", which was not the answer I was expecting. I moved across to the other side of the church, a father had come through shortly after his passing and given evidence to both his daughter and his wife. From the looks on their faces, this was obviously just what they needed.

Towards the end of the service, the spirit helpers, showing no signs of flagging, I began to make my final connections. I moved to a lady in her early fifties, sitting alone. "You have a father in spirit". "Yes", she replied. "He is giving me connections with the police force", again she accepted the information. "You can understand a special". "Yes", she replied, "he was one". I went on to tell her he loved to watch any programme on the police. As he watched he would sit and complain if it was technically inaccurate. "He would state under section so and so, you couldn't do that. That's an offence under the Traffic Act and so he would go on and on, through the whole programme. It got to the point where no-one could concentrate on the programme for his interruptions". A huge smile came across her face as she remembered this and she was nodding and laughing as I regaled her father's habits, his likes and dislikes.

I then went to the two ladies who were sitting together, directly behind this woman. One lady was the daughter from a first marriage and the other lady was her mother, who had recently lost her second husband. "This man tells me he has been over quite a while", I said. Holding my gaze she shook her head. "No he hasn't been over very long". Her daughter leaned towards her and whispered to her. "Your first husband, my dad is in the spirit world". The lady listened nodding, then returned her gaze to me. "Oh yes, I can take that, I had forgotten about him", she said with a big grin. At which point the church burst into laughter, not at her, with her. "Shall I call them number one and two", they laughed even more. Her first husband then went on to say she had a hint of ginger in her hair, trying to be polite I stated "Who was a bit ginger", the audience giggled. The woman looked puzzled and shook her head. A gentle tap from her daughter reminded her, the shaking of the head was replaced by an affirmative nod. My downfall came when I tried to explain I didn't mean to sound ginger-phobic, but he had used the term ginger, not auburn. This did nothing to quell the crowd who laughed even harder. My comment that my partner was once ginger, did nothing to quieten them down. The names began to flow between the tears of laughter. The final name was Dick, "can you take a Dick", I said, in all innocence? This brought the house down. With peels of laughter, the service came to an end. As I glanced around the congregation, many were still drying their eyes and trying to suppress their laughter as we moved onto the serious business of church notices.

When I came off the platform someone explained that there had been some recent controversy with the word ginger and it had been used as a derogatory name for homosexuals. There are some times when you wish you spent more time keeping abreast with up-to-date news stories. It can certainly save you a lot of trouble.

Views & Opinions of the World

I believe this world is not meant to be perfect. Life is not meant to be perfect, if it were would one learn or experience through our journeys in a perfect world? The imperfections of our world help us to define what is right and what is wrong. Each time we enter into a new situation we have freedom of choice to decide what we believe is right and what we believe is wrong. There are no rights or wrongs. It is simply for us to decide and determine what we believe to be right and what actions we believe are wrong. It is these decision-making processes, which help us to develop and expand our own belief systems.

We all have our own views and opinions of the world. Mine changed slightly when I visited Bali in 2003. I arrived at this wonderful island full of beauty, in its buildings, people and scenery. Then I saw an island racked with poverty, where most of the people barely scrape a living. A situation made worse by the bombing, which had all but destroyed the tourist trade. Something the Island relied heavily upon to make their meagre living.

In this spiritual land I developed the view that God held Utopia in his hands and then scattered it across the planet and from that moment there is no one place where you will capture Utopia. You will find places where you feel it is almost perfect, you will see fragments of it everywhere you go. But nowhere contains the perfect world. If it did, we would all live there and what an over-crowded imperfect place it would be.

The whole family became intrigued with Bali after my brother worked there for a while. He fell in love with the island. In fact the whole of Indonesia and for the last twelve years has spent every holiday out there in this fascinating country. He began exporting wood carvings in the early 1990's, directly from the carvers. After the bombing I watched my brother through his little
enterprise, stimulating a little section of the economy on the island. It was almost as if there was some karmic link which had brought Mel to this point and was driving him on to do what he was doing. Yet he seemed oblivious to his achievements. I decided he may not follow the same spiritual teachings as I did, but there was certainly some good spiritual work being done here, if only he knew it.

Shortly after returning from Bali, I left my place at work at Telford in Shropshire. Here I worked with some wonderful people, in a beautiful setting. Unfortunately after my immediate Manager left, I found the constraints of working in a newly formed PCT too much and I spread my wings and moved to work at Sandwell and West Birmingham NHS Trust. Leaving my friends at Telford was one of the hardest decisions I have had to make regarding a work place, and nearly four years on I still miss them.

So I moved from Telford in leafy Shropshire, with a skyline dominated by the ever present Wrekin hill, to City Hospital in Birmingham, dominated by the view of Winson Green prison, there was no comparison really. It was certainly a culture shock and nothing in my life so far had prepared me for this. City Hospital is over 100 years old, set in one of the poorest parts of the region, yet it is full of good kind people.

I had over the years ostracised myself from people by my beliefs. For those who don't believe or don't understand Mediumship or a psychic ability, these skills do not win you friends. It can in fact isolate you, as some people become unsure of you, afraid you have developed some extra-sensory skills which mean you can read the minds and thoughts of those around you. And what do we do when we are afraid of something? We defend ourselves against whatever we perceive to be a threat. They shun you because they are afraid or offended by what you can do or what they conceive you can do.

Believe me, over the years I have heard all the excuses and justifications for the personal attacks to which as a Medium you can become subjected. I decided long ago that despite our 'modern outlook' in society and our acceptance of different religions, it is often all religions, excluding spiritualism. Despite its long history in this country, it is one of the least understood. I also made my mind up that Mediumship and psychic abilities had their place in this world, but certainly not in my working environments. Having been badly burnt in the past, I decided I wouldn't advertise my abilities. I would keep my evening activities to myself.

I have never gone around broadcasting what I do, but at the same time I have never hidden it. This time I decided to not mention at all. Hindsight is a wonderful thing and perhaps I should have taken into consideration that firstly I have a very unusual name, so I am rarely mistaken for someone else. Secondly, as I serve many of the local spiritualist churches, and there are lots of spiritualists in the NHS, a lot of people knew anyway, so really there was no point. Word spread quite quickly and although very few people actually mentioned it to me, they used to approach my colleagues.

In the early days, in complete dismay, as I looked at the area, with its run down buildings, I threw the question into the stratosphere. What on earth am I doing here? The reply was almost instantaneous. I was told I was here to help those would not ordinarily be reached through the normal channels, such as a spiritualist church. Now as I had decided to try and hide my gift, this was going to prove to be rather difficult. How could I help people if they didn't know what I did? We reached a pact. Give me a sign, if they mention anything out of the ordinary, such as telling me they had lost a loved one, or they wish some how they could hear from a deceased relative or friend, then I would respond. This was the agreement and I felt sure I was on pretty safe ground. Believe me you would be surprised how many times people opened conversations with me telling me how they had lost a loved one and were struggling with life. Then they would say 'they didn't I know why they were telling me' and would go on to apologise. Eyes upturned I would cast a glance up and reveal my true gift. The next ten minutes would be history as I gave out words of comfort through messages from their loved ones. At the same time I heard wonderful stories of help and guidance from the other side, which people in churches would have given their hind-legs to have such a venture. But I will come onto that later.

On one occasion I bumped into someone with whom I had being doing some work. We exchanged pleasantries then he went on to explain he was a little down because he was leaving early that day to go to his Nephew's funeral and he had never got over the death of his mother. "Reg are you telling me all this because you know I am a Medium?" I enquired. "No, I didn't know" he said. He then went on to tell me how hard his mother's death had hit him. Without further prompting I went on to tell him his Nephew was fine and his nan and Granddad had been waiting to take him over. I described how he had died following a car accident and all the other occupants had survived. I told him, his nephew had been trapped in the car for 40 minutes. I described his personality, how he liked to spent time in his room, and what his room looked like. I then went on to bring his mother through, while standing on the tarmac on a dull and dreary day. He thanked me profusely and I sent him on his way beaming from ear to ear, with a message for his sister and brother-in-law from their son. As I glanced back at Reg I couldn't help noticing he appeared a lot happier and more settled after I left him than when I bumped into him. With an ability I have fine-tuned over the years, I swiftly shifted from Medium to NHS employee and carried on with my work, switching my mind from the ethereal to assessments and reports.

As time moved on I began to receive phone calls and emails, which often started with "You don't know me, but some-one has mentioned your name, can I come and see you?" On one occasion I was approached by a Manager who asked if I could help one of her staff. Her mother had passed away recently and while Jenny had returned to work she was in pieces. Jenny was not a religious person and had no real opinion on life after death. Prior to the death of her mother, Jenny hadn't really lost anyone really close to her, apart from her nan, who had passed when she was a child. Despite having no views and not really understanding Mediumship she agreed to see me. As soon as I began to give her the evidence, she began to cry tears of joy. "You have a veranda?" I enquired, she burst out laughing, "That's what my mother called my conservatory!" she replied. "You have recently cleared out her flat and hung onto too much junk", I said. "I have", she replied, "I couldn't bear to get rid of anything. "You have one son who has been supportive and two brothers. This crisis has brought you closer together, you were closer to one brother, but now you are all three pulling together to help each other". Jenny nodded her head in confirmation "This is so true" she said. She told me her one brother had for several years stood apart from the family, but her mother's illness and death had changed all that. "Your mother is telling me you no longer want to come to work, but work has been your 'life' for quite a few years." Jenny nodded in agreement. "She is telling me it is walking through the main entrance where you are struggling?" "That's right, I cannot get it out of my head. This is the entrance they brought my mother in through, when she came into hospital. She came in, but never came out". Jenny said, hanging her head, as she

58

recalled how the entrance made her feel. She went on to say, she really didn't know what to do, but it was clear she was struggling with the daily task of facing this door. As there was no other way into her department, Jenny was facing a real dilemma. "Your mother is saying it will get better in time and you must be brave and stick at. She was adamant." The Jenny that entered my office that lunchtime, was a different Jenny who left half an hour later. I saw Jenny and her brothers several times before they were able to face the world without a little re-assurance from the other side. Now whenever I see her, you can see the sadness in her eyes, but she has comfort knowing her mother is close to her. In fact she has developed the ability herself to hear and communicate with her mother, whenever she feels the need.

I began a lucrative business in my lunch hour, well I would have had I charged for my services, but I didn't. It didn't feel right to charge; I had no expenses, so I never did. In my mind I began a web of giving, as Val had given so freely and the Spiritualist churches had given so cheaply, I also gave back. I would like to think in time, I have contributed to a web of giving; where people pay in or give back to society, not for cost or material gain, but merely, because they can. I have over they years watched the web grow, as other's have given back into this web. Why? Because they can. Because they received something from someone at a time in their lives when they really needed it. But more importantly, it was given as a gift, without any kind of payment. This doesn't lessen the value merely nurtures a desire to also give something out, without requiring a reward of any kind, apart from knowing you too have helped another as you were helped when you needed it. I have in time watched the web grow and grow and I hope it will always continue to expand. Not everybody can afford to give their services for free, but sometimes, just a little bit of time, patience or a listening ear is all people need.

I would like to think over the years, my very presence in my places of work has brought comfort and healing to lots of people who would never step through the doors of a spiritualist church, would not have received it, had I not been in post.

You can always tell the ones I have helped, because regardless of rank or position within the Trust, they usually wave from the far side of car park.

Now there is truth in the saying 'what you give out, so shall you receive' and over time they have always tried to help me back in return. This is not favours up and above what anyone could expect, it is to offer help and assistance with understanding and kindness.

Over the years I have spent several years working in different hospitals or in community settings. While it is never my intention to use my psychic skills in my 'normal' working life, you would be surprised the number of times I have utilised it, sometimes with people's knowledge, sometimes without. Although I have to say, the only time I have or will use it without people's knowledge is to utilise healing power or positive energy. I am not a healer and don't credit myself with this title, as I haven't received any training. Neither do I have any desire to, my hands are full with my own work. But what I have done on several occasions is allow myself to be used as a channel, to give positive energy to someone.

One occasion was for a gentleman, who had Motor Neurone Disease MND. He had deteriorated very rapidly and was now unable to talk or move unaided. He was in fact completely immobile and while he couldn't talk the light in his eyes made you very conscious that this dignified man understood everything that was going on around him. His wife had coped exceptionally well, up until this point. She was adamant she wanted to continue to care for this man, but physically was finding it almost impossible to do. Furthermore he was agitated and waking several times during the night wishing to use the commode. As he was totally immobile the task of lifting him on and off was proving too much for this young elegant 60 year old woman.

My role was to provide the necessary equipment and advice to try and help both support and ensure his wife could continue to manage to look after him at home. As I demonstrated the equipment and showed the wife how to move her husband, I had a strong urge to place my hand on his shoulder. As I was standing behind him as he sat in a wheelchair, I could quite easily manage this, without drawing attention to what I was doing. This I duly did for several minutes, as I chatted to the wife. I felt a wonderful vibration surge down my arm and pass into this man's frail body through my hand, and I continued to chat with wife as if nothing was happening. When I removed my hand I moved to the front of the wheelchair to take off the footplates, when he caught my eye. He looked into my eyes and for the first time since my arrival over an hour since, his facial expression changed. He smiled a very knowing smile. At some level he had known what I had done and gave me a wonderful smile of approval.

Over the next week I stayed in contact with the wife, who told me he was a changed man. The agitation had left him and he was now sleeping through the night. She put it down to the knowledge they had the equipment and both knew they could move him, if necessary. I never visited again, but I did hear via the District Nurses, he had passed away a couple of months after my visit, peacefully, in his sleep, still being cared for at home by his wife. I gave a silent 'thank you' to those above.

I hadn't set out to do anything other than my paid job, but the occupants of the spirit world had obviously thought otherwise. They will use any opportunity they can to give us help on this side. On this occasion I didn't mind, as long as they didn't expect it too frequently.

On another occasion, in the distant past, I was in 'Resus' in the Accident and Emergency Department, carrying out assessments, which involved observing staff. This was one of the last places for us to visit that morning. It felt as it I had been on my feet for ages, despite having good quality flat shoes. I couldn't help thinking I would be glad to get back to the office in order that I could get off my aching feet. Just as I was about to depart a patient arrived, a man in his 60's, who had suffered a major heart attack. As the trolley was rapidly pushed in I became aware that a man was walking alongside the trolley, closely followed by a lady wearing a head scarf, with a shopping bag in her hand. I soon realised that the man accompanying the trolley was in fact the man who was lying on it. I strongly suspected this man was not going to survive.

I have over the years been involved in the care of the terminally ill and felt the presence of their souls, external to the patient. But I had never seen one so clearly walking alongside his body before. Despite the brave efforts of the staff in the Unit, who deployed all their skills to bring this man back, they appeared to be losing the battle, although I wasn't there to see the end result. The staff were still working away on this gentleman as we left. Just before we left, I felt a strong urge to send this man positive energy. So from where I stood I visualised a huge cloud of blue energy descending over this man and slowly wrapping around him and sinking through him. As my time had finished I silently walked away not knowing the outcome.

I was intrigued to see if he had survived, as I could see him (in my mind's eye of course), outside his body, I strongly suspected he had not survived. Unable to understand what was happening he had stayed close by his body. Not knowing what to do, he had merely followed his body as it was taken to Casualty. Now I was in a quandary. I could not walk back down the Unit and ask or call to see how he was, as it was none of my business. All I could do was accept the situation, that on this occasion I wouldn't know the outcome. Besides I consoled myself, if it was in my interests to know the outcome, the world of spirit would find a way of letting me know. They are far more resourceful than we realise. In the comfort of that thought, I forgot about the incident.

It would appear on this occasion it was in my interests to know the outcome. Within 2 days I was called to the Mortuary, to deal with another issue. As I walked into the main area of the Mortuary there, attached to the wall was a huge white board with the names of all the occupants of the 'fridges. As I walked past the board one name caught my eye and appeared, for all the world, to jump out at me. I knew it was the man from Resus. I casually asked if they had received anyone from A&E, last Friday. "Yes" replied The Technician, as he waved his hand to towards the name on the board. Which, incidentally was the same name that had caught my eye when I walked in, ten minutes ago. Despite there being another 32 names on the board!

As I walked back to the office I thought about the situation. I was glad I happened to be in Casualty at the right time and was able to send this man healing thoughts. I have always understood healing is not always about curing, and can be used in many ways. On this occasion it had been harnessed to help in his progression across the other side. I had also done my best to comfort him and point out his mother to him and why she had come.

As I walked and thought about the circumstances surrounding this man, I suddenly felt his presence alongside me. Although he was a much fitter and happier man than I had met before. "Thank you for what you did for me he said". "My pleasure", I replied in my head. "Glad I could help", I added. "You really did" he said. As quickly as he arrived he suddenly disappeared. I felt sorry for his family, to have lost some-one so young, but I consoled myself in the fact I couldn't change the situation, but at least I had been able to help this man on his journey home. What was he doing here? Like many people who have passed over, he had no connection with the place he died at. So why would he be here? I believe, as spirits, once we have passed over, we stay close to our families and friends, until we feel able to leave them. I believe a single thought is all it takes for our spirit family to coming to our sides. Unlike us here on earth, when someone needs us we have to physically travel, a spiritual being can cover great distance in a split second. Why would or should he come to me? Normally there does have to be a 'love' connection to reach someone in the spiritual world. But on this occasion he had merely dropped in to say thank you. As we wouldn't normally speak to strangers here, so nothing changes when we pass over.

I don't believe that under normal circumstances we can reach people with whom we have no connection, which is why I am a little reticent when someone tells me they have been chatting to a deceased super-star. Why would they want to come and talk to 'Joe Public'; I'm not sure they would. So why was this patient keen to talk to me? Simply to say thank you. Although I strongly suspect the spirit world were looking at the wider picture. By showing me, through a little 'thank you', that my efforts were worthy and did do some good, would ensure I would continue to occasionally give some healing.

So it was quite worthwhile for me to meet this man in this way. I don't feel he was hanging around the Mortuary. He simply popped in at an opportune moment when, after seeing his name, he knew I would realise exactly who it was saying 'thank you' to me.

On another occasion we had finished training and despite being physically tired we had to tidy up for the next session, which would begin early in the morning. On of the candidates had stayed on after all the others had left. I could see something was bothering her, but it was unclear what the problem was. Unbeknown to me, she was aware of my 'out-of-work skills'. For the brief moment we were alone she hesitantly asked if it was true that I was a Medium? I had to tell her, that yes, I was afraid it was true, I did have Mediumistic skills. She looked at me, then looked away, biting her lip, as if to muster the strength to ask me something. I spared her the agony and gently led her to a small quiet room off the training facility.

Sarah was a professional woman, with an air of confidence about her, quiet with a lovely disposition, tall thin and elegant with long well maintained straight brown hair. Throughout the training she had either stayed quiet or had gently tried to support the other candidates. Once we were alone I gently enquired what I could do for her. "I've lost my dad and wanted to know if he is okay she said", biting her lip, in an effort to maintain her cool composure. "He is fine", I told her. I then went on to describe him. "He is a very tall thin man, who would be quite an intelligent gentleman, who loved to read the paper and he is standing right next to you". I described what he did for a living and gave a few names. I then felt this man become very serious. "He is telling me to tell you to use the money. Do you understand?" I asked. She nodded through her tears and began to look away from me staring out of the window, as she bit her bottom lip. "He is also telling me there is some issue around you regarding a child", I said "and I feel as if there is a great longing. Are you trying for a child?" "Yes that's correct" she said. "Well I have to tell you there is a child waiting for you in the spirit world and this child is going to come to you, by hook or by crook. But I have to tell you the time is not right yet, you must be patient" I then went on to bring lots of information for her from her father. I finished by reminding her to be patient and know that a child would come her way. Sarah looked physically relieved by my comments. She dried her eyes and thanked me for the information. She went on to say she and her husband had been trying for a child for 12 years. They had encountered let-down after let-down. She had recently had IVF treatment which had proved to be unsuccessful. She never discussed her childless plight with her father. Now they were faced with the prospect of paying for their treatment, but they were in a quandary, did they use the money left in the will or did they take out a loan, or did they throw in the towel? I could only really re-emphasise what her father had said, use the money and be patience and know there is a baby out there. Unfortunately the baby is going to come in its own time, not at the time dictated by the parents. As we spoke I felt positive this woman, before long, would be holding her own child. She thanked me again and although you could see she was still apprehensive, I hoped the words would bring comfort to her. The course had ended that day, after five days, which is why she had waited to speak to me. I wasn't to see Sarah again for nearly three years.

Our paths didn't cross again for a long time, then one windy day I was walking across the site, when I noticed a woman looking at me. She hesitated for a while, waiting for me to come closer. As I approached she said hello. I politely said hello back. "You don't remember me do you?" she enquired. She carefully watched my expression for signs of recognition in my face. I was stumped. I didn't recognise this woman at all. I had to admit I did not know who she was. "It's Sarah, I did a training course with you?" As soon as she mentioned training, it all fell into place and I recognised her immediately. Well nearly recognised her, she looked far more tired and care-worn than I had remembered. "Of course, how are you?" I enquired "I'm fine" she said, her head nodding to confirm, she really was fine. "Do you remember you gave me a message about a child?" "Yes", I replied "How did things work out?" I asked rather hesitantly. I do try to always have faith in the advice the spirit world gives out, but faced with the harsh reality of someone standing facing you, can sometimes shake my confidence. She looked at me and smiled, "he is 14 months old now", she beamed. The advice I had passed on from her father had been spot on – 'thank goodness for that' I thought. She then thanked me again and with a face full of sincerity told me I would never know how much my words had helped her that afternoon. I looked at her and smiled and simply said "I know", because

I did. On that afternoon, as she sat listening to me, I could feel the sheer helplessness of her situation. Here was a woman yearning for a baby and after years of trying, was finally losing hope of ever fulfilling that dream, and reaching the point when she was without hope. Then in a strange twist of fate, she happened to attend a course where she had overheard people talking about my psychic ability. While neither a believer nor non-believer the hopelessness of her situation had urged her on and from this she had found the courage to approach me. These strings of coincidence and Sarah's courage in approaching me, meant that the spirit world, through her father, were able give her assistance and guidance; but above all they gave her hope. Because we know when we lose hope we are in danger if losing everything.

As I walked away I smiled to myself. I turned to Sarah and casually threw a comment over my shoulder, "I shall include you in my book I said" as I walked away. "That's fine" she retorted. I hadn't the heart to tell her that no wonder I hadn't recognised her. Her long well cared for hair was replaced by a short bob and her elegant demure was replaced a frazzled look of a woman juggling motherhood and work. But more importantly, she oozed happiness.

Fred had worked in facilities nearly all his life. He had a wonderful sense of humour and the kind of personality that made you want to spend time talking to him. We had lunch together and over a coffee I had given him a message from both his mom and dad, which had really shocked him. Following this we became good work colleagues and Fred would always greet me with a warm smile. Following on from our coffee, I went to see a friend of Fred's and his wife Jean, who had lost her husband to cancer. While he had been over a couple of years, she was struggling to cope with life without him. Fred was extremely grateful for the time I spent with this family friend and apparently my visit had done her the world of good. It had been enough to help her move on, in the knowledge they would be together again one day and indeed the fact that he was just a thought away. She also understood from my visit that all that was required was a thought from her and this would bring him to her side.

I hadn't spoken to Fred for a while when suddenly I had the urge to call him. As our workload often overlapped, it was quite easy to make an excuse to speak to him. So I rang him and we discussed a pressing work issue. Suddenly I found myself telling him I needed to speak to his Wife - some-one I had never met. "Rather strange, you should say that" he said "because she is at home at the moment. We have been to a funeral". He went on to say, "I'm sure she would like to talk to you" and promptly gave me their home number. I duly called her. I needed no explanation. Once I said my name, Jean knew exactly who I was. I went on to tell her why I was calling, which was I had a strong desire to speak to her. What a marvellous woman - she merely took it in her stride. As I began to talk to her I quickly became aware of a man standing alongside me. While I worked with my usual confident manner, he came through rather differently, although I still managed to communicate with him, albeit very difficult. I told Jean this man was concerned about her daughter, who had taken this man's death quite badly. Jean acknowledged this was correct and he advised her to keep a careful eye on her. I felt he was telling me to tell her that he was okay and not to worry, but more importantly to tell her daughter that he was okay and he hadn't suffered during or after the accident. I duly passed on this information.

Keith was not easy to communicate with, rather than seeing in my third eye, everything I gave off I sensed, rather than saw. As I continued to give Jean information it suddenly dawned on me I knew this man. I recognised the energy. How? I don't know, I just did. Something prompted me to ask her his name. As soon as she said Keith, I knew why I recognised the energy. Keith was a very dear old friend of mine, from a long time ago. I felt physically thrown by this, but I duly continued and gave her the message. Here I was trying to calmly give a message to someone, while at the same time feeling terrible that Keith had passed over. This is the only time I have discovered someone I know has passed over, by giving someone else a message, and I hope it is the last. I was also amazed at the inter-connection of our lives, without actually realising it.

Fred didn't live far from me. It would appear we shared some of the same friends, but our paths had never crossed outside work before.

Karen happened to be in the office that day. Still quite shaken by the turn of events, I sat and told her what had happened.

Back in my office, I sensed Keith was close by. In fact everywhere I went for the remainder of my working day, I knew he was by my side. As I drove home that evening the feeling grew stronger. In the silence of the car I began to communicate with him. Yet, as before, this was not in the normal manner and I struggled to use 'sense' as a means of conversing. For most of the journey we conversed in this manner, yet all the time I puzzled as to why I was having so much difficulty in communicating with someone I had known quite well.

It suddenly dawned on me. He had not gone into the light. Keith had parted from his physical body, but he had not actually entered into the light. His death had happened very quickly and for some reason he had not left this plane. Now I understood why we both couldn't use the normal channels of communication - well normal for spiritual connections, that is. He was reliant on impressing a sensation on me, as a means of communicating. Had I not been a Medium, I doubt I would have understood what was happening. In fact had I not been urged to call Fred and then give his wife a message I very much doubt I would have sensed him around me at that moment. When I meditated yes I believe I would have sensed him, but not in paid work mode.

I then began to ponder the question. Had he or hadn't he passed through the light? A strong sense that there was an issue here swept over me. But sometimes practicalities take over. I had tea to cook. I would talk to Keith later.

Once tea was done and everyone settled I went to my meditation room. I sat and closed my eyes. I could still sense Keith was close to me. I decided to take the bull by the horns. 'Keith have you been into the light?' I asked. 'No' came the reply. 'Go into the light' I said. Again I sensed an emphatic, no. At the same time a feeling of fear spread over me. 'There is nothing to be afraid of' I urged 'go into the light. It is where you belong. You can come straight back. You will still be able to come and see everyone'. As I communicated with him, I urged him and implored a sense of urgency to go into the light. Each time I was met with a sense of fear and uncertainty. The more we talked the less fearful he felt. This exchange lasted around10 minutes, they slowly I felt him move towards the light, where I could sense a loving energy waiting to greet him, which felt like his grandfather. Then in a moment, he was gone. I pondered all evening had I done the right thing? I could only hope I had.

Life went on as usual, as it always does, and the next day I arrived at work as normal. No sooner was I through the door when Karen grabbed me, "Sandrea I have to tell you, your friend has not gone into the light". She continued, talking at the same speed as a bullet train. "After you left last night, I had this real urge to ring you as I drove home and tell you, he hadn't gone into the light and needed help". She went on, "But I decided to wait until we were together so I could help". I smiled and told her what had happened and how I doubted my instincts. She then explained how she had also had an overwhelming sensation that he had to go into the light. She did not want to frighten me so had waited for me to get into work to tell me. Soon after Keith came back very quickly and for quite a while stayed around me. I have yet to be given an opportunity to meet his family and give them a message from him. I know in time life will present me with the opportunity and I will be able to tell them that he is okay and still watching over them.

A Mother's Love

There is nothing more powerful on this earth than the feeling of love. To be able to love and feel loved. Within the scope of this wonderful emotion, there are many different types of loves. Without doubt the love of mother for her child has to be most powerful sensation we are capable of feeling.

On a par with this sensation is the pain we are capable of feeling when a mother, or indeed any parent, loses a child. For most of us, we never expect to be in this situation. Our grandparents and our parents die before us, but not our children. Unfortunately, for some they do.

For a Medium one of the hardest readings or messages to give, is to a mother who has lost her child.

Marjorie had called for a private reading in November 2004. She arrived at the house at 7.30 prompt. She was a woman in her early fifties, tall slim, attractive, well dressed and well composed. We settled down in my 'reading room' and I asked her to give me the relationship as to whom she wanted to talk. While I made my introductions she sat looking at her hands which were clasped together in her lap; she paused, as if checking her own emotions, then raised her head and looked directly into my eyes and said, "My son". He was by her side in an instant. As the reading progressed I described his personality, how he looked, his build hair colour etc. He went on to describe her work, then switched to his own career path. How he had changed jobs several times and how at last he had found a job he really enjoyed. He then rather hesitantly began to tell how he died. "This young man did not cope with life on this plane", I said. Marjorie nodded in agreement. Her focus kept shifting from me to the table, where her elbows were neatly folded. Her pain was impossible to hide, yet she remained composed.

I felt very unsure how to give off the next piece of information, in case I had misunderstood what he was telling me, or in case she hadn't known all the facts. I was wrong on both accounts. I gently began to approach the subject. "Mark had been using drugs?" After a sharp intake of breath, Marjorie sat for a moment with her eyes closed. As she slowly breathed out, she opened her eyes and nodded in agreement. "I believe this is heroin he is using". Marjorie nodded again.. "He is telling me he died from an overdose and you must understand he didn't mean to do it. It is so important you understand that mom" I repeated. Marjorie turned her head towards the walls as her eyes began to fill with tears.

"You are very angry with this man and he has bought shame on the family," I said, through her tears she nodded in agreement. I went on to tell her that the problem was no-one knew but her, his mom, that he was using heroin? Again she confirmed this was correct. "You are blaming yourself for this?" Yes, she nodded through the tears. "You had loaned him money, on many occasions" he is telling me. "You felt you had caused his addiction and his death?" She just nodded through the tears. "Mom it is not your fault, could you tell her please it was not her fault?" Mark repeated this several times.

He went on to explain the one thing that bothered him was the impact the whole situation was having on his mom.

Mark had come from a middle class background. For years there had been just the two of them. Mom had always worked, quite successfully to maintain their lifestyles, although the bond between them had always remained strong. At 25 he had left home, at 26 he had started using heroin recreationally. At 28 he was still holding down a job, but his continual financial difficulties highlighted that there was a problem. He had finally admitted to his mom that he was using drugs. Mark had promised to stop, and had kept his promise for over a month, until that fateful night. Then according to his message from the other side, influenced by his friends, he decided to have one last go - this was it and it proved to be his last. He died from the effect of contaminated heroin. It was hard to describe the mother's pain as she re-lived the whole event. What had made things even worse for her was the knowledge that she had given him some money that day. Probably the very money he had used to buy the drugs.

Mark had no excuse for his addiction. He came from a loving stable background. He had always appeared sensitive and had struggled with life in general. Unfortunately the drugs gave him what he had never managed to find on his own - peace. The drugs gave him a sense of safety and peace within, and it was this desire which had taken him back to heroin several times. During the reading he repeatedly told her she was not to blame, how much he loved her and how lucky he had been to have her for a mom. His quirky personality went on to describe some of the antics he had got up to when he was younger. She slowly began to smile then laugh as she remembered all these events. Some of which you could see she had clearly forgotten.

By the time the reading was over Marjorie was still smiling. You could see and feel how uplifted and elated she was by this experience. She left the house far happier than when she had arrived. No doubt the experience wouldn't last, who knows? But the reading with her son had given her hope, some relief and comfort to know his soul had lived on and if she wished to she could speak to him again. I doubted I would ever see this lady again. She was someone who didn't appear to have an interest in spiritualism or the after-life, just a mother looking for help, guidance and re-assurance that her son had lived on. The spirit world certainly achieved that on that particular evening.

We arrived at Bromsgrove Spiritualist Church on a bleak November evening. It is always easier to serve Churches when the Sun is shining! I glanced around the congregation. There were around 15 people in the Church. In the early stages I used to get upset when there was hardly anyone in the Church, believing no-one had come as they didn't want to see me! There is the ego within me rearing its ugly head. I had learnt over time, whoever was meant to be there would be there, this was nothing to do with me, I was merely the messenger.

So despite the size of the congregation I was quite uplifted, the smaller the size the larger the percentage of the congregation are likely to receive a message. The link for Matt came through quite early on, but it was towards the end of the service when I went back to his mom and dad to deliver the message. I could feel their burning need to speak to their recently departed son. Sometimes when anyone is desperate to speak to someone who has passed over, they can actually push them away, but not in this case, this lad was too strong to allow this. He came through with volumes of evidence, his condition, how he spent time in hospital and a series of names. "He is showing himself riding a bike" I said. Yes he had received a bike shortly before he died. He is showing me his legs? This bought amusement to both of them. He had lost a leg before he died. Mom and dad left the Church that evening, very happy people. Matt was my last link and the Service was drawing to a close. "Can I speak to you afterwards?" I asked. I arranged to see mom and dad at home.

Judging by their dress it was obvious money was not issue, but I had to insist on seeing them without payment. Matt wanted to give both his mom and dad a Christmas present as this was to be their first Christmas without him. I arranged to meet them both at my house the following week. Matt came through instantly. He was such a good communicator. He went on to chat to them for 45 minutes. They left happy and uplifted. He talked about his grand-parents, his bedroom, his brother's room and the food he liked and disliked. He described what his parents did for a living, including his mother's office and what his dad had done at work the previous day. Christmas would not be easy this year or for years to come, but at least they left happy in the knowledge he was still around them.

Over time I gave several of the family messages from the platform. On another occasion as I walked onto the platform Matt whispered in my ear, 'look that's my brother, sitting by mom and dad' he was quite excited to see him and although he wanted to be the first link, I left it for a while to allow his brother Chris the chance to settle down. As soon as he could he regaled the family with information upon information, about his stay in the hospital, what he did, but more importantly what they had been doing since. This gave them clear evidence that he was still around them. Shortly afterwards Chris the brother came to see me and again he repeated what he had been up to, what he was wearing and described his journey to work and what he did with his friends and where they went. He described his new girlfriend and what the inside of his car looked like. He was in his element to talk to him.

It was to be a while before I saw the family again. The next time was a reading for mom at a day of sittings for the Church. Elaine his mother jumped out of the crowd, Matt whispered very excitedly to me, look it's mom, she's over there. As I glanced across I could feel her pain. As soon as she sat down he was there. He began describing issues around the family, how Elaine was feeling. "Ask her about my photo, she always carries it". I understand you have a picture of Matt in your bag, "yes that's correct" she said. "Tell her how different she looks", which I repeated. He was so

69

pleased to see her, we were both crying. He told of stories of former and forthcoming holidays, skiing without snow, Chris's new girlfriend, her age, how he could never keep a secret and used to tell everyone what he had purchased for them for Christmas. He gave her family cars, current and past, family names, a DVD of him which had been transferred to from tape to disc and Kodak cameras. The 30 minute reading came to an end and we were both sad to see him go. Finally he added ask mom why dad hadn't come, Elaine explained he was at home watching the Rugby. ' When you get back ask him if he, had a thought about me, while watching the television, with a drink in his hand', he prompted "I will" she promised. I couldn't help feeling this was a very special lad who had brought so much sunshine into the lives of those around him, that now he was gone, a hole had appeared in every-one's lives, so deep, it could not be filled...not at this moment.

Nothing prepared me for Holly that Sunday evening at Walsall Church. A little girl, barely four years old, who had come to speak to her nanny and grandad. You could feel a wonderful energy around this small child, who came so close, the tears streamed down my face. I spent the first few minutes continually sipping water as I tried to get her to move a way a little, so I could gain some composure back. The closer the spirit person comes, the more I can feel the painful emotions and sometimes it overwhelms me. The love bond between Holly and her grandparents was so powerful. As she moved in too close, I could feel their pain. My own throat contracted, while the tears streamed down my face. Once I had the balance correct between Holly and I, the information flowed. This little girl gave the names of the immediate family, how she passed and when she passed. The look on the grandparents' face made all the hard work of serving churches worthwhile. This wasn't the last time I saw Holly, who in time came through for her aunties and nana on many occasions, but more importantly she came through and chatted to her mother. A young woman who, when I saw her, looked as if the bottom had fallen out of her world. With several other children, she had no choice, life has to go on, but it was plain to see the loss of her beautiful Holly was almost too much to bear.

The last time I saw nana was when another member of the family was tragically murdered leaving two grieving children. On the same day she died I gave a brief message to pass on to the family. I later visited her brother and gave irrefutable evidence that she had lived on, including describing her last moments and the terrible argument which ensued between her and her long term partner, which ultimately led to her death. "He didn't mean to do it", she said "it happened all so fast. It was accident." She also talked about the children's hair and that the family needed to understand how to look after their hair. While she was white her children had inherited their father's strong African-Caribbean hair and she was worried they may not know how to manage their hair.

Holly's death didn't end here for the family, led by the grandmother they used their grief and the short life of Holly to spur them on to set up a charity to help children like Holly. To date they have raised thousands of pounds.

I first met Wendy and Derek when they came for a reading, through a personal recommendation. While Billy their son had been over in the spirit world several years now, they had never come to terms with it, choosing to bury it away. The loss of Wendy's mom had brought the intense grief they had felt, following Billy's death, to the forefront again. While they were both desperate to talk to the mom, you could sense their longing to talk to Billy at the same time. We chatted briefly to Wendy's mom long enough for her to bring evidence through that it truly was her. She thanked Wendy for all her care prior to her death, and the wonderful white lilies. She explained Billy was there to meet her when she finally fell asleep. With that, he flew out after 15 minutes of marvellous evidence. "Tell mom all my hair has grown back and it's still orange!" he said. Wendy and Derek exchanged glances and Derek began to smile. He chopped and changed from one subject to another. "I have all the pigeons here, with granddad". Derek smiled, "I used to keep pigeons" he said. "He is giving me the names, Paul, Peter & Richard". "That's his brothers' names", they said in unison. "He is telling the age 8 and 10 and saying he had funny blood, that couldn't be fixed". As they sat, they held each other's hands and continually looked at each other to see how the other was responding to the evidence. This time Wendy answered, clearing her throat before she spoke, she said. "He died from Leukaemia, after 2 years, he was ten years old." The youngest of five, he talked about life at home, when he was down here, and then moved on to talk about what the family had been up to, including the birth of three cousins in quick concession and the death of the family dog.

At the end of the reading, both of them seemed and appeared lighter. Like many people Wendy and Derek didn't really know much about spiritualist churches and what bit they did hear, they didn't know where to find one. And they were afraid to go as they didn't know what to expect. I readily gave them the details of a local church and for a couple of years I used to see them sitting in the congregation, whenever I served the church.

Then when I went back to the church neither of them were there. I was rather disappointed to see the vacant seats where they had previously sat. It was the same on my next visit. I casually asked the President where they were, "I don't know" came the reply. They haven't been for a couple of months now. In fact I never saw them again.

I knew they would never forget Billy or Wendy's mom. But Like many people who frequent spiritualist Churches, the church had served a purpose, it had been there for them in their hour of need. Now they had moved on which is what some people need to do. The need for the church and the qualities it can bring was not to be theirs forever. Just at that window of time while they came to terms with their pain. This is not to say they forgotten their beloved Billy, but through the Church they had received enough help, assistance and guidance, to enable them cope. They hadn't moved any farther away from their son, or forgotten him. They had received enough information to know he was well, safe; living in another dimension, which was closer enough for them to be able to either feel, see, or know he was there, whenever they needed him.

They had restored there faith enough to know at Christmas, birthday or specials day would not pass without a visit from him or mom.

This is what often happens with the congregation of the spiritualist churches. Some will stay for a short period of time. Some will continue to come for a significant period and a small minority will stay on forever ensuring the survival of the church for others.

Another sad event occurred at Wolverhampton Spiritualist Church which is my home Church. I and two others were doing private readings at an open day to help raise funds for the Church. The collection plates from the services rarely bring in enough money to keep the doors open. So other events, such as this one, are vital to keeping the churches open and in a well maintained condition. The open day was a busy event with lots on for people to see and do which left little space for the readings. Now unfortunately, like you do with family, I ended up with the worst room - the office (although Terry did have the toilet!). So surrounded by filing cabinets, chairs, computer, etc. cramped into a very small space I stayed for four hours giving readings. At one point this included answering the telephone. I didn't mind at all, as it was for a good cause.

My fourth sitter that day was a young woman, in her thirties. She was well dressed, confident and gave an air of someone who was completely at ease with themselves, happy and contented. Which goes to show how well we can hide how we are truly feeling, when we so choose. As soon as she sat down I became aware of a small child coming very close to his mommy. In an effort to ensure she had some choice in who she wished to speak to I went through the process of asking her if there was anyone she wished to speak to, so to give me the relationship, not the name. Immediately and directly after I finished talking she said my son.

I began to give her evidence names etc., This child was of school age, "yes that is correct" she replied, "he would have loved reading?" Again she confirmed this was correct. He described his blue school uniform, with white shirt and grey trousers. "This child would have passed over very quickly with a heart condition?" Again she confirmed, "this was something he was born with, but no-one expected him to pass so quickly?" He then went on to give his own name and names of close family members, how long he had passed over and his bedroom and toys. "He keeps taking me back to school regarding his passing and he keeps showing me the playground" I said. "I feel his death is associated with his school". "That's correct", she said, "He died in the playground". He then showed me the harrowing scene of his mom running towards him as he collapsed in the playground and picking him up and holding his limp body close to her, while screaming for someone to do something. I saw how she had fallen to her knees crying for help. The First-Aid person who bounded from the school, and later the paramedics, could do nothing, and that is where little Ben died. In his mother's arms in the playground of the school he loved.

I valiantly fought the tears which formed behind my eyes as this scene unfolded and I could feel the hopelessness of it all, as the mother fell to her knees holding the limp, lifeless body of her beautiful son.

Now mom wasn't new to loosing children, at 39 he was the fourth. Three others had been lost during pregnancy, one miscarriage and two ectopic pregnancies. She had been advised the possibility of conceiving naturally was zero. Four years on, when all hope had gone, Ben had come along. They had thanked their lucky stars. Now he too had gone.

For several years following his death they had been trying for a baby, but the situation felt quite hopeless. Ben had explained that mommy and daddy were not talking to each other about this, living their own existences, in their own small worlds. He begged her to stop hardening her heart and talk to daddy about their future. "I will try" she reluctantly agreed.

Once the reading was over she explained she had been a great believer in spiritualism who attended a Spiritualist Church on a regular basis, until this had happened four years ago. Now she had lost her faith.

As I watched this woman walk away I couldn't help feeling what an advanced soul must lie behind this exterior. What kind of soul could agree to take on such pain and hardship? To me this was a very special person and if she finished this journey intact, not wrapped or embraced by bitterness, she in turn would re-discover spirituality. She would give hope to others by demonstrating she had survived such terrible pain and hardship, in fact. So could they.

On another occasion I went to a young couple sitting at the front of the church at a service at Darleston Church. It had been a lively service with a full congregation. I had given them both lots of evidence, including the fact that the young woman was in the early stages of pregnancy. The young man's mother had come through and despite being over a few months and this being her first time, she communicated extremely well. I suddenly said "there is someone pregnant?", a little unsure of myself. "Yes" the young man replied. "Over here" a woman shouted from the rear of the church on the opposite side. There, I was soon to discover through his mom, sat the other brother and his partner. I duly gave him a detailed message with clear evidence his mom was still watching over him. While I was talking to the young man, the woman alongside caught my eye. She was in her late 60's and clearly related to these boys, who were not sitting together, due to the lack of space. I then instinctively became aware she was the grandmother to the two boys and the mother of the woman who was currently communicating with me. She had not a care for herself. All she was interested in was these boys receiving comfort. To know their mother was okay and she had made it to the other side. At the same time I could feel her pain. When I finished I turned to this lady and said, "Your daughter says thank you for looking after the boys, you are doing a fantastic job, but she always knew you would". She is telling me "her father was waiting for her when she died". The tears cascaded down her cheeks. I felt the mother's tears, the daughter's tears for her mother and her Husband's concern for her. I was overwhelmed. I couldn't speak, and I began to cry with her, as I felt this pain as if it was my own. I reached for a drink of water. As I sipped I quickly asked the daughter to stand back a little so I could gain enough composure to continue. With the spirits back in check, I turned and continued with the link. "Your daughter has been over less than four months?" Correct she said. "Your husband has been over much longer". That's correct. I gave both conditions, of how they had died. This was followed by a lively banter with the husband that lasted several minutes.

Several months later I gave this woman another message. I didn't recognise her immediately, which is often the case. I gave her messages from her sister, daughter and husband. Afterwards she came up to me in the coffee room and reminded me of the message I gave her, several months ago. She was clearly full of admiration for my work. "I cannot tell you want you have done for me" she said. "The last time you gave me a message was our first night in the church. I was at the end of my tether and didn't feel I could carry on. Your message gave us all hope". "I come every week now" she added. She held my hand and looked into my eyes and thanked me from the bottom of her heart. I accepted her gratitude and tried to radiate love back.

It didn't seem right to break her bubble at that moment and tell her that it wasn't me. In fact it was her family and her openness which made the communication possible. As we drove home I couldn't help but feel that this was what it was all about. I didn't need or want the thanks, but it was lovely to know that my gift had helped someone in their hour of need. I felt very humbled and glad I could use my gift in such a positive way. I never fail to marvel at how much stress and strain the human body can take emotionally and come out the other side.

One of the reasons people cite when vilifying Mediumship is that Mediums are preying on vulnerable people. Taking advantage of them when they are in a weakened state. To these people I say you are misinformed. Go to a spiritualist church and see the comfort that can be given from the platform and the hope it gives to people, when they need it most. There are no doubt charlatans out there, who do prey on the needy and vulnerable. But you most certainly won't find these people in a spiritualist church.

Negative emotion – Feeling Guilty

Guilt is an extremely negative emotion. It is one of the most damaging emotions we humans are capable of feeling. It impedes our progression and ties us to situations. When held by guilt we are unable to move forward. Until we deal with these feelings, we will inadvertently keep creating situations which are 'guilt related'. Unfortunately sometimes feeling's of guilt are not of our own making. Other people are capable of making us 'feel guilty', both intentionally and unintentionally.

This is normally associated with a feeling that we have let someone down. When it involves someone who has passed on, it is very difficult to deal with. We feel we cannot rectify it, as they are no longer here, in our world. So we cannot talk to them, or apologise and explain we didn't mean to hurt them, or neglect them. For many, unless they seek the services of someone like myself, they are left with this deep-seated guilt for many years, unable to release it through words of regret to those they have perceived they have wronged.

Sarah was a young girl in her early thirties, well dressed, well spoken and someone who had done extremely well in her career in social care. Through a friend of a friend, she had made an appointment to come and see me at home. She had an air of confidence around her, a wonderful soul, which clearly shone through. A figure to die for, blond hair and large blue eyes that barely masked the pain, she was clearly trying to hide.

We sat down in my small meditation room and chatted for a little while I tried to make her feel at ease. "I would like to talk to my nan please" she asked, before I had chance to ask her. I could immediately see her standing alongside her. "Your nan is standing alongside you and she has her brown shopping bag in her hand, a blue rain coat on, a multi-coloured head scarf and cream shoes. These would be a wide fitting, she is telling me, and she is off the shops to get some shin of beef for the stew for tea tonight". I said, before pausing to catch my breath and giving her a chance to respond. Her hand flew up to her mouth, as she exclaimed "Oh God, that is just how she would dress and she loved going to the shops". She went on to tell me she loved her stew, which her nan made for her once a week, during the cold winters months. "You were a very active girl she is telling me and that you have won medals for swimming". You swam for both the school and represented the County, She is saying". She nodded in agreement. I went on to say "she is telling me you loved her very much and she loved you too, but you are eating yourself up over something to do with her death, where you are blaming yourself?" The tears began to flow down her face, biting her lip she nodded in agreement, unable to speak. I handed her a tissue and gave her a few moments to compose herself. "I wasn't there the night she died, I went to the pub instead" she said. It came to light this wasn't any ordinary trip to the pub. Sarah had recently gained a promotion and was leaving her current office and moving to another district. The staff had all contributed to a collection and they had thrown a surprise party for her down at the local pub. This had really put Sarah in a dilemma.

Her nan was currently in hospital and she had been visiting her, without fail, every night, and was due to visit that night. In fact she had promised her nan she would be there the next night. She had also told her she would bring her nan her favourite chocolates, quality street, which she was going to pick up on her way home from work. But on the other hand she felt unable to let everyone down in the office who had taken a lot of trouble to arrange this event. Her mother had scolded her and told her to go, telling her there were other nights she could go and visit her nan. After all 'she was going nowhere'. So taking her mother's advice she had gone along to the party and had thoroughly enjoyed the evening. She had not arrived home until after 11.00pm exhausted and laden with gifts. She had gone straight to bed.

Unfortunately for Sarah her nan rather unexpectedly died the same night. Her heart was broken. Six months on and she was no further on in her grief than the day her family had broken the news to her. To make matters worse her mother had received a call in the early hours of the morning from the hospital informing them that the nan had taken a turn for the worse and that they were advised to go to the hospital immediately. Everyone but Sarah was contacted. Her mother had decided Sarah was too exhausted and needed her beauty sleep, so they had dashed off to the hospital leaving her at home in bed, not wishing to disturb her sleep. This factor had only made things worse.

Sarah had always been close to her nan, in fact far closer to her nan than her mother. Her mother had always worked full-time, so after school and during the holiday periods all her time had been spent with her nan. But more importantly her nan understood her. At its best her relationship had always been a little strained with her mother, at its worst there had been distinct hostility between them. Her mother was extremely outspoken to the point of being rude at times. This did not always go well with Sarah's sensitivity. Her nan on the other hand understood Sarah. Now she was gone and Sarah had not been with her in her hour of need. Her nan spent a lot of time trying to soothe her and asking her to let this go. What probably clinched it for Sarah was her nan telling her she had gone when she did to try and make it easier for Sarah, not harder as she didn't want Sarah to see her suffer. She comforted her by telling her she would always be there, whenever she needed her. She would only have to think of her nan and her nan would be by her side. To show Sarah she had been around her, she described Sarah's new office, its location and the untidy state of her desk. She admired her new car and recently purchased handbag from River Island. Although she did say she preferred the black one to the brown. Sarah was amazed - she had indeed purchased a new bag last week and couldn't decide at the time between the black and brown one.

Before she left she thanked me profusely for the information I had given her. She was brimming with happiness and elated to know her nan had survived death and that she was still around her and didn't blame her for not being there the night she died.

I waved her off and quietly watched her as she sat in the car calling her family to tell them the good news. Before she left she asked me if she could come back, again and how soon. Not wishing to make her too dependant upon my services I suggested she waited a year. I have never seen her since. Mine must be the only trade where I am pleased when I don't see people. It shows I have done what I was supposed to do quite successfully and the person has moved on. This is what should happen, in an ideal world. Unfortunately life isn't always an ideal world and some carry the guilt for the rest of their lives.

Coping with negative emotions is something I often address through inspired talking, during a divine service. Sometimes the easiest way to get a point across is to tell as story. Here is one I occasionally use. It is story I adapted from one I heard on a radio.

It is the story of two monks, a young novice and an elder, who one day set off on a 20 mile hike. The monks belonged to a devout order which forbade the physical contact with females, in any way shape or form. At the start of the journey they had to wade across a deep wide river, with a powerful current, that took all their strength to overcome. As they arrived at the river, there on the bank sat an old lady. Unable to mast the strength of the current on her own and with no other means to cross the river, she had sat for days, merely looking at the water, unable to move on. She was eternally grateful when the older of the two monks, recognising her dilemma, walked over to her and said 'climb upon my back and I will carry you across'. This she gingerly did and using all his might and strength her carried her across the river. On reaching the other side she thanked and thanked him, she had nothing to give him but her thanks, which he accepted and set off on the long walk to the nearest town. They continued the journey in silence. As they walked the youngest monk fumed - here is a devout monk. Had compromised everything they believed in by allowing this woman to climb onto his back. Still they walked in silence. As they approached the town the young monk could contain himself no longer. The elder had not apologised or offered an excuse for his behaviour. He could stand it no more. "Father, please tell me, why did you compromise everything we believe in for that old woman". He continued "does our faith not dictate that we should have no physical contact with woman? Why have you ignored this?" The elder, tired from the physical effort it had taken to carry the woman across the river and now more tired by the journey, looked with earnest at the young novice. "Yes it is true I did compromise what we believe in". The elder hesitated for a moment as he searched the young mans face for a reaction. He then added, "Yes I carried her, but across the river. But you my son, have carried her for 20 miles". The novice hung his head as he contemplated the words of the elder.

It was true. While the elder may have compromised his beliefs, for him it was over as soon as the deed was done. He had made his decision and had seen the needs of the old lady as being greater than his beliefs. Once the deed had been done, it was forgotten. Whereas the young novice could not let go, he carried it with him, churning it up and turning it over in his mind, re-living the event when really it needed to be left where it belonged in the past. Unfortunately this is what many of us do, when we are unhappy with an outcome. Our first response is to try and change it, but when this involves the finality of death, changing an outcome is not an option. So we continue to either re-live the event, scrutinising and analysing it over and over again or we bury it deep inside, replaying it, only when a memory or an event brings it back to the surface.

How do we deal with the guilt when one person survives an incident and another dies? You bury it. Anthony came to see me at a party booking at someone's house. I had arranged to see seven people. Due to his shift patterns he had come in quite early. He was a big built powerful man of whom you would not have wanted to get on the wrong side. He oozed an air of defiance. This was re-iterated by close cropped hair and tattoos the length of his powerful arms. Despite the time of year, it was in the middle of December, he strolled in wearing jeans and his vest top. Not wishing to stereotype, but he was not the usual clientele associated with spiritual readings - for a start, the biggest proportion are usually female.

As he sat a huge smile spread across his face revealing a warm, kind character, with a heart of gold. No sooner had he sat down when I felt someone standing alongside him. I still went through the formalities of asking him if there was anyone he wanted to talk to, and before I could go any further he immediately said his nan and his brother. "This boy was in his early teens when he passed over; he is telling me you would understand the significance of 11½" "Correct", came the reply. "He passed over very quickly, and he is showing me a sign saying fragile roof". You could see he didn't expect me to pick up this information as he moved a little

uncomfortably in his chair. I then went on to tell him his brother had followed him, as a gang of children clambered over a roof. It had given way underneath his brother. He had fallen 40 feet and died instantaneously. "He's telling me, your mother blamed you for his death?" This bulk of a man fought to maintain his composure, as he nodded, head bowed. He quickly wiped his eyes with the back of his hand, trying to disguise the tears. "It wasn't your fault Tony" the lad answered "you told me not to come, but I wouldn't listen". As the story unfolded, Tony's (every-one called Anthony Tony) mom had worked full time and children were left to fend for themselves or go to their nan's. Tony had always looked after his younger brother. He was heart-broken when he died. To make matters worse, on one occasion, one too many, strangled by her own grief, his mother had spat at him that it was his fault. "You should never have taken him with you. You knew better" she had shouted at him. Once spoken the words which had tortured him could never be retrieved. In Tony's eyes she had accused him of causing his death. He may as well have killed him with his own hands. He still carries the guilt to this day.

After this event he had spent more and more time with his nan, who loved him as if he were her own. Her death 18 months previously had triggered all these deeply buried emotions relating to his deceased brother. She regaled him with stories of fish & chips and favourite meals, children's games of knock-and-run and lazy sunny afternoons drinking lemonade, paddling pools and garden hoses. Once lulled into the security of these memories, she also emphasised to him it was not his fault and more importantly, it was John's time to go. "He had never planned to stay a long time" she said. She also reminded him how his mother, to this day, was deeply ashamed of what she had said and had told everyone who witnessed her outburst, thousands of times, that she would sacrifice her own life if she could only take back those angry words she had spoken that day. With his head on one side he didn't speak for a moment, as if hearing these words for the first time. His nan continued "go and see your mom" she urged, just as she had during her time on earth "she misses you". It would seem Tony had not seen his mom for a long time.

So 15 years after that fateful day, Tony had hopefully received enough evidence to help him move on. John's final comment to his brother before he left was "tell him I know what he did to my bike". Tony looked quizzical, unable to work out what he was talking about. "You know - my wheel". In seconds the biggest grin came over his face. He explained to me that the last Christmas, before John's death they had both had bikes for Christmas. Within a week Tony had punctured his tyre. Now John, only 2 ½ years younger than Tony, had always been his mother's favourite, so Tony had sneakily exchanged the wheels on the bikes so that John had the puncture. With laughter in his eyes and on his face he got up and heavily shook my hand. "Thanks mate". I felt honoured.

I read once that to bestow blame on others is a failure on our part to accept responsibility for our actions or inactions, which is exactly what happened in the next case.

Despite being in a very crowded church Ian managed to shout above all the others to get my attention. As soon as I looked at the woman I knew I had her son with me. "Tell her happy birthday" he said. "It's some-one's birthday today" I said. Immediately the tears began to flow. She nodded and told me it was her birthday today. Ian had been over ten months and this was her first birthday without him. "He's mentioning a bike being involved in his death and I understand this was an accident", she continued to nod and wipe away her tears. Sitting close by was his older sister who held her mother as close as she could, as if she was trying to shield her from the pain. "He was knocked off his bike" came the reply. "He is telling me he didn't suffer and it was over very quickly and that he was 17". Again she nodded. "He was killed doing a paper round and his father is still angry regarding his death". Again she nodded in agreement, scarcely able to talk for the tears. Ian was a good communicator and he went on to say his own name, his sister's, mom's and dad's. He talked about his room, which he informed me remained unchanged. Everything was exactly the same as the day he left it and his dad couldn't talk about it. His mom and sister nodded in agreement. Mom looked like she had the whole world on her shoulders. I thanked them both for talking to me and moved onto my next link.

Afterwards the mom and sister approached the platform to thank me. As they chatted they told me his dad blamed the mom for allowing him to do a paper round. He didn't want him to do it, but had said very little at the time. Now he was consumed with anger and blamed his wife, Ian's mom, for Ian's death. He had subsequently moved out of the house and was drinking quite heavily. He refused to even discuss his dead son. The Wife was beside herself but there was nothing she could do. I listened attentively, merely nodding my head and trying to make the right sounds. What could I say? Not only was she trying to deal if the death of her son, but on top of it the failure of her marriage and a consuming hate from her husband towards her.

The saddest part about it was she was accepting the blame he was bestowing on her. Tearing herself apart over and over again as to why she had allowed him to do this and if he hadn't taken on this paper round he may still be alive today. I gently and firmly told her that it was his time to go and it wasn't her fault "he is telling you, it's not your fault" He is almost begging you not to blame yourself, I said. I then repeated him, word for word. "Mom please, don't blame yourself" he then added "Dad will come round before Christmas". "He will?" she asked with hope in her voice. "He will" I repeated. She thanked me again and gave me a big hug. I don't normally predict the future. But the spirit world obviously felt she needed to hear this. As she walked away a beautiful grin covered her whole face. What a lovely birthday gift he had given his mother, a message of upliftment and hope of resolving this family crisis. As it was now the beginning of November, a change for the better wasn't far away. Hopefully given time, his father would find the comfort his mother had, through the church, or at the very least he would accept the mother was not to blame for his death. No-one was.

It is almost impossible for families not to feel angry and bitter when something has directly caused the death of a loved one, either through something they did do, or something they didn't. In the early days I remember meeting a very special lady in her early sixties. By anyone's standards she had not had an easy life. He daughter had been diagnosed with MS when she was in her later twenties, a mother of two toddlers. Her husband at the first sight of a wheelchair had gone off with her best friend, and heavily supported by her parents, life went on. In three years her husband never visited or contacted her once. Then suddenly out of the blue the husband arrived and demanded to take the children with him. The boys were terrified, now nearly four and half; this man was a complete stranger. A struggle between the strong healthy husband and the wheelchair dependant daughter, broke out on the landing of the flat and as a direct result, the daughter fell down the stairs and died. The husband was eventually acquitted of causing her death. Once this was over, he came for the children. The mother and father vowed to use everything they had to keep them, as they were the only family they had known. They lost the fight and their father was awarded custody. His victory was short lived. His new partner had given birth to another child and had no time for the boys, so within four months the husband had dumped them back on their doorstep. The children were much thinner and it took months to settle them back down again.

In her early sixties mom was now a widow caring for two dependant lazy young men, but Mary was incredibly proud of these two lads and all they had achieved. Even when her deceased husband berated her for mowing the lawn, while they both watched from the comfort of the lounge!

The interesting thing about Mary was she bore no anger towards her former son in law for abandoning her daughter or contributing to her subsequent death. She brushed the incident off. With a flick of her wrist she dismissed the whole incident as something that happened a long time ago and it belonged in the past. It had been 16 years since it all happened. What she had done, for the boy's sake, was to let go of her anger and put it all behind her. As she walked away at the end of the reading, I couldn't help thinking, would I have been able to show such understanding towards a man who had contributed towards my child's death, then tried to take her children from me? I very much doubted it.

Fear

Alongside love and possibly of equal power is the feeling of fear. Without doubt this is a negative emotion, yet it also has some qualities that serve us well. Love can throw us into a state where we are carefree. Throwing caution to the wind and unable to see potential harm. Fear can be our saviour in moments of wild abundance. Fear makes us cautious, distrustful. In fear we are still and focused while we assess the situation. While fear can instinctively protect us, it can also hold us back.

In its negative sense in holds us back, stops us from progressing and ties us to situations that may no longer serve us.

As human beings we are creatures of habits. Routine gives us security. We are sometimes reluctant to change, especially when the impetus to change is not coming from within, but from an eternal force. For example, many of us will change jobs several times during our lifetime. We will move with relative ease from one working environment to another, as we slowly progress through our career pathway. However, when we are forced to change jobs that is a different matter. If we lose a job through redundancy or closure of the business the effect is far more dramatic. We are moving on because we have no choice. The decision has been made not by us, but for us. Our automatic response is to feel fear. We become afraid of a multitude of issues. Will we ever find work again? How will we find it? How will we manage? This is a very different response from when we have decided to move on to another job. When we decide to move, we have the control. We have made the decision. This is not to say we don't feel fearful of the situation. What if I don't like it? What if they don't like me? We feel fear in nearly everything we do, but we have ownership of the decision and therefore have a feeling of being in control, so our fear is nowhere near as great as when we have had no control over any given situation.

As human beings fear does not bring out the best in us. Some of our worst deeds occur when we allow our negative emotions to get the better of us. One of our greatest fears is to lose control of any given situation. We spend a large proportion of our time throughout our lives trying to maintain our own feelings of power and control over our lives. Yet at the same time we need to be extremely cautious and ensure the pursuance of this goal is not to the detriment of others. Power struggles in relationships are often battles for dominance over another. Imbalances in power within a relationship can result in one party having power over another, thus empowering one and disempowering the other. Yet we only behave in this manner when we feel threatened or challenged. In others words we feel fear, for whatever reason.

One of the major areas where we will, at sometime, experience fear is in our love relationships. We know we loathe change unless we are in control of the changes. As humans one of our greatest fears, is the fear of rejection. Often when faced with rejection by a Partner our first response is to try and work it out. In our desperate attempt to try and hold everything together, we will often compromise our morals and core values in an effort to try and hold our lives together.

When we resist change we will alter our base beliefs or justify our behaviour to others, in order to maintain our 'status quo'. This justification validates our actions. For example we hear statements, such as, 'he didn't mean it, he was under a lot of pressure', or 'she threw herself at him'. It is very difficult when faced with a crumbling relationship to determine the best course of action. We are gripped by fear. What will people think of me? Will they think I am failure? How will I cope? What if I am left on my own forever? The list is endless. We rarely can look at the matter from the heart and ask am I truly happy in this relationship? Or is it meeting my needs? Why? because fear gets in the way. It is only when we learn to conquer fear, can we begin to move on.

Jodie was medium build with short brown hair. She was quietly spoken and clearly lacked confidence in her self. She had been married to Paul for 6 years. The surprise pregnancy has brought the marriage forward and put all Jodie's dreams of nursing on hold. They now had two children, both whom were of school age. Paul had been unfaithful to her on several occasions. He was a bully who dominated her whole life and she allowed him to do so. Jodie had a mortal fear of being left on her own with sole responsibility for the children and the running of a marital home. She had no formal occupation and didn't feel she could sustain a household single-handedly. The recent death of her mother left her without any family support. Paul on the other hand had a well paid position in the civil service. He maintained his own supremacy over Jodie by keeping her at home and playing on her fear. The whole situation came to head when Jodie, with the help of a friend, made the decision to enrol in a nursing course. Their family complete, she felt she could cope with a part-time course. Paul, seeing the possible consequences and doorways this could open for Jodie began to flex his muscles. He applied immense pressure on her, not to take this opportunity.

When this failed to have any effect, he issued the final ultimatum. 'It's me or the course'. To add weight to his words he packed his bags and went to stay at his mother's, while Jodie made decision.

Jodie was beside herself when she came to see me. She came looking for guidance about what should she do.

Apparently her mother, who was normally meek and mild, came through as a tower of strength. After 30 minutes of chatter, she gave Jodie the courage to stand her ground. This she duly did, as I found out when I saw her 12 months later. In fact not only did she stand her ground, she refused to have him back! Paul and Jodie did eventually become friends, then lovers and partners again. Only this time the relationship was on equal terms, with both partners views being taken into consideration and Paul never strayed again. Had he done so, Jodie now had the confidence and courage in herself that, without a doubt, she would have been able to respond from her heart, not from fear.

Had Jodie have not found the courage to stand up to Paul no doubt the situation would have continued indefinitely. On reflection we can see the experience here was to help Jodie to face up to her fear of responsibility. Jodie was inadvertently giving away her power, to try and ensure Paul didn't leave her. Yet in some ways, she was creating exactly what she was trying to avoid. The more power she gave away, the more powerful and domineering Paul became. Her nursing course went some way to help her overcome her fears. It gave her confidence and financial security. This helped her to turn her life around. This is not to say all her challenges are over. No doubt in time other experiences will draw near to her and their reasons for them would remain equally as vague.

We do know resistance to change is a waste of time. What we resist will persist. As with any challenging life experience there comes a time when we have to stop and face our fears, otherwise they will keep presenting themselves to us, until we do.

As humans we sometimes give our power away in many ways. We allow people to tell us what we can and cannot do. We give permission for them to make decisions on our behalf. In other words we shun responsibility. Sometimes by asserting what we want can hurt those close to us, if the goals are not shared. But we cannot live our lives for or through others. God gave us this life. It is our responsibility to live it. To welcome the challenges life presents to us and face them, head on. Not try to avoid them, for they will not go away.

For many of us, one of the experiences we will face is the parting of the company - with partners, friends etc. This is unavoidable. But whether you are the instigator or the recipient, the challenge is difficult. One of the many questions we ask ourselves is 'am I doing the right thing?' Unfortunately we never know the answer until after the event has passed. The only positive thing you can do when faced with this prospect is to be truthful to yourself, open and honest. Deceit has no place in this scenario, even deceit masked as kindness. It is still deceit and to deceive will, in turn, bring deceit back into our lives.

Emma was in her late thirties when she came to see me. She had been with Kevin since her late teens. When they met she was nearly 17, while he was in his late 20's. As far as her family was concerned it was not a match made in heaven and it had taken them several years to accept him. Emma was a very gentle person with very few opinions in life. Had she been born in the 50's she would definitely be one of the flower people. Kevin on the other hand had very clear ideas and values so deeply entrenched, they could have been set in stone. Emma's family often believed that Kevin suppressed her. What Kevin wanted Kevin got. In other words, he dominated her. For example, Kevin had two grown- up children and had decided long before he met Jodie he didn't want any more children. A vasectomy many years ago ensured he didn't have to consider more children. What's more he didn't believe in fertility treatment or adoption. Emma on the other hand did want a family, as I would soon discover. But as he had made his mind up, there was nothing to discuss.

Emma came to see me with her mother, following her father's sudden death, without Kevin's knowledge or permission. Apparently he didn't believe in the afterlife, neither should she. As soon as she sat down I felt her father draw near to her. I described his height, size and how he passed. "Your father is showing me a fairy circle". Emma wrapped her long arms around her thin elegant frame, placed her hair behind her ears and nodded excitedly. Her father added, "tell her she always does that when she gets excited" he said referring to her tucking her hair behind her ears. "I do" she exclaimed. "He tells me you have recently had a promotion at work and he likes your new office, but stop over-watering the plant". She continued to nod and laugh with amazement as he gave her evidence after evidence of her past and current situation. I gradually began to notice a difference in what he was saying. He suddenly stopped his banter and showed me himself tenderly holding a baby close. I relayed to Emma the scene. Suddenly her sparkling blue eyes began to mist over. She looked directly at me titled her elegant head to one side and with all the control she could muster, asked, "is the baby for me?" Her father looked up and nodded, I repeated this information. She shook her head and began to cry. Then her father showed two heels firmly dug in the ground. He was adamant. I rounded-up the message and finished by telling her not to worry, there was a child waiting for her and that she was to stand her ground over a situation relating to this child. Through her tears she thanked her father. She then explained how she was desperate for children, but as far as Kevin was concerned he had all the family he ever intended to have. She could feel her biological clock ticking away. But she found herself in a quandary, desperate to have children, but unable to get Kevin to even discuss it with her. "The trouble is I have always given in, over all major issues" she said. "But I cannot over this one and I really don't know what to do". What shocked her more than anything was the fact her father had instigated this discussion. So here she was discussing her very intimate secret thoughts with a complete stranger. All I could do was pass on the advice her father gave. Follow your own dreams. I repeated this to her. After she left I couldn't help but feel, for once, she would stand her ground. She would be surprised how much Kevin would compromise in order to keep her. But on the other hand, if she continued to let his views overshadow her own, she would remain childless, unfulfilled and no doubt in time would become embittered by the whole scenario.

I sometimes see life as being back to front. We are expected to make decisions without knowing what the consequences or benefits of are of the decisions we make. For example, when we decide to move house, we have no way of knowing how we will settle into the new home or how we will get on with the neighbours. Or indeed, if the move is the right move for us. Only after we have moved will we know the answers, but then it is too late.

We function better in life when we have a balance between our emotions. When we are not driven to wild abundance by love or held back from pursuing life's challenges through fear.

Ghost Stories & Clearing houses & People

As a Medium the ability to b able to communicate with those who have moved on from this world offers numerous work opportunities. One of the least expected is 'ghost busting'. Without doubt there are and will continue to be homes that have unwanted guests. Guest's who are difficult to see, yet make their presence felt in a variety of forms. Such as strange noises which cannot be unaccounted for. Scents and smells that do not appear to come from any source and sometimes sightings or 'intruders' or at least glimpses of people who disappear as quickly as they have appeared. For those inexperienced or uneducated in the field of spiritualism, the whole event can be extremely frightening, although some people do cope quite well and live with the knowledge they have an unwanted lodger. But not everybody is comfortable with sharing their property with someone they cannot see.

While house clearing is nowhere near as glamorous as some popular television programmes have made out. it is one of the areas where I have been a reluctant participant. I am not the bravest of people. In fact I am afraid of the dark, something which has puzzled my partner for years. As I have developed my skills the fear has lessened and is certainly better than in my younger days. During the 1970's and early 1980's, I did several stints of night work in homes for older people. Not only was I afraid of the dark but I was terrified of ghosts. Every home had a ghost story to tell, with my latent psychic ability and vivid imagination, this was for me a recipe for disaster. All my reasoning and pleading not to hear any of these stories always seemed to fall on deaf eye. The carer would look and nod sympathetically and then tell me, "I know, but let me just tell you this" and in great detail they would regale me, sparing no details of the ghostly events that occurred with assured regularity.

On one occasion it was the mist in room 13. "Nobody likes this corridor" she told me with pursed lips and an air of knowledge about her, as we began to walk down the dreaded corridor. As my eyes grew wider she carried on. "Nearly all of us have seen a white mist in there". She said. "No resident will stay in that room. They complain they feel they are being watched" she told me. Then she leaned forward and informed me it was okay at the moment; the lady in there was blind. "Come on" she said as we began the hourly checks. Every door had to be opened and a quick visual check was made to see the residents were okay.

"You do that side I will do this" she told me. Off we went. I had odds she had evens. I was at room eleven before I cottoned on. I opened room 13, but couldn't open my eyes. With lids tightly shut, "are you okay?" I whispered "Yes thank you" came the reply. I closed the door gently, before I dared open my eyes. I made sure from that point on I was always one step ahead, on the even numbers.

Another issue I had to deal with was the old wives' tales, which held a sinister twist, or at least appeared sinister to me. "They never die alone" I was told on numerous occasions, by the older staff who always had an air of superior knowledge around them when they shared their wizened words. When we were caring for someone who was ill I would invariably be told to leave the door open or a window slightly ajar. When I foolishly enquired why, I would be told "there times up, someone will be coming to fetch them tonight". I remember on one occasion in a home run by Social Services in Dudley Wood, hearing footsteps walking slowly and deliberately above our heads. The mature Mrs Bailey raised her eyes to the ceiling and listened intently, as she sat peeling and eating her orange. As she stood up, she said, "come on, they've come for someone, lets see who". I scurried behind her. Sure enough someone had passed unexpectedly in their sleep. I was terrified.

Such was my fear, at times I would even stand outside the toilet door waiting for my work colleagues, facing the wall and refusing to hear or see anything.

I realized over time they were correct, people did not die alone; someone always came to fetch them. On one occasion I sat nursing a very frail man in his late 70's. The doctor had visited earlier that day and felt the cancer was getting the better of him and he was 'not long for this world' as they used to say. With the knowledge in hand we took turns to sit with him throughout the night. My turn to sit came at around 2.00 am. Harry was extremely alert and I sat fascinated as I watched him for nearly an hour talk to someone I couldn't see, although I sensed them in the corner of the room. It was quite clear he was talking to someone. It would have been impossible to have the conversation he had with himself. He was chatting to an unseen guest. The conversation went something like: "I know, I know I shouldn't have done that", "You know what I did", "yes", "ashamed", "I don't think she did, if she did she never said". He coherently chatted away in this manner. I knew then most definitely Harry wasn't alone. What frightened me more, was that I wasn't alone either as I sat caring for him. Harry was still chatting when my duty finished. The next morning he died.

Over the months I began to recognise the signs. I didn't have the knowledge and experience of the different staff I worked with who could walk into a room, take one look at the ailing patient and give a knowing nod in my direction. I on the other hand would just watch and observe. After a time I began to recognise the signs. They would begin to talk to someone I couldn't see, ask who that person was in the corner, when no-one was present or begin to call out the name of a deceased relative. In fact when my own mom was dying she asked on several occasions who the figure was on the stairs. I knew then she would not be with us for much longer. These were all signs that someone was here to take them home.

As I have matured with age, I find this fact very comforting - that when we are ready to go home, someone we loved very much will be waiting to lead and guide us home.

As my career in residential care in Social Services progressed I had to participate in the sleeping in Rota. At that time there had to be a senior member of staff in the building 24 hours a day, 365 days of the year. You would go off duty at 9.30 and come back on at 7.30 am. In between times you couldn't leave the building although you did have a sleeping-in room, for your sole use. If you were lucky you had television and a sink. If it was luxurious accommodation you even had a toilet, although these were few and far between. You usually had to pad along the acres of corridors to find the staff toilet.

I have slept in too many rooms to recall them all, but none were as bad as a home in Stourbridge and the Woodlands, which was a home I managed. I was asked to cover at the home in Stourbridge, as a favour, at very short notice, and as there was no cover I reluctantly agreed. At the time I had my hands full with managing the Woodlands. It was a really old building with a history which dated back nearly 200 years. The room was located at the top of the house, in the old part of the building, in a self contained flat, with a bathroom, kitchenette and a bedroom area. It was bliss. I went upstairs almost immediately after the shift finished, made a cup of tea and settled down for an hour of television. As I sat unwinding, I felt a little uncomfortable, but couldn't really put my finger on it. I turned everything off, except the light in the hallway (remember I am afraid of the dark) and got into bed. As soon as I closed my eyes I was aware someone was watching me peering over the bed at me, trying to get my attention. A battle of the wills ensued. Whatever it was spent the whole night willing me to open my eyes never! I vowed. Even the gentle pulling of the quilt, tapping on the wardrobe door and the pressure on the bed as if someone was sitting on the bed, could not persuade me to open my eyes. I can honestly say I can never remember being so afraid as I was that night. I didn't feel like I had slept a wink. I'm sure I did, but as soon as I dozed the different sounds around the room quickly roused me. When the noisy dustbin cart arrived at 5.30 I was still awake, although now I would open my eyes as it was light. It was funny really because after that night I never slept there again. Help out yes, sleep in, never, I was always too busy.

Months later I realised I wasn't alone in my experiences at this home. Two of my senior staff had also given cover to the home. One had sat up, downstairs all night, refusing to go back in the room after an unseen finger had physically tapped her on the shoulder. Another was always busy when asked to cover shifts, after suffering similar experiences to me.

In many ways the Woodlands was no better. Staff complained the taps to the sink turned themselves in the middle of the night and air would gush out instead of water. Yet visit after visit from Plumbers never detected any air in the system. I woke one night to the feeling of someone sitting on the bed and being unable to move. This was far better than what happened to a colleague who woke abruptly to the sensation of someone dropping on them, followed by a thud, as if a person had rolled onto the floor.

On one occasion I had my dog with me and she refused to go into the room. When finally persuaded into the room she lay on the hard shower room floor, refusing to lie in the actual room.

When the home shut for four days and nights, for security purposes the night staff worked as normal. Despite being in the building on their own, they reported hearing furniture being dragged across the floor, the lift operating and hearing footsteps walking on the floor above them as they toured the building.

Looking back I know both places were haunted. The buildings were occupied or being visited by people who had long departed this world. At the home in Stourbridge I think it was someone merely trying to get my attention for whatever reason, but I didn't understand. What do we do when we cannot understand something? We fear it. I most certainly did. The situation at the Woodlands was very similar to that situation in Stourbridge, although I think the ghost there was a little aggressive and would have required expert handling.

With my past reputation and fear of the dark, it seems hard to work out, how I went from 'scaredy-cat' to 'ghost buster', but somewhere along the line this is exactly what happened to me. As my Mediumship developed, so did the call to offer assistance with unwanted guests. Fortunately I had accompanied Val on such excursions, so I knew what to do.

Over the years I have tried so many different ways to lose weight, tone up and trim down. One form of exercise was the toning tables. During the process I met some wonderful people, including the staff. In fact long after I bored with the tables and lost heart, I was still going just for the company. Tammy was one of the part-time staff who worked there. I'm not sure how my unusual talent came to light, but over the months I had given them messages in and outside of the Centre. Tammy was one of those people and when her brother had a life crisis, I willingly offered to go and see him. He had recently lost his best friend and was quite distressed by the whole episode. Now Tammy's brother lived quite close to my house. In fact it would have been quicker, using the short-cuts to have walked, instead of driving. I had noted this earlier and had decided to walk. Yet I seemed to have jumped into the car without thinking and as I drove I really questioned my laziness, although later I thanked my lucky stars I had taken the car.

The friend had committed suicide less than a week ago. During the visit I was able to give lots of evidence regarding what they had done together, including camping and days out, names of their friends, girlfriends etc., I know my words had brought comfort, as Lee was convinced he had let his friend down. I was able to tell him that he had died through asphyxiation and that he really didn't mean to do it. I was also able to comfort him by telling him Scott had made it to the other side. I emphasised to Lee even if it was suicide this would never affect his passage to the spirit land.

For those friends and family of people who have committed suicide I can only repeat what I have been told by the world of spirit. In every case I have communicated with (and there have been a lot), they have always made it to the other side. They are welcomed, nursed and nurtured back to full health.

For all those who may ever be considering doing this, remember there is always a consequence for an action. As a spirit in the before life we welcome the opportunity to experience life on earth. When we arrive home, the only person who judges us is ourselves. We will re-live, if only in a flash, all our experiences on earth, including how we felt and how we made other people feel. A life on earth is deemed as a gift, a wonderful opportunity. When we commit suicide we prematurely end that gifted experience. Once home we will have to face our own inadequacies and will choose to come back to earth to finish what we started and what we had planned. I suppose in a way it is like returning to have another go and we often return to earth quite quickly. This concept is addressed quite well in Michael Newton's work 'The Journey of the Soul'.

Lee was very pleased with the evidence I gave him and we chatted for a little while. His home was a downstairs flat and had anything but a welcoming feel to it. In fact it felt dark and oppressive yet looking at the visual appearance of the flat, there was nothing physically present to create such a feeling.. He went on to explain his girlfriend didn't like the flat at all and was quite frightened by it, especially the living room. In fact they spent most of their time in the bedroom.

Now, I hadn't noticed this when I arrived, probably because I was concentrating on bringing Scott through and holding his energy. But also I am great believer in protecting myself. As stated previously I am not the bravest of people. So I use quite stringent protection which means I cannot see, hear or speak to dark energy. This is a little bit of a problem when trying to remove these energies.

Just before I left I became aware of a sinister female in the corner. She was in her very late forties and appeared to have suffered from some sort of mental illness during her life on this earth. She didn't seem to know she had passed over. While she had not lived in this flat she certainly had connections with the people who had occupied the flat before.

I began to open up and ask for assistance and I knew immediately I could not deal with this on my own, I needed help. The situation was too powerful for one single Medium to tackle by themself. I decided to leave the flat and go back to the house and call my dear friend Karen, a fellow Medium with whom I had worked in the past, in clearing properties. I said my goodbyes to Lee and promised to be in touch later to tell him how and when we could clear the property.

Pleased with my work and the comfort I had given Lee, I waved goodbye and set off home. I got in the car, put my seat belt on and started it up. I leaned across my shoulder to reverse the car and with what appeared the backing of a 48 piece orchestra, I was immediately stung with the reality. She was with me. There on the back seat dishevelled with long unkempt and a strange smiling face, sat this demented woman. I was terrified. The spirit world spun into action and I followed their instructions "ignore her, she cannot harm you and will soon be gone". I did as I was told and I refused to acknowledge her and calmly drove home.

As I made the short journey I became very ware of the dark short cut by the disused railway and long alley I would have had to walk along had I not have brought my car. I said a prayer of thank you as I made the four minute drive, which felt like three hours.

I walked into the house, picked up the cordless phone, pulled the living room door shut to cut out prying ears from my phone call, and from the kitchen I calmly called Karen.

After quickly enquiring about her health, knowing she had a nasty cold, I asked her if she could sense anyone with me. Yes she replied and went on to describe the lady I had seen in the flat, including her dishevelled look. This confirmed what I suspected. I had inadvertently brought her back to my house. I understood that, somehow, this situation had been engineered, so we could both deal with it together. This was quite handy really as it avoided a further night out for me and a one and half hour round trip for Karen. Believe me I didn't feel grateful at the time, all I wanted to do, was deal with it.

Quickly and deftly we created in our minds a wall of white light. Within that wall we created a door and asked for assistance; very quickly I felt White Feather come down and with one swoop she was lifted by him and carried over to the other side. I have no doubt I my mind that when she arrived over the other side there would have been a little army of loved ones, angels and spirit nurses waiting to heal and nurture her back to full health.

I really felt Lee had value for money over this one. Two for the price of one and the first one was free! Through his sister Tammy I found out the flat, after that night, was a changed place. The feeling of darkness and suppression had lifted and no-one was afraid to be there any more; in fact it was turning out to be quite a nice flat, where he still lives today. Tammy reported everyone felt the place was physically lighter after that visit.

A few years later history repeated itself. As I had sat giving Jamie a reading from the local hairdresser's, I felt very uncomfortable with the opposite wall in the lounge. With all my energies concentrated on the reading, I didn't have time mentally to find out what was wrong. As soon as I finished the reading Jamie asked what I thought about the flat. My immediate response was they were not alone in the flat and I didn't like the energy that was around it. As I wouldn't be able to return for a couple of weeks, I didn't like to say what I really felt. Jamie had two children and the eldest who was five often talked about the nasty man. Recently a coat hanger had come flying out of the bedroom into the living room, barely missing one of the children. This time the intruder had gone too far and help was needed.

As usual when we returned - Karen, Martin, David and I - I told the others nothing. That way when they pick something up, we know they have truly got a link and are not influenced by what I have said.

We walked from room to room; all three felt exactly the same as me there was something about the back wall of the lounge. You could feel the energy running along it and it didn't feel nice. While the energy in the children's room appeared alright, it was the atmosphere in the parent's bedroom which was the most oppressive. There was an older man in his late fifties, who most definitely didn't like children, especially children who were noisy. Hence he threw the coat hanger. He was a dark demanding, domineering energy. There was a feeling of alcohol dependence around him and family connections with the flat. The back wall of the flat we felt was a ley line, which had quite a negative feel about it. We walked around the flat and as usual whispered and nodded what we were about to do, in case he heard us and disappeared before we could send him over. We created a box of white light around the walls of the flat. We then pulled it in until he was encased in a small box of light. We then called for help from the other side. Before we disappeared we pushed the ley line outside of the flat, so it ran around the outside of the building, to avoid anything re-entering.

As with Lee, there was a noticeable difference in the light in the flat. This is something I have witnessed first hand on many occasions following a clearing. It is as if a light has been put on in the room. Apparently when the eldest child returned to the flat he turned to Jamie, almost immediately and said "The nasty man has gone now daddy".

Over the years Karen and I, her partner Martin and David, have cleared numerous properties together. Some have been easier than others.

Holiday House Clearing

Another time I worked with Karen over the telephone when together we cleared a holiday cottage in Southern Ireland. In 2005 we visited Ireland for the first time. Wishing to cram as much of Ireland as we could during our holiday, we travelled all over Ireland staying at various locations. We finished the holiday by staying in a cottage in the district of Connemara in County Galway, an area of outstanding beauty, which like the rest of Ireland, I would love to visit again. We stayed in a lovely white-washed cottage, which began its life as a barn, but was converted to a single storage dwelling in the late 1960's. It was located at the end of a long lane, set in its own grounds, with a front lawn that stretched down to sea. It was idyllic and we loved every moment we spent there.

As we had arrived quite late in the evening with a tea to cook and lots of unpacking we had very little time to get a feel of the place before it was time for bed. The next morning, I awoke and began to cook breakfast for all five of us, in a very small galley kitchen. At the end of this long thin kitchen, which resembled a short passageway, was a small passageway running across it, forming a 'T' shape. At one end was the back door, with Beverley's bedroom at the other and a bathroom in-between. The boys' bedroom was off the kitchen, close to the lounge and our bedroom was at the far end of the cottage off the other end of the lounge.

I had been rather surprised when, as I cooked breakfast, I opened the door of the boys' bedroom and found my daughter asleep in with the boys, instead of her own.

As I began to cook, rather pre-occupied with trying to work in a kitchen I didn't know, with equipment with which I was unfamiliar, in a very confined space, trying to cook with calor gas. As I cooked I slowly became aware of a banging noise, which over time appeared to be getting louder and louder. The sound was coming from the bedroom to which Beverley was 'assigned'. Curiosity got the better of me, so I turned off the gas and went to see what was happening. As I turned the corner the sound completely stopped. I checked the back door, which was a modern sturdy type, which snugly fitted against the walls. There were no gaps. I checked the bathroom, the small window was shut. Then I checked Beverley's vacant room, the window was firmly shut. I closed the door behind me, rattled it to make sure the latch was firmly over the catch. As I took the few strides back to the kitchen I began to get a little suspicious. Back to the cooking I went. Bang, bang, went the door again. This time I mentally asked who was there. I sensed a young female presence. So I began to ask her what she wanted and why she was banging the door? Not only did I not receive a response I was suddenly very aware the banging had stopped and I couldn't sense her anywhere in the cottage. I had really felt I frightened her. For the first time, probably in a very long time, she was around someone who was not only aware of her existence but was able to communicate with her. In some ways it was rather funny, the tables were turned and I had frightened the ghost!

For several days we didn't hear from her at all. During my brief encounter with her while I burnt breakfast for five I discovered she was a young girl who had died from a contagious disease in the late 1800's. She was 17 and it was shortly before her marriage. She felt very deprived of the opportunity to be married, as this is all she had ever wanted out of life. It was this deep emotion which had tied her to the cottage and the earth plane: a feeling of being cheated out of what she wanted most.

As soon as we were alone I asked Beverley why she was sleeping in the boys' room. Beverley went into great detail as she recalled the events from the night before. Apparently Beverley had woken quite abruptly in the middle of the night to the sound of the door banging. She got out of bed. Closed the door firmly and got back into bed, only to be woken by the same occurrence of events. After the third time Beverley carefully said if someone is doing this, do it again. Slowly, without any human intervention the latch raised itself and the door began to open. It was at this point Beverley bolted into the boys' room, where she stayed all week. The disturbance of the boys and their antics was obviously far more attractive than sharing the room with the ghost.

We had a holiday to enjoy and gave very little thought to this matter, as after my first encounter I had not seen her.

I was convinced following my conversation with the resident ghost that she had lived here, where the barn stood, in a hovel. This was confirmed on the day we left when I discovered, from a local woman whose father farmed across the lane from our cottage, that hovels had in fact stood where the barn was.

On the last day of our holiday I felt a strong urge to help this young girl. I didn't feel I could do it alone. I knew Beverley could help, but I needed the assistance of another Medium. So, on the off chance I rang Karen, who happened to have her phone on at work and happened to be on a coffee break. As usual I said to Karen "can you pick up anyone around me?" "A woman" "how old?" I asked "Around 17 years old I feel", was Karen's reply. I knew then we were both on the right track. We built a wall of white light and as usual, created a doorway in the wall and saw her sweetheart and mother come to collect her. As she left all three of us felt a lovely cool breeze sweep around us. All this happened on a very sunny day, with the sun shining through the window. Yet despite this Beverley noticed immediately that the room became even brighter as the young woman left the confines of the cottage.

In some ways I felt a little guilty removing someone from a property without the owners' consent, but I doubt they even knew of her existence. On the other hand when spirit asks for assistance to help a lost or trapped soul, I do and will always feel obliged to help. Ghosts are not for amusement or as a tourist attraction and sometimes we all have to do what is right, and this was one of those moments.

Ireland is a very magical land which is steeped in folklore, which tells stories of little people and strange animals. Before we were to leave this wonderful place we had another ghost encounter. Within the confines of Connemara national park there was a road which ran across a bog and which was aptly named 'the bog road'. According to local legend the road was haunted and locals were reported to drive miles round rather than use this road.

Like many holiday-makers we relished the local history and stories, although we didn't take the story seriously for one minute. However, as we negotiated the road for the fourth time, I suddenly became aware of a black figure running directly in front of the car, as it dashed from one side of the road to the other. Within a split second Ben my eldest grandson asked in a somewhat alarmed voice what was happening. He then went on to say he had just seen a figure run across the road. He described a female figure in a black cape. This is exactly what I had seen. I believed we had both seen the ghost of the bog road that day, my first proper ghost, without being frightened!

Business for Sale

Since moving into the village I had always used the same hairdressers. I was a little disappointed to hear the shop was to close. My sadness wasn't to last, they were moving to bigger premises, two doors away. The business was owned by Pete and Dave. After donkeys' years in the trade Pete decided to pull out. Dave was to take over and move to bigger premises. Both partners were aware of my spiritual connections. When Pete asked if I would check it out, I readily agreed. Work was currently being undertaken, so there was no rush. With Christmas out the way Karen and I went to look former florists. As no activity had been reported we were merely going to look and check it out.

Keys in hand and a refusal to allow a posse to come with us from the hairdressers we wandered round. The building was extremely cold, with no heating on - what did we expect. Yet there felt another kind of bone-chilling cold, which appeared to be in the very material of the shop. We knew it had been a Florist's, a mini-freezer centre and butchers for many years, but nothing else. Yet almost immediately on the one half of the shop we could feel the slaughter of animals taking place on the premises. We could sense the fear of these animals, everywhere, but only in the one half (we later found out, the other half was actually a cottage until recently). For some reason there appeared to be a residue of negative energy that was perpetually suspended in the atmosphere of the shop. The energy hung quite heavily and gave the feeling of repulsion, of not wanting to be there. A need to get away. Not exactly the kind of atmosphere you want when you are selling a service.

This sensation began from the rear of the building and spread all around, but again only in one half. The other half was calm and peaceful. We sensed an elderly lady bringing in tea. We both felt she was someone who had lived here a long time ago and popped back occasionally. We later discovered this was in fact correct.

We decided to concentrate our efforts on the side of the shop where we had detected the negative energy and set about clearing it. Once we had cleared it, we then placed a series of small vortexes around the room to try and fill the building with a positive charge. The effect was instantaneous and we could immediately feel the bright light, as we always did.

We went back to the hairdressers' and reported our findings. Local research discovered an early butcher had slaughtered animals on site. It was this energy we could feel.

Once Gillis Rowlands opened the place was as warm as any normal shop, too warm in fact! It would appear even when it was a mini-freezer centre, with all the motors from the freezers running, the shop was always ice cold. Not now - it had a vibrant feeling, somewhere you wanted to be and, in fact, still is to this day.

Had we not cleared the shop before the business was transferred I doubt they would have done very well. People would have felt uncomfortable, wanting to cut their stay short and not coming back, without understanding why.

Harnessing Dark Forces

There are powers out there in this world that are far greater than we can imagine and this unfortunately includes dark energy. There are many people who believe they are greater than the dark forces and they can harness and control such forces. These people are fooling themselves. These energies rarely impact on the lives of ordinary people unless they try to use it for their own good. Unfortunately this is what is in the next story.

It has become a kind of ritual that I take the closing Christmas service at Darleston Spiritualist Church. After one such service I was approached by a young woman asking for help and guidance. The previous evening, all the doors and drawers in her kitchen had begun to open and shut, and were slamming and banging in the process. Leah had recently split up with her boyfriend and was now living alone, with her young daughter. Several incidents had occurred in the property, but this was the worst one. Leah was extremely frightened by this episode and feared for her own safety and that of her daughter. It was this fear that had sent her to find assistance in a spiritualist church. After the service a rather frightened, shy Leah approached me, while I was still on the platform to ask if I could help her in any way. She explained about the kitchen incident and how frightened she was for her own safety and that of her daughter.

As all four of us were present at the church that night, we decided there was no time like the present and agreed to go to the house straight away. As her infant daughter was staying with friends this seemed like and ideal opportunity, so off we set, full of mince pies and Christmas cheer.

As soon as we entered the property we were aware of a dark gloomy atmosphere and a bone-chilling cold, despite the heating being full on. As soon as we arrived we decided to go straight to work. We began by touring the house. As we entered the living room a small ornament by the television seemed to catch my eye; I thought no more of it as we made our way upstairs.

The first room we felt we needed to clear was the bedroom. It was difficult to determine what was in the room. There seemed to be a dark energy crouched in a corner by the window, alongside her ex-boyfriend's black candles. Feeling a connection between the dark energy and the candles, we gave these to Leah and asked her to dispose of them, outside of the house. Why we needed to do this only became apparent towards the end of the clearing. We stood in all four corners and between us created walls of white light which filled the room, including the ceiling and floor. In moments the whole room was covered in white light and whatever was hiding from us, in the corner, disappeared, engulfed in this brilliant white light.. It is at moments like this where I am extremely grateful for my protection. In this case the energy felt so uncomfortable and challenging, I was glad I didn't need to communicate with it.

Convinced we had dealt with the problem in this room, we checked all the other rooms upstairs, they felt fine, and we all traipsed back downstairs. The next room we felt needed some attention was the lounge.

As we began to spread ourselves around the room, none of us wanted to stand near the television for some reason. Karen and I were the first to object to it, followed closely by David and Martin. Karen suddenly said, "It's that ornament, I don't like it". She was pointing to an innocent looking black and red angel, a gift to the girl from her ex-partner. David echoed the same view, while Martin and I nodded in agreement. This was the only time I have ever suggested to someone they needed to throw something out. We all felt the dark foreboding energy we could feel in this house had emanated through this innocent looking toy. While it looked innocent at first glance, when we focused our attentions upon it, you could feel a more sinister side to it and the dark energy which emanated from it. This was the same ornament which had caught my eye earlier.

The girl removed the ornament from the room and threw it into the garden. We then repeated what we had done before in the upstairs room. It was difficult to ascertain what was in that house that night. Was it merely a dark energy that had enfolded the property or was it something far more sinister that we had helped remove? I really don't know and I wasn't prepared to remove my protection to see for myself. I was glad our protection had shielded us from seeing exactly what was present in that property, because if we had, I doubt Karen would have been able to deal with it, as fear would have taken over. As it was it wasn't an issue. The spirit world were able to harness our earthly energy to remove this presence while at the same time protecting us from harm and catching sight of what we were dealing with. As soon as she had removed the object and we had cleared the lounge, despite it being 10.30pm on a dreary winter's night the place appeared lighter as if a dark filter had been removed. Almost instantaneously the whole house began to feel warmer. The young woman who owned the property was the first to comment on this physical change. We stayed and spoke to her in general for a little while before we left, leaving a contact number for her to call should any other problems occur. We all felt quite sure this would be the last we heard of her and we were right. I have never seen her in Church to this day, or heard anything from her. We can only assume, between us and the world of spirit, we had cured the problem.

Before we left Leah told us her ex-partner had been dabbling into black magic. He felt he had the gift to call upon these energies to work for him and was going to use it to make himself money. It was something with which he had only recently become involved. In that short time his relationship had broken down with his girlfriend and they were now estranged and he was not seeing his little girl. She also said he had changed almost overnight and this was the reason they had broken up. It sort of gets you thinking, who is controlling who?

There are no short cuts to life. I am sure, without doubt there are dark forces out there that can promise and deliver many perks in life, for those willing to listen. But dark energy does not work for the good of mankind or for the good of the helper. It works for its own means and will promise you anything to get your assistance and to get what it wants. My advice is to keep away or learn at your peril, as did the people in the next short story.

Ghost Busting People

I had met Carol on several occasions, on the first occasion in a spiritualist church, then on several other occasions when I was giving private readings. Over time I had got to know her quite well.

Carol herself was quite gifted psychically although she had never developed her gift. I received a frantic phone call from her and a friend at 6.45 am, while I was in the shower. The phone had switched to the answer machine. The message was heartfelt, two people crying and pleading for help.

The paid job has to come first unfortunately. I rang back and spoke to Carol explaining I couldn't come until the evening. I suggested they try and stay calm and stay out of the house, until we could all four get there together. Fortunately for them, all four of us were free that night and able to respond.

The four of us duly set off early that evening. We were not sure what to expect or if there really was a problem. It soon became apparent that there was most definitely a problem and it was not of this world. In fact it had never been part of this living world.

The problem had started with Carol. She had felt something had attached itself to her, after spending some time at a friend's house, where use of an Ouija board had become a daily activity. As a believer in the spiritualist principles and a regular member of the local spiritualist church Carol should have known better, but as she wasn't using it, she felt protected. How wrong she could be.

Carol and Lisa had recently become friends, hearing her plight Lisa offered to help to try and shift it. Unfortunately Lisa had no experience in this type of work. She had completed a crystal healing course and had some experience in reading cards. This was her sole experience of esoteric matters.

Without the experience, knowledge or a strong link with her guide, she was unable to deal with this. In fact she had been drawn into the situation. Their efforts to try and rid themselves of the problem had in fact made it much worse. Unfortunately if you lack the experience and knowhow of how to deal with these beings, it is very easy to be overcome and inadvertently make the entities more powerful, by feeding from your fear. This is exactly what had happened here. It had been more powerful than Lisa and she had given in to fear. The entities were thriving on it.

It soon became apparent Carol was in fact correct in her assessment something had attached itself to her and now similar entities had also attached itself to Lisa. In fact there was more than one - we detected at least two or maybe three on each of them. So the problem lay with the two women, not the property.

They had received physical marks to their bodies as they tried to overcome and defeat these entities; these were clearly visible. They looked like bite and scratch marks, which were evident on both the inside of their forearms, their backs and shoulders. These had suddenly appeared over several days. They were both terrified and it took quit a lot of time to make sense out of what had gone on. They had tried to clear whatever it was bothering them together. They had said their affirmations and prayers and asked the angels to help them. Yet at the same time, they felt like they were being physically attacked. They believed the attacks were an attempt on the entities behalf, to try and stop them removing them. As the scratches and bites had begun to appear, they had both physically felt pain as the unseen beings physically attacked their bodies.

We began by trying to calm down and relax. As soon as we tried this they both began to cry out with pain. Physical marks began to appear before our eyes. We decided drastic action was required.

I cannot recall ever seeing anyone as afraid as these two women were that night. Whatever had made a home with them was living off this fear and the more afraid they felt, the stronger it was becoming. At the moment I have used the singular term, but as the clearance progressed we didn't feel it was a lone entity, but several beings, on both women.

We walked around the house, into every room, there was definitely nothing in the property. We were only aware of these entities when we were near the girls. As they showed us these scratches and bites we saw they had every type of crystal strapped to their bodies to offer protection. Both Karen and I felt this was making the situation worse.

Having removed all the paraphernalia they had taped to their bodies, we got the girls to sit back-to-back in the dining room where there was ample space, to allow us to move around them. While they sat we formed a circle around them.

More so than ever before, we carefully planned what we were going to do, sometimes by nods or occasional whispering outside of earshot of the girls and their unwanted guests. You could feel their menacing presence clinging onto their backs, like skinless 12 inch monkeys, with razor sharp teeth and long talons. I was acutely aware that if we talked out loud they would realise what we were going to do and try to foil our plans. Fortunately we had taken this into consideration and with our forward planning knew what we were going to do without talking out loud to each other.

With the girls seated back-to-back, the four of us encircled them and joined hands together, to make a continual link between each other. With precision uniformity and without speaking a single word we all called for assistance through our guides to remove these entities from them.

We held the circle close and used minimal spoken words, except to decipher what was happening. The biggest danger was we would stop the process prematurely and would not succeed in removing them completely.

On this occasion we used a tried and trusted method we had applied before, which is for Martin to offer his energy field to move the beings from wherever they are. For many entities the temptation is too much. The next stage is for the rest of us to remove them from Martin while he stands perfectly still. How this works we have never been entirely sure, but we have used it quite successfully in the past and tonight was no exception. Knowing they were defeated and had no choice but to leave their hosts, they jumped from the girls onto Martin. Now all we had to do was remove the entities from him. David provided the power, while Karen and I did the communication and execution of the removal with guidance being giving from the spirit world. After quite a while Karen felt the entities had left Martin.

I knew there and then we had achieved what we set out to do, the girls were free, although I did have to return twice to convince the women of this fact. The difficulty in this type of situation is there is a real risk you can attract back whatever has been removed by continually talking about the circumstances surrounding the event. You really need to just forget about it and put it behind you. If you keep reliving it there is a strong possibility you will attract the energy back to you. This is exactly what was in danger of happening here. They had lived with the problem for two weeks, living together 24 hours a day to support each other. Once we had finally left they continued to re-live the episode. Several phone calls later and two further visits did finally convince them that they were truly rid of the problem. It wasn't as if they had experienced anything wrong, they were in a state of constant anticipation and fear of a re-occurrence and it was these anxieties that would prompt a call to me.

Once we had removed the entities from the girls we then moved across to Lisa's property just to make sure there was nothing in her house.

We had arrived at the property from our respective homes, so we were in two cars. As it would be easier for both couples, we agreed to travel in our own cars to the next property. I had a really strong pull to travel in the car with Martin, so Karen and I swapped partners, for the journey. As soon as we pulled off, Martin asked if I could sense anything around. He said he still felt uncomfortable and uneasy, as if he hadn't fully been cleansed of the negative energy associated with these little demons. He asked what I thought. Martin and I have done this together numerous times and had it down to a fine art. But on this occasion I had let rank of marriage stand before experience. I sat and I sensed the energy in his aura and around him. As I did, I could feel something attached to his back like a black dark lump.

With no verbal communication passing between Martin and I, I sensed and listened carefully to White Feather told me to do. I was told to place my hand onto his shoulder (this was the opposite shoulder to where the problem lay) which I did. I felt a surge of energy flow through me, down my arm and into Martin's body. After a very short while Martin said he felt better. I knew from the feeling White Feather was giving me, that we had removed the problem.

It was quite obvious what we had done. On this occasion we had been a little premature in ending the circle and a residue of energy was left in Martin's aura. As a very competent sensitive and Healer Martin could feel this. So could our Guides, which is why I was prompted to go in the car with him.

Lessons were learnt all round for us that night and as a group, we never made that mistake again.

These young women also learned a short sharp lesson they could have done without. Never try and take on something that is bigger than you. Always ask your guides and helpers advice before attempting a clearance. If you are not trained, or a strong experienced Medium, then leave well alone or the same could happen to you. There are spiritualist churches dotted all around the country and they will always offer their services in situations such as these.

Ouija boards

I have never charged for a house clearance and have always tried to respond as quickly as I can, treating these experiences almost like an emergency. I remember too well my own experiences as a child and how my own parents had no idea who to turn to when an experience with an Ouija board went badly wrong.

When I was 14 years old, the craze at the time was to play with Ouija boards, for those who could afford them, for others it was a home-made one. We fell into the latter category. Five of us decided we could do this. We created a circle of the alphabet made out of paper, on the table. We got a stemmed glass out of the cabinet and away we went. We had hours of fun at first, amazed that it really did work. We were sold, hook, line and sinker. For nearly a whole week that summer holiday, our afternoons were spent talking to the glass. At first we accused each other of moving the glass, especially when it spun around the table.

We all took it in turns to remove our fingers off the glass. The idea was if it stopped when one of us had their finger off, we would know they were pushing it around the table. While it slowed down a little, especially when my finger was removed, it still continued to move. On several occasions it appeared to develop a life of its own and continued to circle the table after we had removed our fingers.

How silly and naive we were. If I had fully understood what we were doing I would never have taken part. When it told us a friend was going to die, we felt duty bound to tell him and off we went and solemnly advised him he would he dead by the following May. Years later, he told me how it had made him feel. How the worry had made him ill, and how he had, with fear and trepidation in his heart, waited for the month of May to come. He was really convinced he was going to die and the fear stayed with him a long time. With friends like us, who needed enemies!

Our makeshift board went on to tell me it was coming for me in the night and I was going to die. I never said a word until ten o'clock that night, when advised it was time for bed. I became hysterical. It all spilled out, what we had been doing. My parents didn't know what to do and despite doing their utmost to try and calm me down, telling me everything was going to be okay, they couldn't talk to me on a level I needed to hear. They couldn't talk with knowledge of the world of spirit. They couldn't explain to me how the board had worked or what the consequences were of our actions. Above all, they couldn't tell me how they could stop it or how they were going to protect me from it. They finally persuaded me to go to bed, but I didn't feel absolutely safe. In fact it was a long time before I ever felt safe alone again, especially in the dark. I never forgot the incident and I never went near an Ouija board again.

Over the years I have realised how these boards or makeshift boards work. The concentration of attention and energy through the glass or planchette somehow provides a conduit for communication to take place between the two worlds. More importantly, by concentrating our energy and asking if there is someone there who wants to talk to us, we are giving permission for anyone to come through and talk to us. This is the overriding factor. We are giving away our protection. We are using our free will. This opens the doorway to anything, including unsavoury characters who will pretend to be anyone to get you to talk to them. There are no short cuts, if you want to speak to beings who have passed over, go to a church and learn to do it properly.

I believe when we die the majority of us will go through the light and re-join our friends and loved ones in the world of spirit. Once through the light and reunited with our soul group, our true abilities emerge. However, until we have made that transition, deceased beings are no different from you or I. They have not re-joined and claimed their wondrous gifts. They are merely an entity without a body.

The only difference is that most human beings cannot see them and in some ways they have an advantage over us. They can frighten us and they can live off the fear. The more afraid we are, the more energy they can draw from this. We cannot see them. As the majority of us have not developed our psychic abilities, we are unaware of their existence. This gives them an unfair advantage over us. But they can very rarely harm us.

My advice for any budding Mediums out there is, remember the adage "there are no short cuts to learning the art of communication with the after life." For every action there is a consequence. When it involves an Ouija board, there is a real possibility that you will attract some very unsavoury characters. These entities can hang around you and listen to your conversations. They can then use this information to pretend to be a loved one in the spirit world and give credence to what they say. A smattering of truth in any deceit makes it very plausible and therefore very dangerous. So my strong advice to any 'would-be players', is to keep well away from these boards ands save yourself from a potential horrible experience. If you want to receive communication from the other side, go to a spirit church or centre, they can advise you of a reputable Medium.

House to Let, Partly Occupied

Emma had found the move into her own flat quite traumatic. She had recently split with her long term partner, who appeared to keep everything they had accumulated including their flat. So in a short space of time she found herself breaking up and moving home. Somewhere in the middle of it she had also managed to change jobs.

Emma and her two dogs had settled in well, but over a couple of months she found herself beginning to feel increasingly uncomfortable in both the bedroom and the lounge. A very good indicator is how pets respond and she found the dogs were at times reluctant to come in one or the other rooms, preferring to lie close to the front door as if trying to avoid something. The little dog had begun to bark, something she had never done before. It had got to the point where she was unable to leave the dogs in the property on their own.

Emma reported cold spots in the flat, vile smells and a sensation of being watched. She had also seen orbs in two of the rooms and an old lady in the kitchen. With very few days left before Christmas, and not wanting to leave someone with an unwanted guest, Martin and I went alone, somehow squeezing the visit in between Martin's healing and my group night. We had asked Emma to take the dogs to her mother's for the evening. I was quite content to leave Emma in the flat while we attempted to clear the property, but those upstairs had other ideas. As soon as she mentioned staying, before I could nod in agreement, I had a stern White Feather standing with his arms folding shaking his head. I gently asked her if she would mind leaving, knowing Emma was a keen follower of all ghostly matters. I felt very guilty, but I have learnt the hard way, to listen and take notice when I am given advice or an instruction. They really do know best. "Come back in 20 minutes" we advised. So off she set riding around aimlessly, while Martin and I got down to the task of ridding the property of this entity.

We wandered from lounge to bedroom and back again several times as we tried to sense this entity. It soon became apparent that he didn't like Martin and found him a threat. Whereas with me, a female, he was far more comfortable. I could sense he wanted to dominate and control me. As soon as I sensed this urge to control me, we both understood why we needed to remove Emma from the situation. Her vulnerability and her inexperience would have made her any easy target and the task much more difficult. Our energies would have been weakened as part of our resources would have been spent trying to protect Emma from this dark entity.

After several trips to and from the lounge and bedroom we were convinced that the easiest place to reach him was in the living room, as this was the point from where he seemed to flit in and out.

In whispered voices and nods and looks we formulated our plan. The entity was avoiding us. He knew what we were there for. He was quite happy in his current environment and had no intention of going anywhere. Clearances take very little time it is the sensing, investigation and detective work that takes the time. We also have to make sure we have got the culprit, not a friendly family member who has popped in for company. This incidentally was exactly what the figure in the kitchen was. It was a grandmother, who was doing her best to protect Emma.

This being did not want to leave this world. He had lived a life of debauchery. Excessive drinking and drugs were a way of life for him during his time on earth. He couldn't resist displaying his involvement with young teenage girls, who hung around his flat and were obviously being exposed to things young girls of their age should not have seen.

In order to capture him Martin and I needed to entice him out. Martin stood close to where we had felt his presence several times. With his arms outstretched he offered himself, as a sacrifice, inviting this entity to join with him. The temptation was too great, arrogance and greed over took caution and he took the bait. I stood watching Martin who stood perfectly still with his head bowed and I began to sense and see physical changes. Martin began to slowly raise his head. His was physically changing. A Dark shadow of stubble appeared to cover his chin, he jaw became squarer. Physically Martin appeared to be growing taller and more solid in his appearance. Martin was transfiguring into this man. Still Martin held his energy perfectly still and allowed the intrusion to take place. Slowly he began to open his eyes. The appearance was commanding and unnerving. As the entity nestled fully into Martin's aura it began to exert its energy at me. This is just what our spirit helpers were waiting for. Then in a swoop I saw in my mind's eye a huge feathered wing sweep through Martin and magic the being away. At the same time the change in Martin was miraculous. In a split second the physical changes that had taken place were no longer visible. Martin's energy had reverted back to his own.

The entity had been lured and captured by his own desire. He wanted something he couldn't have. A few moments later we called Emma to tell her it was all clear and she could return. As soon as she walked in, she immediately commented on the difference in the whole feel of the flat. The sinister feeling was no longer present. The flat remained clear and to this day she has had no further problems with it.

Patience at Breaking Point

Walsall Church had given my telephone number to Jean. She was a pleasant woman in her late forties, who lived in an ex-council house with her teenage daughter, husband and a son in his early twenties. Jean had had problems and issues in the house for around five years, but it was getting more frequent and it was beginning to get her down. She had recently started a reflexology course and did something she had never done before, she told a fellow student about her problem, who mentioned the church and this was how she came to call me.

Jean would never have moved this forward but two alarming things had happened. Her son was beginning to receive visitations during the night. He was waking suddenly to the sensation someone was in the room. But more disturbing her daughter was beginning to see, hear and feel this being. That was the trigger for her. While she didn't mind being inconvenienced and had learnt to deal with this encroachment into her life, he was now treading on very dangerous ground. He was beginning to bother her children. The protective instinct of the mother had taken over and this was the driver for Jean to sort this problem out, once and for all.

As Jean explained the problems to me she told me she had heard voices in her head for years. Alarm bells began to ring in my ears. I was just about to suggest she see her own doctor first, Jean had obviously pre-empted this and told me the whole story. She had been to see the old family doctor on several occasions to discuss this. He had in fact put it in writing that mentally there was nothing wrong with Jean, but perhaps something physically was happening to her, from a source which was external to her. I couldn't argue; with mental health issues aside I sat and listened to Jean's story. After talking to her for 20 minutes I decided this was a job for the whole Team, so David and I called upon my dear friends Karen and Martin for assistance.

We had recently met up with another person Gary who had been involved in ghost detection from a different angle. Gary's speciality was detection through the scientific route, by the use of EMF and infra-red cameras, to detect activity. With Jean's permission we invited Gary to join us.

This was probably one of the strangest clearances we had ever attempted. In the corner of the room, right alongside Jean's chair, there appeared to be some anomaly in the ether. It was almost as if there was a default which was allowing free access from the lower planes of the spirit world, directly into Jean's living room. If anyone else had tried to explain this to me or suggest it, I would probably have dismissed it entirely out of hand. But we all reached the same conclusion, there was definitely some sort of energy warp in the corner of this room.

We walked the house several times and each time we were drawn to the space directly by her armchair. In the kitchen there was a small area where a similar sensation could be felt, although not as strong as by Jean's chair. This confirmed our theory. This space, while in a different room, was in fact inches from Jean's chair, separated only by the kitchen/lounge wall.

As we talked to Jean the voice talked to her. As he (Jean knew it was a male) talked we were able to ask questions, which he answered through Jean. We were able to establish he had no connections with her or the house, somehow he had just wandered in and made a nuisance of himself ever since.

This being was very plausible. As Jean relayed the conversation, he made comments such as,

"Tell them to go, they can't help you". "..they will make you ill". "..this will make your daughter ill".

Everything I said he immediately counteracted. Listening to him for a moment, I was beginning to doubt myself. I could feel and see how he had managed to manipulate Jean.

We decided to deal with this in stages. Firstly, we concentrated on cleansing the house, just in case we had missed anything. Then we shut and capped the warp in the ether, to stop him coming back again.

We then concentrated on removing him. This was without doubt the hardest task and it took two visits to finally get rid off him.

What became apparent was Jean had a very powerful latent ability to receive spiritual communication. Unfortunately her sole communicator was this dark entity and I doubt if anyone would want to receive a message from him. His language was appalling - one look at Jean you instantaneously knew she would never use bad language. Over the years he had used every swear word she knew and in the process she had learnt a lot of new ones too.

Removing him appeared quite easy, but he somehow had developed such a good communication channel with her the difficulty was shutting it off. Each time we removed him, he came back. We would sense he was gone, within ten minutes he would be communicated through her again. We were baffled, but only for a very short while.

On the second visit we removed him again. But this time I was drawn to the side of Jean's head. In my third eye I was shown an intricate pattern, approximately 4" across. The pattern was similar to a snowflake. This appeared to be attached to Jean's head. It was almost as if a transfer had been placed here and this was the means by which this entity was communicating directly into her head. Through this pattern. While we had removed him, he was still managing to communicate albeit from a distance. I still don't understand it, but I do know White Feather was showing me this for a reason. I also understood if we blocked this, we would cut off his means of reaching her. So using a combination of psychic ability to remove this pattern and healing to seal it, we severed his links to Jean. It took a couple of days to get the full effect. Over this short period the communication got weaker and weaker, till it finally stopped all together. It was as if we had cut off the energy supply, by doing so, it slowly petered out.

I do hear from Jean occasionally and last time I heard she was still free from this entity - he never returned.

The readings taken by Gary were quite interesting. But what was more interesting were the photographs and the orbs which presented on the photos, but that is for the next book.

Marie's Tale

I have always tried to allow the spirit guides to direct the course of events in any of the Circles I have led. I usually begin by sharing any experiences I feel will help them, followed by any spiritual experiences they wish to share with the group. Either as an example of achievement, or something they want to share or receive guidance on.

This is what we doing one evening when the conversation somehow turned to house clearances. I shared one or two of the clearances I had done as examples. The group were enthralled and so we talked and discussed. What was apparent was several group members had or were having problems of their own. One, in particular, I felt I had to go and deal with as soon as possible.

Marie had experienced several disturbing events in her bedroom. One was the trooping of a 16th Century battalion diagonally across her bedroom, in the middle of the night. As she looked in amazement and watched the event unfold, her Partner, without opening his eyes, raised himself onto his elbow and said "Have them lot finished going past yet?" He then promptly fell back to sleep. Marie said he had no recollection of this the following morning. I felt immediately that this property had been built across a ley line or spiritual path, which would account for the term of events. I had visited another property north of this house, where similar accounts had occurred. While this story amused the group, I found the following events quite disturbing.

As we chatted and I shared my experiences, including the different ways to deal with these entities, Marie sat forward in her chair. It was clear she was contemplating whether or not to speak. Elbows tucked into her side, her hands joined as if in prayer, with her index fingers resting against her lips, she sat posed. Then she opened the conversation to posing the question. 'Is it possible for a spirit to try and have intercourse with you?" My straight answer was "Yes, unfortunately it is possible, although this type of 'haunting' is extremely rare". Once I confirmed what had happened to her was possible, rather hesitantly she shared her experience with us.

Marie told us the event occurred after she had split with her long term partner. She explained she always slept on her stomach. This was the position which she found most comfortable, unfortunately for her, considering what happened to her, this was the worst position she could adopt. Marie went straight to the point. She had woken in the middle of the night, for no apparent reason. Slowly she became aware of the sensation; there was an undefined pressure above her and across her shoulders. Her immediate response was to try and push herself up off the bed. Somehow or other she was pinned to the bed unable to move.

In moments Marie felt unseen hands pressing heavily onto her back. Without giving too much detail she described how this entity, tried to perform a sexual act with her. Her screams of no, appeared to have the desired effect and the entity stopped. Panicking she sat up in bed. She pulled the quilt around her, huddled her body in close and began to cry. Out of nowhere an outstretched hand appeared at the bottom of the bed. She could clearly see the hand and an arm. Marie hesitated for a short while. Through her logic she felt this was a friendly being and felt she had to trust it. She leaned down the bed and offered her hand to the entity. In a split second she found herself, suspended up side down, in mid air, with the sensation she was being held by her ankle. The whole event lasted for less than a minute. Marie couldn't work out what was happening. Was she awake or was she asleep? Moments later she found herself sitting on the floor in the corner of the bedroom sobbing. She knew without a doubt, what had just occurred wasn't a dream. Somehow or another, this entity had managed to physically pull her from the bed and hold her upside down in mid-air.

Anguish, distress and a strong desire to forget the experience meant she had only ever confided in one person about this incident. Marie probably would never have mentioned this again, had it not been that quite recently a similar event had occurred. After an absence of nearly a year she found herself being woken by the entity again.

As before, without warning she woke to the sensation of being pinned down onto the bed by an unseen force. As she lay consciously awake, what felt like hands began to roughly massage her back. There was without doubt something on top of her. This time her anger overcame her fear and she shouted out "Oh no, you don't". With that command the pressure released her and the being was gone and Marie was able to sit up in bed and grab her little angel from her bedside and ask for protection. What was apparent for her was it was capable of coming back. It was this driver, which gave her the courage to talk about it openly that night.

Our open discussion in this little group allowed her to share her experience, and by doing so we were able to help. As she spoke I gently asked her guide to give me a sign. As Marie talked I saw a dark green shadow, sickly in nature begin to cover her head and side. This was all the information I needed.

I knew immediately we had a serious problem on our hands and this required an immediate response. So with hastened diary check we all convened outside the property the next day. This time we added another Medium to our group, Judy, as a learning experience for her. No doubt in time Judy would be called upon to carry out such tasks, so now was a better time than ever to learn the ropes of the trade. Judy had arrived first and gone into the house. We quickly called her out to discuss our plan of action. Judy said she felt there was a connection to Marie's sister Jody. It wasn't until the end of the evening that we were to discover how true this was.

We then called Marie outside and asked her to get everyone except herself out of the property, including the dogs. We checked we had all done our protection and recognised this might not be as easy and straightforward as we believed, as I felt it would evade us.

We all trooped into the house and as the other occupants collected their belongings. We talked about our plans for the remainder of the evening. In fact we discussed any subject except what we were about to do. All our planning had been done prior to entering the property, to avoid the entity pre-empting any action we may take.

With the dogs and people safely re-located outside of the house we began to walk and sense the property. Because all the activity had taken place in the bedroom, this seemed an obvious choice.

I asked Marie to show me the line and direction the soldiers had marched. I was a little concerned to see the battalion had trooped across into another room, rather than outside wall to outside wall. If this entity was entering through this spirit path, then there was a strong possibility that the occupant of the adjacent room (Marie's recently divorced sister, who was temporary staying here), may have been effected by it. With other matters to deal with I let this matter slip, for the moment.

Marie lived in a modern detached house, on a modern estate, and as with lots of new properties the rooms were quite compact, but well laid-out. We circled the room, all changing places with each other as we felt the energies in the room. There were some incredibly strong sensations in this room, ranging from fear, sickness through to anger. It was soon evident if we were to lure this entity out, we needed to place Marie sitting on the bed. While Marie was still developing, she was a strong Medium. He was clearly attracted to her. We had the perfect trap. More importantly, Marie was trained in trance work. It was this ability which would be of most benefit in luring him out into the open, by using Marie's energy field as bait.

The energy to right of the bed, where the troops had marched in felt quite angry. This we all agreed upon and this was the access point to the room. The energy to the left of the bed was so strong it made everyone feel a little nauseous. We decided to seal the room, with a small doorway to the right of the bed. With us all strategically placed, we began the process. But before I started I insisted Marie share my protection and asked her to recite it out loud. Assured she had adequate protection and with us all strategy placed, we protected the whole room. We then stood and waited, in moments we could feel the entity begin to join with Marie.

As I stood at the foot of the bed with Karen alongside me, I could feel the energy begin to overshadow Marie. While nothing was said, you could feel its venom. Karen gently asked if we should let it fully join with Marie. I had no intentions of making it that powerful. I began to talk to it. Telling it Marie had not invited it into her home and it was not welcome. Marie didn't want it here and she was asking it to go. For a momentarily second the scene from the Exorcist appeared in my mind where the girl projectile vomits green matter over the Priest. Now, if one film bothers me, it is this one. I have often tried to watch it, but never fully achieved it since I went to the pictures as a teenager, then I had spent the whole evening with my head buried in my hands. I knew instantly he was trying to invoke the feeling of fear within me. If I was fearful I would be significantly weakened. This was why Karen had asked the question earlier - he had tried to make her fearful. As I was leading the process, if I gave in to feelings of fear, this would have had a detrimental effect on the whole event. In an instant I knew what he was doing, I tossed the scene of the film aside and looked and challenged the being, with a greater force than he could manage at this moment in time. With the help of the others I was able to overpower him.

As far as he was concerned he was going nowhere. At one point Marie's face moved as if to growl. Later I learnt she had suppressed the word Bitch, from being directed at me. I wasn't surprised. The four of use sent wave after wave of white and silver light, while imploring him to go away. I turned to look at Martin and recognised the signs there; he was inviting him across. In a very brief moment, this being with a human-sized head, with pointed features and sharp teeth and a body like an octopus leapt from Marie, onto Martin. As he did so, he took with him all but one of the long tentacles which had firmly been attached to Marie's solar plexus region. As it left we psychically severed the link between Marie and the entity.

We were now faced with the task of fully removing it from Martin. This we achieved with relevant ease. This time we took the time to ensure it had gone completely and sealed any holes in the process.

As usual the house began to feet physically lighter and warmer as both Judy and Marie commented on how light the rooms were and how the house appeared to be getting warmer.

While we had removed the entity we now felt we needed to ensure that the doorway was firmly shut or diverted to avoid a re-occurrence. So we spent a few moments shifting the spiritual pathway across into the street away from other properties, not into the next door neighbour's house! We also agreed the computer needed to be moved. It was directly in the corner where the doorway had been. This was the area where we all felt angry. As we advised Marie to put it elsewhere, she said she would be glad to as every time she went near it, she felt angry.

I couldn't help wondering if the source of electricity had in some way contributed to the magnification of this doorway.

As we all stood downstairs chatting we couldn't help but comment how much better Marie began to look. While we had concentrated on getting the entity off Martin I had, at the same time, given her some healing and her cheeks had begun to look quite rosy. Just before her sister and her new boyfriend came back into the house, Marie shared the events that occurred before we arrived.

She had explained to her sister of our pending visit and why she had invited us along. Her sister had listened intently then asked her if she had also been bothered by dreams of a sexual manner, which were so graphic they appeared to be actually happening. Marie said as she looked at her sister she realised for the first time she wasn't alone in her experience, her baby sister had also been suffering from a similar fate. Possibly because of her lack of psychic experiences she didn't realise what was happening to her, although she did feel like she was being violated as these were not erotic dreams but sensations of being debased, with no control over the situation. Before we left Martin gave Jody some spiritual healing and like Marie a glow also appeared in her cheeks immediately.

As we all walked out we felt confident that we had dealt with the problem and it would not be coming back. We also felt as if the land had in some long-lost time been sacred in some way and should not have been built upon. It was thought that in the time of King Charles this area had been a battlefield; maybe so. But we felt we would need to go much farther back to find the answers. Back before the history books began.

What this shows is that there doesn't have to be a cause for unwelcome occupants to move into or be resident in your home as soon as it is built. It doesn't always have to be something we have done to for these events to take place. There is an awful lot about the land and the energy paths that zigzag across it that we in modern society don't understand.

We all felt that it was the existence of the energy path running through the bedroom and the source of electricity, at the point of entry, which had allowed this entity to cross the boundaries of the two worlds. While quite rare in today's society, the concept of beasts from another world attempting to have sexual intercourse with humanbeings, is not a new concept. In middle ages there was a name for these beasts. The male form was called an Incubus and the female Succubus. It was believed that these entities would prey on their victims during the night, or while their victims were in a dreamlike state they would attempt to have a sexual encounter with their victims. These beasts are thought to have adopted a variety of physical forms to achieve their desires. There is no doubt this is exactly what had happened here, but in a modern detached house, to a very modern family.

Whether we believe in another dimension so vast that it can accommodate beings from the lowest realms to the highest is immaterial. To these people these events, without doubt, occurred. No matter how bizarre and unbelievable they appear, for the people mentioned in this chapter they did occur and for some they had the physical evidence to show for their contact with these entities. This chapter is not designed to be scaremongering, but merely a sharing of experiences. More importantly it here to show people these events can and do happen.

Should it happen to you now or in the future hopefully these stories should give you hope that there are organisations out there, such as the spiritualist church that can help. They have within their churches people who are experienced in dealing with these matters and should be able to help you to rid your home of this property.

For the 'would-be ghost-buster' I would say, leave this job to those who know what they are doing, for without Mediumship skills it is hard to see what is happening. But more importantly it is harder to hear what the experts from the other side are trying to tell you, as they take over or lead the task of removing someone who is not of this world, and therefore should no longer be in residence here. Remember, Mediums are what their title implies. They are conduits for those of the greater realms to use to put things right that have gone awry in our world.

Sceptics

Not everybody believes that we survive or that we can or should communicate with people who no longer occupy our world. Some people have never considered it. Death has not yet been a part of their lives and there has been no event that has challenged them enough to contemplate their own mortality. So in short there are those who are sceptic of the possibility we could survive death; those who believe we should not disturb the dead; and finally those who have not even considered it.

I learned long ago never to enter into a debate with people who are sceptical about Mediumship. It is very easy to rise to the bait. But experience has taught me otherwise. I remember in the early days. I was eager to show off my skills and desperate to convert the world. During a conversation with a work colleague after hearing of my extra-sensory skill went something like. "Go on then, tell me, who is with me?" "Your dad" I replied. Giving no sign of recognition in their in face they ventured "What is he saying to you?" "He is giving me the name Bill, Jack and John" I said. But before I could say anything else, she looked at me rather quizzically and replied "They are his brothers' names, but you could have overheard me say them at sometime or are just lucky, as they are popular names. Is there anything else you can give me?" I apologised explaining I was due somewhere else in a few minutes and suggested another time. I felt exhausted by the encounter and vowed never to rise to the challenge again. I did. It took several attempts before I stopped rising to the bait.

Through these experiences I discovered that it is very easy for people to sit back and say 'show me'. Very little effort is required by the person throwing down the gauntlet. They merely need to sit back and allow the Medium to 'perform' as they give evidence after evidence to try and convince the sceptic that there is, without doubt, life beyond life. However, remembering the universal laws we know, no-one can take away the free will of another and this also relates to belief systems. To believe or not believe is a personal choice. There is no evidence which a Medium can provide which will change this view. What we see or what is presented to us, can challenge our views or force us to re-evaluate them, but they will not change overnight. So the engagement of 'show me' and attempting to do so, is futile. After discovering this 'fact of life', through experience, sometimes good, sometimes not, I learnt how to deal with it. I discovered by telling the curious "If you ask me I will look to see who is around you and if you ask me, I will pass on a message from them to you". I subsequently engaged the enquirer and ensured they contributed to the process, in some way or another. In other words, instead of the sceptic sitting back, with arms folded, contributing nothing to the exercise. Waiting to prove you wrong and a charlatan, they had to give something in return.

On another occasion I remember approaching a woman in her mid-forties, in the congregation of a small church. She sat looking at me with her arms folded, her body completely closed. A stony look on her face greeted me as I asked her "can I come to you? You have a father in the spirit world?" "Yes" came the reply. "He was 5ft 10inches tall". "I don't know". "Did you know your father?" "Yes", "but you don't know his height?", I asked a little unsure where this line of questioning was going. "Don't know" came the cold response back. "God bless and thank you for working with me" was my response as I quickly moved onto the next link, which was gladly received.

As we left the centre where the service had been held on a cold December night, some of the congregation didn't realise I was behind them. "It serves her right" came the comment from one of the women, obviously talking about my disgruntled recipient. "I have been dying for someone to do that to her" came the response back. Suddenly they noticed me walking behind. All three turned and smiled, knowing smiles.

As we got into the car David asked what was going on. "Well, David", came my reply "I give my time willingly to these churches and centres and serve them for next-to-nothing, but I will be dammed if I am going to waste everyone's time when someone clearly is not going to accept my message". I then added I wasn't here to prove myself, merely to prove life after death. He looked at me, searching my face for a moment, and then nodding in agreement added "good for you". That was the last we said on the subject.

Over the years my attitude hasn't changed, when someone stone-walls and blocks, I gently move on to the next. Majority of the people don't do this deliberately, they just don't understand the process. For Mediumship to work successfully the recipient needs to be open, warm and willing to receive information. If any of these elements are missing, the exchange is fruitless and pointless. The recipient must want to receive a message and be open to it in order for the communication to take place.

There will always be those who believe in life after death and believe there are people around who have the ability to communicate with people in other realms, and there will always be those who don't believe. For the latter I have and will always have a healthy respect. We all have own belief systems and no-one has the right to force their views on another or believe they are superior because they believe something the majority does not. I have therefore made it a habit never to try and convert the unconverted.

On the other hand there is another type of sceptic, those who don't really believe, but have an open mind to the subject. You are more likely to come across this type of sceptic's at events such as 'suppers with Mediums', where they have been persuaded to come along with friends.

During one supper with Mediums, my second table was extremely large. It soon became apparent that only one of the group had ever been in a spiritual church before. The body language and behaviour of the others clearly showed they were unsure what to expect and a little nervous.

As soon as I sat down I went to a young man in his early twenties, blond, good looking and certainly capable of looking after himself, he was anything other than a 'softy' to look at. It later became apparent his girlfriend had persuaded him to come and the look on his face when I asked if I could go to him showed he was not expecting a message. "You have a brother in spirit" I said. He was a little shocked that I had picked this up. "He has been in the spirit world for 4 years" "spot on" came the reply. I then went on to say he and his brother hadn't always got on. His brother was older than him and at times could be a bit of a bully who often hit him. "Don't put me on a pedestal" he said "I could be a right ar****ole", clearly as I was in a spiritualist church I didn't relay this word, just intimated he was using choice language! "Stop feeling guilty you lived and he died, it was his time to go". At this the young lad began to cry, tears cascaded down his face, his fiancé holding his hand tightly joined in, so did I and his future mother-in-law. It was a very emotional moment, which was only broken by the joining of the mother-in-law's father who was an extremely lively character who brought evidence for all his daughters and granddaughters.

Several weeks later I met the family again, when I visited them at home for private readings. They explained the brothers had not always got on. The young man was feeling guilty because he had survived and his brother hadn't. They said the information I had given had been such a relief and they said he was a different person because of it.

My assessment of him was correct as a few weeks after this event I saw him working away as a security guard, at a very large store, in quite a challenging area. I looked away before he noticed me, not wanting to cause him any embarrassment. The next time I visited he was still there, as I stood queuing at the check-out and he stood beside the doors. Our eyes caught, not wishing to embarrass him, but before I could look away he waved across to me; he was obviously not bothered or embarrassed to see me.

119

I Never Said Goodbye

For most people, the prospect of loosing a Partner through death is something we don't contemplate, until our senior years in life. We reserve thoughts of death to our later years. The departure of someone is difficult to cope with on its own. But nothing can be harder than the sudden exit of anyone dear to you. We seldom appreciate what we have in life and we rarely take the time to tell our partners how richer and fuller our lives are made by their presence, until it is too late. We then live a thousand 'if only's. Someone sent me a lovely email and into it, a verse said " ....you can buy a clock, but you cannot buy time". How true, I thought then and still do. You cannot turn the clock back and have it all again. Once a moment is gone, it is lost forever; it can be imitated and repeated, but never re-lived as it originally was. David would often repeat a couple of lines his mother used to say to him when he was a child:

"Pleasures are like the poppies spread,
you seize the flower the bloom is dead
or like the snowfall in the river,
a moment white, then gone forever"

It is the finality of death which makes it so difficult. It cannot be changed, altered or amended no matter how many times you hear people say "they're not far away", or "they are only a thought away". Many of you will know this and need no reminding. Yet it is still not the same as having someone in the flesh, to cuddle you when you feel insecure or someone to offer re-assuring words when you are in doubt.

Glenda was a tall slim woman, with a weathered face that showed all the appearances of too much sun. Her face was further lined by the continual half-scowl she appeared to wear. She was visiting friends in the area for a few days, when someone had recommended she come and see me. As she was only in the area for a limited period I agreed to see her at short notice.

As soon as Glenda sat down I could feel the presence of a very gentle loving soul alongside her. I did my usual opening and asked her if there was anyone in particular to whom she would like to chat. Her reply was "Anyone" shaking her head, as if at a loss to think of anyone to talk to. "Do you want to talk to your husband?" I enquired "Oh yes please" she answered immediately, moving to the edge of her seat to ensure she could hear me. As he moved closer, I sensed a tall man with a big frame, prematurely grey hair, a thin moustache and a broad smile. "This man is giving me 56 and is telling me that he has not been in the spirit world for very long". "That's correct" her face grimaced, as if recalling her current painful circumstances. "He tells me he has been in the world of spirit for 4 months and you will understand the 24th and the month of April" "Yes I do", came the reply. "He is saying 10 days to go". Her hand flew to her mouth, as she nodded she appeared afraid to speak, as if this may break the connection. I went on, "He is giving me the name, Cheryl, Paul, Anthony and Beryl and he is talking now of a coming birthday". She continued to nod. He was a fluent communicator I said. As I spoke Glenda sat on the edge of her seat her face set in concentration as she hung onto every word he said. He described his own personality, their likes and dislikes and how he had passed, with a crushing blow to his head. "Tell her I never felt a thing, one minute I was walking around the yard and the next thing I knew, I was standing looking at my body!" By the end of the sitting she had laughed, cried and chastised him for teasing me. The sitting was all but over when Glenda asked if she could ask him a question. Of course I replied. "Am I doing the right thing?"

Unfortunately, there is a very curious person within me, to function as a Medium I have to keep myself out of way. When someone asks a question and I am intrigued, I really do struggle to keep my nose out. With great restraint I managed to keep my mind still as I rummaged for her answer. I need not have doubted, within seconds I saw a huge grin pass across Ken's face and he raised his thumb up to her. With a wink of an eye he was gone. I repeated the scene to her. She smiled and thanked me. With her eyes raised towards the ceiling, smiling she half-spoke and half-mouthed "Thanks Darling".

Glenda and I sat and chatted for a moment and she explained that they had holidayed in Portugal for 20+ years, spending all their time out there. Ten years ago they had brought an apartment out there. Two years ago they had decided to move out there permanently when they retired. They had sold their own home and had a villa built a few miles outside of Faro. For 18 months they had lived with Ken's elderly mother, while they worked towards their dream. With ten days to his retirement and 14 days to realizing their dream, Ken was tragically killed at work, when he collided with a reversing artic. The blow to the head had killed him outright. He had died at the age of 56, four months ago. Glenda was distraught over the loss of Ken. Initially no mention was made of the villas and Portugal until recently when, to her families anguish, she had decided to move to Portugal anyway. "Ken and I dreamed of moving to Faro, all our dreams are there" she said, she then added "but they are my dreams too and its killing me to be here, homeless without him". She sat silently turning her small hankie around in her hands. She then looked up and asked if it would get any better. I tried to re-assure her as much as I could. But we all know it is the first birthday, first anniversary, first Christmas which are the most difficult. Then it is the second round and so it goes. We never forget a loved one, but in time life will fill the void that was once occupied by a spouse and people go on to other relationships, which will be equally loving. Each relationship has it own uniqueness and holds its own place in our hearts. We never forget, but in time the pain lessens. We will all reach the stage when we are able to look back at our relationship with a deceased love, with love and fondness, without being racked with pain and heartache, although some will take longer than others to reach this stage.

The belief that we survive death is a strong part of spiritualism and for many, it is this strong belief which helps us to cope in our hour of need and gradually move one, but not all.

I met Sheila during a church service, when Eric her husband came through. She cried throughout the whole message and received the information as if this was the first time she had spoken to him. I was a little hesitant when he gave me 17 years and I realised that he had been over this length of time. Sheila had found the spiritualist movement shortly after his death and still attended weekly services, always in the hope she would hear from him. All the messages and healing in the world, could not help her to move on. She was happy and her life appeared content, so who are we to comment.

Brenda on the other hand had lived eight years in torment. She had been married to Tommy for 26 years, he had always worked hard and lived his life for his family, his wife and two sons. Unlike his own father, who had spent all his time in the pub. The pub and his friends had always come first, with his wife and children coming a poor third. Tommy always vowed to be different and he was. His weekends were filled with activities with the boys, fishing, camping, BMX tracks and as they grew older motor cross, these were some of the many things they did together. He even became a Boy Scout leader, so he could accompany the boys. Brenda in the meantime, received very little attention as Tommy spent all his time trying to be everything his father wasn't. She was left to her own devices. In her loneliness she succumbed to the advances of John, a single man whom she met at work. Through his charm and attention, something she missed so much at home, he coveted and wooed her. Brenda loved Tommy with all her heart, but she didn't feel loved. Having fallen for John's charms, in a moment of weakness, she packed her bags and went. Tommy was heartbroken and realising what he had done in neglecting his wife, he set about winning her back. After six weeks realising how much she loved Tommy, she packed her bags and asked him to come and collect her. They were staying in Mid Wales. Tommy set off immediately. He never made it. He died in a head on collision on the A5, just past Llangollen. Six hours later Brenda received the news. Tommy had died in the process of collecting her. She left John that day and headed home, without Tommy. Eight years on, she was still tormented by her loss. "I never had chance to say goodbye" she sobbed during the sitting. "If only I hadn't gone or came back sooner, he would be alive today", she informed me solemnly. For eight years she had harboured this thought that Tommy was dead because of her. The boys were without a father because of her. She was only opening her heart now because a friend had bamboozled her into filling a place at an evening of readings. I was glad she was the last person of the night, because I could spend the amount of time needed, which was quite a lot of time. I explained to her that when it is our time to go, we pass over. It had been Tommy's time to pass and nothing she could have done would have changed that. Tommy also reminded her it took two to tango, he gave her numerous memories of how she had asked to do things with Tommy and he had put his own and the activities of the boys before their own relationship. Including the time he had left her to go on holiday alone, because something had come up with the scouts. While he joined her for the last three days she had spent four miserable days sitting alone in a caravan in Devon, waiting for him to join her. He was able to show her it was not her fault. If he had been more attentive as a husband, she would never have strayed. Each time he made fresh revelations, she listened, as if hearing it for the first time. As if this was the first time she had seen it from this angle. As Brenda rose to leave the room, she looked as if the weight of the world had been lifted from her shoulders. She looked taller and younger. No doubt now she had released all the guilt, Tommy would at last be able to reach her and she would be able to move on with her life.

Brenda's case is not unique. There are thousands of people in this country alone trying to come to terms with the loss of a loved one they never had chance to make peace with before their passing, as death from this physical world came too quickly.

There is some truth in the words, 'once it's gone it's gone' and never more true are those words when talking about our relationships with those around us. Ask yourself when was the last time you looked and evaluated your life together with your partner. When did you spend quality time together, telling each other how much you mean to each other? Well do it now, don't wait until it is too late. Don't wait to enjoy weekends together and meals together, do it now, or next time you could be communicating to them through someone like me.

Messages from the other side – How soon?

People often ask the question, how long is it after a loved one passes over before they are able to come through? My initial response was to say I don't know. I don't believe there are strong and fast rules. If I had any pre-conceived ideas of how long it would take this was quickly eroded away in time, as I saw people, time after time, come through and speak to their family and friends after very short periods of time.

Spiritualist Churches cannot survive on general services alone, the proceeds from the plate collections do not bring in enough money. Throughout the year they lay on different types of events, to ensure the doors always stay open, such as private sittings, specials and suppers with Mediums. Throughout the West Midlands these suppers are very popular. For a small fee the participants, who sit at tables of no more than eight, will have three or four Mediums join them for around 30 minutes. Every effort is made to ensure everyone receives a message. This is followed by fish, chips, bread and butter and tea or coffee.

This is how the majority of these events flow; that is until there is some catastrophe with the fish and chips, like them arriving late, which happens very occasionally, as these events are organised with military precision. When this does occur the Medium usually stays on the last table until they do arrive.

This is what had happened in December 2004 at Walsall Church. I had gone onto my last table, which consisted of six young very vibrant women, who were eagerly participating in the event. I could sense as soon as soon as I sat down that they were open to the idea of spirituality, as a Medium this does make life a little easier, although I had difficulties immediately, something which had never had before. For the first time ever I couldn't place someone from the spirit world. I felt sure I was with the attractive young women on my right. "You can understand a woman in the spirit world, who would have been quite ill before she passed over?" I asked, looking directly at her. "No" came the reply. I felt sure I was with her, so I pressed on. "She would have lived in a Nursing Home?" "No" came the reply. I glanced around the table to see if anyone else was showing signs that this may belong to them, although I was convinced I was with this young woman. On I pressed. "She was unable to communicate, due to her condition and was nursed from bed?" "No" came back the reply. One last attempt, I added: "she has not been over very long?" "No" came the reply, as she shook her head empathically, she could not take any of this.

At this point I gave up, quite despondent, but I applied the Terry Cotterill (a wonderful Medium from Telford, who has worked the circuit for years) rule of thumb, three strikes and I am off, in fact on this occasion I think it was more like five! For the remainder of the time on the table everyone took everything I gave out. Unfortunately tonight was going to be that very rare occasion when things were not going to go according to plan and the food was delayed. So as usual, we stayed on the table and kept working. Towards the end, I felt myself flagging slightly and prayed the food would arrive shortly. I continued to give messages out, although at a slightly slower rate. I was talking to a woman on my left, when I suddenly became aware of the bleeping of a text message. I glanced back to the woman on my left and she intently read her text message and began to respond. Her finger deftly flying across the keys, with a speed and expertise I envied. I jokingly asked her if my talking was disturbing her. Not looking up from her phone and in rather a quiet voice, she shook her head and said "No". The young woman who sat directly opposite her kicked her gently under the table and added. "She was being sarcastic, she is trying to give me a message and you are disturbing her". She looked up from her phone glanced at her friend and then towards me, then directly back to her phone. She was clearly pre-occupied with the message she had received. Suddenly realising what her friend had said to her, she then began to apologise and explain. Her friend and I exchanged glances and smiled at each other, as the woman still hadn't cottoned on we were joking. She placed the phone down on the table and said "I'm so sorry, it's just that I've had a bit of a shock. My cousin's nan has just died, suddenly 30 minutes ago", she explained to everyone on the table, paying particular attention to myself and her friend who sat opposite her. To me it suddenly became apparent. Just at the moment the double doors at the back of the church burst open as the posse arrived with boxes of chips in hand, and everyone immediately began to talk. The first part of the evening was officially over. The food would be distributed, by the Team of helpers in minutes.

Desperately trying to compete with the sudden noise that filled the church I leaned forward and said to the girl, in a voice loud enough so the rest of the occupants on the table could here, and said "you mean the elderly lady who was being nursed from bed in a nursing home?" She looked at me, astounded by what I said. I then went on to tell her the name of the husband and how he had come to fetch her. "This lady was unable to communicate for a significant period of time". "Oh God", she said "that's correct, she's been really ill". I then added "well she has briefly popped in to say, tell everyone I'm okay and thank them for what they did, but tell them I am on my way". In my mind's eye, as clear as a bell, I saw her waving goodbye as she walked away arm in arm with her husband. I repeated this information to the astounding lady. She again repeated "My God, I cannot believe this". Before I had arisen from the table, her phone was back in her and again and she was frantically texting her cousin to tell her of the visit from her nan, to offer her re-assurance that she was okay and off back to the land of spirit.

To me this proved several things. If they wish to, some spirits can come back very quickly and communicate with this world.

In a quest to decry the art of Mediumship, I have over the years heard and read many theories on how Mediums allegedly obtain the information they do. One popular theory I have heard many times is that we read people minds. For all those sceptics who believe this, please explain this one. If all we are is merely mind readers how come I received the information, before this young woman actually knew her cousin's nan was dead?

This was not the only time I had received information from spirits who had recently departed this world. In fact this has happened to me on numerous occasions. Here are a couple more examples of early communications.

On another occasion, a similar thing happened to me. It was December 5th 2006 and my last service of the year at Kings Heath Spiritualist Church, although oddly enough, as it sometimes happens, my next service was booked for early January 2007. It is quite unusual to have two dates in one Church so close, considering a Medium may serve some Churches only twice a year, but with the change-over from one year to another, this does occasionally happen.

The evening was going well, I had numerous connections already open and very little time left when I moved over to the left-hand side of the room. I suddenly became aware I had picked up another connection. I asked a lady if I could come to her. "You have a mother in the spirit world, I asked?" "Yes that's correct" came the reply from both the younger and older woman, who clearly looked like mother and daughter. The younger woman held her mother's arm, by threading her own arm through her mother's, as if to give her as much support as possible. "She is mentioning warden controlled accommodation and that someone had not been in this type of accommodation for too long?" They both looked at each other, as if to say this is definitely her, then turned and nodded to me in agreement. I then gave a list of names, all of which they could take. "She is telling me she hasn't been over very long?" "Yes that's correct, she died yesterday!" I could not believe my ears on receiving this information and struggled to hold the link. The lady was undeterred by my moment's hesitation and continued to chat to her daughter and granddaughter. She explained she was very well before she died and she had met several of her friends since arriving here and, as usual, she finished off with several names of close family members. She then went on to tell the family she was fine and not to worry, even confirming some details they had been discussing about the funeral.

In January 2007 I am again at Kings Heath and before I realised I was again delivering a message from this lady. Only this time the mother and daughter were accompanied by several other family members. With the same determination and expertise she again brought evidence beyond belief that she had survived her physical death.

Some people may find it a little strange to come to church so soon after the death of a loved one. But as spiritualists we believe in life after death. To seek solace in a church service is a very natural thing to do.

On another occasion, towards the end of a service I was drawn to a gentleman sitting on the back row. "You have, I understand, a mother in the spirit world?" I said to him. He hesitated for a while, as if he was reluctant to accept the information I had presented to him. Urged on by the gentle persuasion of his female companion, he clears his throat and confirms this information. "This lady passed quite quickly and with little warning, following a long illness" I added. Again he cleared his throat and looked to his partner for assurance before confirming this was correct. "This lady was dependant on oxygen" "yes" again came from the man. "You will understand emphysema and a heart attack" I said. "Yes, yes I do" said the man rather nervously. "The name Stanley?" "That's my name." "Margaret?" "My partners name" "and Joan?" I added. "That's her name". As the message finally ended she gave several other names, towns and street names. I thanked the gentleman and moved onto the next recipient.

As the service ended I watched the gentleman and his partner stand and leave their seats. They seemed really unsure of what was expected of them. I felt compelled to stop and speak to him, as he had appeared so nervous during the delivery of the message. I wanted to check he was feeling alright

They both thanked me for the message and his partner added that it was their first time ever in a Spiritualist Church and that they had been very unsure about actually coming into the church, not knowing what to expect. I tried to re-assure him, adding that the church was an extremely friendly place and suggested he should come back. He then went onto say the whole experience of losing someone close was very new to them and his mother had only passed on five days ago. But after looking after her for three years, without warning she suddenly passed over after suffering from a massive heart attack. He was desperate to know that she was safe on the other side. Hesitantly, he moved from one foot to the other and cleared his throat. Before the question could form on his lips, I quickly told him that she was with her father and he did come to fetch her and had safely led her over to the other side. The man and woman exchanged loving glances with each other and with tears glistening in their eyes they thanked me. With collars upturned and scarves tightly wrapped around their necks, they set off into the cold air. There was no need for further words. It was clearly the answer he wanted to hear, she was safe, she hadn't died alone and she had met up with her husband. As they walked out of the door, I couldn't help smiling to myself.

It has been events such as these which have helped me to form the idea that there are no thick and fast rules when it comes to the world of spirit. There are factors in play, which govern when people can come and speak to people of this world, but they are factors that I and many other do not understand. But who knows in the future.   These were not the only times I have given messages to people who have departed this plane very recently. There have been countless times when I have communicated with spirit shortly after their deaths, but these are a few which I felt emphasised the situation nicely.

Waiting for Evidence

I was just beginning a service, had several connections open and was just about to launch into my work, when a young woman at the rear of the church caught my eye. I felt instantly drawn to her, but I couldn't for the life of me, work out who was trying to get my attention. All I could feel was this very strong emotion exuding from almost every pore of this woman. 'Speak to me please', came the plea. I stopped and spoke to her for a second, "Can I come back to you I asked?" She nodded, with deep sadness in her eyes. Towards the end of the service and with no time left, I suddenly became aware of her again. Why hadn't they reminded me, they usually do. "Can I come and speak to you afterwards?" I asked "Yes", she replied. I went and sat down with the woman and her partner, I was still struggling to see who it was she was so keen to speak to. I told her I felt she was desperate to speak to someone and this was making it difficult for me to reach them and asked who it was; as soon as she said her name I felt her mother draw close. I gave her a short message packed with information, the condition her mother had passed with, how long ago it was, her perfume, what she looked like, personality etc. "Your mother is telling me you have a particular question to ask her" I said and she says to tell you she is standing alongside you holding a little boy's had. "That was my question" she said "To see if she had found my little boy and to check she was looking after him". Her mother suddenly appeared quite anxious and began to shake her finger at the daughter. "You are thinking of doing something really silly?" I said. 'Yes' she nodded. All the time her partner sat listening, with a feel of helplessness as she admitted she was thinking of committing suicide and she didn't feel she had the strength to keep going. The loss of her mother 12 months ago had proved to be the final straw and she was struggling to cope. As I sat I soaked this woman, from head to foot, in blue healing energy and I visualised an endless flow. I gently explained to her if she committed suicide she would only be with them for a short while as she would have to come back down to finish her life's journey. She looked at me with sincerity and a deep inner knowing. As my words slowly sank in, she knew I was right; there are no short cuts out of life. Once we are here we need to complete our lives. I suggested she stay for healing, as this followed the service. The healers we already set up and a small crowd were gathering to receive healing. I gave her a huge hug from her mom and left to join David in the large room at the rear of the church.

When we are quite needy, it is sometimes very difficult for the spirit people to penetrate this energy. This is one of the many reasons why some people seen to wait an age before they receive a message from the other side. There are also those who don't hear when they are given a communication, because they are desperate to hear from someone special. Unfortunately it is not always possible to 'order' who you would like to talk to. I remember visiting a Spiritualist Church years ago, at a time when I needed guidance and praying my nan would come and talk to me. I had her focused in my mind. When the Medium came and spoke to me he brought

through a distant aunt, not my nan. I struggled to accept a lot he was offering me. It is only after I looked back on the message did I realise the importance of the evidence he had brought through. Because I was focusing on my nan, when he asked questions, I looked around my nan and my memories of her for the answer, instead of casting the net farther. Just because I wished to speak to her didn't mean she could arrive to order, probably because I kept the thought and kept re-thinking it, over and over again, instead of letting it go. By
releasing it, we realize the wish and allow it to happen. We can only achieve this, when we release it.

People will often and speak, after the service and ask questions. After one particular service a woman came up to me and said she had waited 9 years for a communication with her mother, yet despite all her asking and pleading she had received nothing from her, not a sausage in 9 years. I could feel her mother standing alongside. "Are you sure you have never had anything from your mother?" I questioned. "No. The other week I sat in my car and said Mom where are you? It's your birthday, I thought you would have come through". She went on to tell me she didn't know why but she felt the urge to turn on the radio and there was her mother's favourite song, 'Are you lonesome tonight' by Elvis. "See mom, even the radio station is playing your record and you still haven't come through". I listened for a moment, trying to work out how to address this. "Hang on" I said "you were sitting thinking of your mom?" "Yes I was". "So if you were thinking of her, what made you put the radio on?" I asked. "I don't know I just did" came the reply. "So something prompted you to put the radio on, just at the moment your mom's favourite song is playing and you didn't think this was a sign or a message from her?" "Oh my God" she cried out, covering her mouth with her hand "This has happened loads of time, I never thought of it that way. You mean they can prompt you like that?" "Yes they can. The spirit world will use whatever means it can to reach you. We just have to learn to be open to many possibilities".

I remember casually thinking I hadn't heard from my own nan in an age and let the thought go. One of my fondest memories of my nan, was her love of the tune 'Amazing Grace'. I can fondly remember my step-granddad Jack, at Christmas and New Year parties, being cajoled to stop enjoying himself and to go and get his accordion and give us all a tune. Jack was always a very quiet shy and reserved man, and for many people they were at a loss to understand how someone as outgoing as my nan had ever partnered up with him, who was exactly the opposite to her. But there was no doubt that she loved him very much and he brought her great happiness. Eventually he would give in to the requests and would go and get his much loved machine. I remember as he played his accordion he would sway from side to side, his flat cap on and a woodbine perched in the corner of his mouth and a beer close at hand, which he would drink in the short interludes, between tunes. Uncle Jack, as I addressed him, was a slightly built man and the accordion appeared to swamp him. It seemed to all the world, as if he struggled to wrap his arms around this enormous machine. Once in place the only part of Uncle Jack you could visually see was his head, legs, forearms and fingers. The house would be packed with party revellers, in the lounge and kitchen. He would stand in the corner, by the doors to the stairs, barely able to fit into the room for all the other people, and he would go from tune to tune. The only time people noticed him was when he stopped, then after a few minutes of cheering, clapping and cajoling he would re-commence his round of endless tunes. When the 'old favourites' were played people would spontaneously join in. No matter where my nan was in the house the tune 'Amazing Grace', would bring her running. She would stand alongside him and sing her heart out to this tune. Periodically she would pester him to play it again and the scene would be repeated. The tune was played for her funeral and both of her sisters, which by the age of 25 were the only funerals I had ever attended. It is no wonder I associate this tune with my nan.

After my casual thought, for six consecutive Sundays 'Amazing Grace', was one of the hymns we sang during Sunday service. For the one evening it was not selected the hymnal (a machine that can be programmed to play music), accidentally played the tune and we ended up singing it anyway! For those who think this is not unusual, I can honestly say I hadn't given a service anywhere in the last two years where they had played this tune, until my thought that is.

As we drove home from one of these evenings David and I discussed the frequency of this hymn in relation to my request. Despite all the odd things that have happened over the years, the coincidences etc., both of us felt the same, a kind of sense of gratitude that the people of spirit still take the time to give the signs and the evidence to show that they are close to us and hear all our requests and wherever possible respond with a sign. As we drove I silently gave a 'thank you' to her for hearing my thought, but above all showing, me through the selection of 'Amazing Grace', just what lengths they will go to and what abilities they truly have to reach us in a manner which, should, leave us without doubt that they heard us.

Following on from this I couldn't help but think that to ask for a loved one to draw near and give a sign that they can hear us is the easy part. The most difficult part is to have the courage to believe when you are presented with evidence. The next is to acknowledge it.

Call Signs

We are never alone in this world, as I have stated before there are an army of beings from the other side queuing to help us. All we need to do is to believe. I rarely receive evidence in the physical world from White Feather, so when I do I take heed. White Feather's calling sign for me, surprise, surprise are small white feathers. On a recent holiday to Gozo, we went across to Malta and visited the underground war shelters. These are set deep underground and consist of a series of narrow tunnels, which still contain benches tables etc. At one point we had to get through a very narrow gap, which required a certain amount of manoeuvring to achieve. I was the last one and the small party were waiting patiently while I attempted to negotiate this narrow gap, with as much dignity as I could muster. However, just as I was about to attempt this I watched a white feather slowly float from the low granite ceiling to the ground. I looked with anticipation at the small group, expecting a response, nothing. I quickly ascertained they had not seen what I had seen and I had no intentions of trying to tell them. I looked up the roof. There was nothing from which it could have fallen. I then looked down at the ground and it was gone. I was amazed as I know what I had seen. As soon as I could collar David I asked if he had seen it. "Seen what? Where? How could a feather fall in there and if it did where was it?" "I don't know" I mumbled "but I know what I saw".

The day was incredibly busy, with many other museums to see, followed by a journey across the island and a ferry ride back to Gozo. The coolness of the villa was welcoming. After much deliberation about this holiday we had decided to settle for the relative quietness of Gozo, rather than the lively Malta. We had finally chosen a villa through Gozoway, on the internet. We were not disappointed - the villa was located just outside Nadur, it spacious rooms, large sun decks and pool, made it idyllic. As I walked across the lounge, there in the middle of the room was a white feather, just like the one I had seen earlier that day. I knew it was a call sign from my White Feather, but I hadn't got a clue was he was trying to tell me. I pondered for a while, nothing came to me, and with a meal to cook and lots to do, I soon forgot about the gift of the feather. Yet over the next few days I realised why he was trying to get my attention. I, like half the population, suffer from allergies. I had in recent years developed a salicylate allergy. I had been ill for several years, over an eight year period I had begun to suffer from a variety of symptoms. I developed asthma-like symptoms, which meant on a regular basis I would get out of breath just walking upstairs. Yet on other occasions I would be fine. I could also sneeze for England. I would begin sneezing and this could last for several hours. When I finished I would feel physically ill, like someone with flu'. I bloated, put weight on and could lose it, suffered from boils, abscesses, rashes, an acidic stomach to name but a few of my symptoms. When I was diagnosed I had never even heard of it. Salicylate is a natural preservative found in all fruit, vegetables and flowers, some more so than others. Apparently it is quite rare. Now I have to say I have had very little sympathy for my condition, most people smile, when I tell them I am a vegetarian who is allergic to vegetables. Believe me, it has not meant an easy life, quite the contrary, and for majority of the time I follow a very limited diet.

It is very difficult to diagnose and this is usually achieved by a process of elimination. I cannot deny I have at times doubted this diagnosis and despite how ill I have felt when I have ignored my diet for any period of time (salicylate builds up over a period of time), the niggling doubt is probably more a longing for it to be wrong. I cannot also deny that I have said I wish I knew for definite, not the brightest of things to have wished for, but I can actually remember the moment I said it. I was moaning to Karen at work, after eating the same meal again. "I wish I knew for definite" I said "I don't blame you" came the reply, before we moved on to talk about something more interesting. The seed was sown and I did the one thing you need to do, to make wishes come true: I wished it, then promptly forgot about it and my wish certainly came true.

The peace of Gozo certainly agreed with me, the blazing heat didn't, and midway through the holiday I developed an allergy to the sun! We went into a local Pharmacy and carefully explained my allergies. The pharmacist, with an air of knowledge, explained he understood this allergy and I believed him. Unfortunately the cream he gave me was salicylate based. It burnt my skin, and made me intolerant to any heat, a little difficult to avoid on a Mediterranean island - and finally I needed treatment at the hospital. I sat on the sun terrace as the sun was setting trying to understand why this was happening and back came the wish. I heard it as clearly as when I said it. We were determined not to let this upset the holiday, a thin cotton top and a parasol meant we could still go out, even if I did have the inconvenience of people mistaking me for a holiday guide. At one point unbeknown to me I had around ten people all walking behind me in single file through the market place, with the proper guide desperately trying to call her party to a halt. Well at least I now knew.

On returning back to England I had one last appointment with the dietician. She had excellent knowledge of my allergy, advising me, supporting and sharing her knowledge with me. I think I probably did more talking than she did, but she was a sounding-board, confirming what I thought, or putting me back on the right track. During the appointment I gave her numerous recipes I had created in my pursuit to eat something other than egg and chips. Tracey sat and wrote these all down. When I finished she told me I was the only vegetarian she had known to have a salicylate allergy. She went on to tell me that no doubt I would inspire many others, through my recipes. I thanked her and walked away.

As I walked down the long corridor I reflected over the last twelve months and what my allergies had brought to me. I knew the experience I have worked through had more than one component.

In the first instance my allergies had forced me to explore and re-visit my earlier decision, not to eat meat. I knew yet again I had to make the choice whether I was going to eat meat again, or whether I was going to try and survive my new diet without it. Because of the dietary restraints I would now face my Consultant who had suggested I would be better off eating meat. I pondered for a short while and weighed up all the factors. I knew I could never eat meat; I would go home first, I dramatically announced to the family, but after serious thought, I decided I would compromise and eat fish, which is where I still am now.

Don't assume I am a staunch vegetarian, who hates all meat-eaters. Quite the contrary. I believe it is the personal choice of each individual to choose to eat meat or to choose not to eat it. I will buy meat and cook it, but don't expect me to eat it. I gave up meat because as a Medium if I placed my hand on a piece of meat I could tell you the colour of the animal's nose, fur or skin and their personality. Hence I don't eat meat. I also believe animals die in fear, when killed in a conventional way. We in turn eat that meat and absorb that energy. When I gave up meat, within two months my fears began to recede. They have never disappeared, just lessened.

The second lesson for me to learn through my allergy was to overcome the problem, work through it and become more tolerant of it. As I thought back I felt I had come a long way. I had become ingenious in my recipe ideas and flair for cooking bland food, with bland ingredients and creating tasty masterpieces. But I knew I still hadn't overcome it; I still avoided it. The road is long!

The final stage was to inspire others, through my recipes. As I walked down that long corridor I had a certain sense that I had achieved one and three and now needed to finally overcome the second.

He was to give me another feather shortly afterwards. Having arrived home from Gozo and having, like most people, spent more than I wanted to, I was drawn to look at touring caravans. This seemed totally illogical. I had nowhere to store it, I could not afford it and had very little capacity to use it, but still I felt compelled to look for a caravan. My urge wasn't, unfortunately, shared with my long-term partner David, who had stated rather abruptly he didn't want to own one, go in it or tow it. There was certainly no room for mis-understanding here. While he was over at his house in Birmingham I pursued this drive. The first one I liked, they were out, the second one was already sold, the third available. So off Beverley and I set off to view it. The current owner went to great lengths to show us the different features of the caravan, including the folding down bunk. As she began to unbolt it, a feather slowly drifted from nowhere. As it slowly floated down it landed briefly on my chest. Both Beverley and I looked at it, then at each other, in total amazement. "Did you see that?" she asked, "did you?" I enquired. "Of course" came the reply. We looked down at the floor and to our utter amazement there was no feather anywhere to be seen. We just looked at each other.

So not only did this caravan feel mine and so right to buy, I had been given help and support from my daughter. We had seen it on the Saturday, by the following Monday, we were kitted out, with everything you could need, table, chairs, cutlery, water butt, awning etc., The tow bar had been fitted and we were on our way to Wales. More time had been spent trying to decide where to go, rather than collecting the equipment. We had deliberated between Devon and Anglesey. We finally settled on Borth. Firstly, because it was quite near, secondly, because we all held many, many happy memories with Borth. My parents had owned a caravan at Borth for a long time and had only parted with it a couple of months before my mother's death.

So full of fun, laughter and some trepidation we had set off to Borth, not sure how it would be after all this time. Part of the fun was getting there and by the time we arrived at the site, next to where mom and dad's caravan used to be, I had realised I was brilliant at going forwards, but reversing was another thing. After the sixth attempt to get it in the pitch, I got out the car, trying to muster all the pride I could and would have done well if it wasn't for my laughter. At one point the young lad from the site quietly advised me I needed to leave space between the vans. Space - I was so close they couldn't have got out of their van had they been in it. The burly man jumped in my car and in one movement had the caravan perfectly lined up in its pitch.

The next mighty task we faced was to erect the awning. Our plaintive looks at the diagram, explaining how to pitch our awning brought more men to our rescue. It was wonderful to see the way in which people helped each other on the site, and then went back to their lives, expecting nothing back in return, no invasion of privacy, or expectation of invites for coffee. I could see why people enjoyed camping.

We visited all the places my parents had gone and had taken us, and we did the things the things we used to do together, even down to eating the same breakfasts, boiled eggs and fresh bread and Welsh butter. We searched for crabs and shrimps in the tidal pools down the cove, walked up and down the beach, even in the rain and listened to the patter of rain on the van roof, just as I had done as a child; then my daughter and then her son. We went and sat on the spot where their caravan had stood on the Pen-y-Craig site, which was now no longer a pitch due to the gradient. You could clearly make out the outline of where the van stood and the small paving slabs, which led to the door, were still embedded in the grass. I carefully walked up each set and remembered how we all had done this.

We sat and talked to her, and had our pictures taken by the pitch and fought back the tears, which choked both our throats as we recalled these happy memories. No matter how we looked at it a chapter in our lives had closed forever. But the memories will always live on. We both thoroughly enjoyed this week as we did things which cost next to nothing and once again I felt in touch with nature, just as I had all those years ago.

Beverley and the boys were fine. Convinced they could cope okay without me, I came home and left them to enjoy the next few weeks. After my return my daughter made a whole circle of new friends down in Borth. Now, had I not purchased that caravan she would never have gone to Borth, due to the cost and the memories associated with Borth. I had followed my instincts and again new doorways had opened up.

Dreams

I believe far more information than we realise, is filtered to us, through our dreams. I have over the years received advice, warnings and assistance through my dreams. Majority of the time, the information is presented in a very clear form, but the meaning is always open to interpretation.

Of the hundreds of dreams I have had here are few that have had a deep affect on me, in one way or another. One of these dreams unfortunately predicted the pending death of one of my cats. The dream happened several years ago and on a Tuesday night. In this dream I was observing a very old lady, lying in a Queen Ann bed, she lay in crisp white sheets and I knew she was well cared for, but she was very old, very tired and nearing the end of her life on earth. She was ready to make her journey home.

As I awoke the next morning I knew that old lady was in fact my cat, Monday, I don't know how, but I did and I knew this dream was warning me; this was how the cat felt, old and tired and ready to depart her existence on earth. Yet at the same time I was puzzled, the cat was fine, old in age, but she was as fit as a fiddle. As soon as I got out of bed, I went and had a look at her. She was fine, fast asleep on the settee, lying without a care in the world. I let the matter go.

That night I came in from work and suddenly the cat didn't appear too grand, there was nothing I could put my finger on, but she wasn't right. Now some would say Monday had lived a good life really, she had always been well, which was fortunate as she hated Vets. We had only taken her once, but she had become so distressed by the whole episode, that I vowed I wouldn't take her again. It wasn't the small injury to her leg that nearly killed her, but the shock of being taken somewhere she didn't want to go and the effect of being around all other animals was too much for her, emotionally it took her months to recover. We vowed that unless she would benefit from visiting a Vet, we wouldn't take her again.

I decided to keep a very careful eye on her. The next night as I got in from work she didn't get up to greet me, she just lay in front of the fire. Again there was nothing I could put my finger on, but I knew something was not quite right with her. Experience had taught me to hold faith in my dreams. So I contacted the children to tell them she wasn't well and I felt she wasn't long for this world. Both of them visited that evening. They fussed over her, told her how much they loved her and recalled wonderful happy memories they shared with her. As I watched them take turns to hold, love and fuss over her, I thanked the dream.

Ben, on the other hand, my Grandson, does not cope with the death of any pets. Five years after her death he still mourned our lovely Labrador Megan. As Ben lived with me, his inability to deal with death posed as a real concern for me. I wondered how he would cope when she finally left us.

The next day, as usual, I called to collect him on my way from work, from my father's house, who picked him up from school every day. As I walked through the door I was greeted with "Can I stay, please?" My brother had offered to take him somewhere. I readily agreed. As I walked out of the door, I knew Monday would pass that night and felt divine intervention had ensured Ben would be kept out of the way.

As I turned the key in the door and began to open the front door, the smell of Dettol hit me. I braced myself for what was to come. As I walked into the lounge I saw her. She lay, as I had left her that morning, snuggled in a blanket, in front of the fire. Only now she was gasping for breath. I stroked her, comforted her and held her for a little while, concerned she maybe in distress, as she fought for every breath she took. I decided to call the local Vet. As I spoke through my tears I asked for a home visit for my dying cat, explaining she was too ill to move. "I'm sorry", replied the receptionist "home visits are only done between the hours of 11.00am and 1.00pm". Before I could answer, she asked me to wait a moment. I suspect, feeling very sorry for me she had gone off to see if there was anything else she could offer. She was back on the phone in seconds. "Coincidentally someone has just cancelled, the Vet will be with you in 10 minutes". I thanked her, then thanked her again, and putting down the phone down, I went and lay alongside Monday on the floor telling her how much I loved her. The Vet, a young woman, arrived in minutes. She carefully lifted her out of the blanket and examined her. She handed her back to me and merely nodded her head, indicating there was nothing she could do for her. There was no need for many words. "What do you want me to do?" Through the tears I nodded and told her to put her to sleep. I held her in my arms as the Vet quickly and deftly injected her in the hind quarters, and within moments I felt the life leave her body. I could actually sense as her soul merely slipped out of her body. Her fur was wet with my tears. As the Vet left I rang and told the children what had happened. Both were glad not to be there, to see her struggling to breathe, but on the other hand glad that they had come over the night before and spent some quality time with her. Ben I would sort out later, face to face.

Unfortunately that night I had a church booking, not wanting to let them down, I washed my face and off I set. My heart was hurting at the loss of our beloved cat, who had been with us for 15 years. As I negotiated an island in Wolverhampton, I had a vision of my mother, in my mind's eye. She never looked up or acknowledged me she merely sat with Monday on her lap, lovingly stroking her. I felt at peace, she was safe and had made the other side and my mother was looking after her for me. I dried my tears one last time and continued on my journey. I felt contented in the knowledge that I had been given the information and had been able to decipher it. As a result the grown-up children had been able to say their goodbyes to her, telling her all the things they would have wanted to say, before she passed. I have no doubt that this opportunity helped them to deal with her death more easily. The dream and my spirit helpers had moved Ben out of the way, so we could help him, in a managed way, deal with the loss of the cat. The very next morning I stood part-way up the stairs, combing my hair in the mirror, while Ben looked on. Suddenly I felt her brush against my legs, as she had done a hundred times, when I stood in this spot. I knew Ben had felt her too, because immediately he began to talk about her. There was no need for words; we both know she had run past us that day.

I vowed no more cats. That was it, until the next dream. Two weeks after Monday had passed over, my daughter decided she wanted a cat, but a mature cat, not a kitten. Having heard someone at work talk of a cat rescue centre in Wednesbury I promised to find the number, while I was at it I decided it wouldn't hurt to give them a call, to find the opening times and as I explained what she wanted, he described a couple of cats, including a young male cat called Basil. While we all sat around the table at a family gathering, I shared my thought that Basil sounded like a cat we had lost, several years ago, when he was run over by a car. As I shared my views, I convinced myself that this idea was foolish and dismissed the idea of visiting the Centre, with my daughter, out-of-hand. That night I had a very short dream, of Tom sitting on an old dustbin. With his mouth moving in the most unusual way, he actually spoke to me. Nothing to write home about, he merely said "I'm here". Before I had chance to fully understand the significance of the dream, the Centre called. They were very sorry but they couldn't remember when we were booked to visit. I decided all the signs were there, I must go if only to dismiss it out-of-hand.

Now as strange as this may seem to some of you, as soon as I saw Basil, I knew it was Tom. He had come back to us. Both Tom and Toby the dog had arrived into the household within weeks of each other. They were best buddies, they would play fight from dawn to dusk. When Tom died Toby mourned him for weeks. Now apart from Tom and Monday Toby loathed cats and if one strayed into the garden he would menacingly chase them off. So when we arrived home with Basil, who from now on would be called Tom, we knew this would be the telling sign. We gingerly placed the cardboard box onto the table and lifted the flaps up, to release him. Toby stood at the foot of the table his tail wagging. Tom jumped out and rubbed himself against Toby, as if to say, 'I'm back'.

Probably the most telling sign was the first. Tom would follow you when you took Toby for a walk, always keeping his distance he would follow you, staying close to the houses. coincidentally his mother used to do exactly the same. Guess what? Our new Tom did exactly the same; as we walked he followed, at a distance, close to the houses. Welcome home is all I could say.

On another occasion the house had been on the market for several months. I didn't know where I wanted to go, but I knew it was time to move. As I awoke one morning, as clear as if I was looking at a picture, I saw the old parish church in the village of Wombourne. I hadn't been there for nearly thirty years. I lay awake puzzling over this scene. As the busy day unfolded, I thought no more about it. Within five days of this dream someone had viewed the house and put an offer in, as a first-time buyer, with a mortgage offer in hand so it was all stations go, to try and find a property I wanted in the right area. Suddenly I was under pressure to find somewhere, but where? Then remembering my dream, I set off to Wombourne.

I collected the details of numerous properties and out of the pile of those I could afford, in the areas I liked, I selected two and made appointments to see both consecutively on a Saturday morning. As soon as I walked through the front door of the first house, I knew it felt right, I couldn't afford it, but it felt right. I went to view the next one out of politeness, as it was too late to cancel. I decided to do nothing about the property except ponder over it for the next few days.

Five days later no sooner had I woke up, when I decided today was the day to try and buy the house. During my lunch break I contacted the Estate Agent and enquired if the property I viewed on Saturday was still available. "Yes it is, in fact we have just lowered the price by, £8,000 pounds"' she added. Now I could afford it. Within eight weeks, I was nestled into my new home.

On another occasion my daughter had been quite ill with a flu virus that had literally knocked her off her feet, for nearly two weeks. Not quite fully recovered she had returned to work, although complaining of pains and a funny sensation in her leg. We had all told her to go to the doctors, but she had fobbed it off and in truth I didn't think any more about it. Then out of the blue I had the strangest dream. There was a little brown tree with wonderful silver leaves on it. An angel had come down from heaven to care and tender to this tree, because they realised the little tree was dying. The tree had looked perfectly normal to me, but when I saw this wonderful silver angel tending to the soil that surrounded it, covering it with love, I realised that the angels knew this tree was dying, but nobody else had noticed. When I saw it through the angel's eyes I could see the leaves were curling up and it was indeed dying. I cannot describe the love this angel showered onto this tree. She loved it purely and sincerely for what it was, not judging the tree, just loving it.

When I awoke the next morning I knew this dream was trying to tell me something. The angel had loved this tree with the love of a mother and I knew the angel called the tree a she. I suddenly realised the angel was referring to my daughter. While she appeared to have recovered something was not quite right. I got out of bed and called Beverley and begged her to go to the doctors, explaining to her about my dream. She agreed to go first thing Monday morning when the Surgery opened, which she duly did. Consequently they discovered she had a large blood clot in her groin, which gone untreated could have killed her. I again gave thanks for the information I had received through this dream. There are very few perks in working for the other side, the pay is chronic the hours are long, there can be times where there is little gratitude, but with help like this, who cares.

Some people tell me of never or hardly ever being able to recall there dreams, whereas me, I dream, all night and every night. It got to the point where I would wake up exhausted, having slept very lightly all night, watching scene after scene. Often of people I didn't know and of worlds I would find it hard to describe. I used to see places where all the travel was done using the waterways. There were no cars, just a variety of different water vehicles in a world that didn't appear as dense as our own. Time upon time I went to a place where the houses were built right alongside the sea and there was barely 2 metres from the edge of a tideless sea. Then suddenly the sea would go out and within seconds it would disappear and display a wonderful scene. Hard sand would almost vertically lead to a hand sand beach, with light brown ragged rocks and caves to explore. As quickly as it would appear so it would disappear, but never putting the people at risk; it was as if everyone would know when this would happen and they would vacate the area. The wonderful colours would disappear and the sea would return right up to the edges, always grey in colour as if the sky was overcast. It was as if the Sun only shone when the sea was out.

I would have dreams that lasted seconds, of scenes of the next day. I soon learnt that when these were shown they were forewarning me of some forthcoming event. When the event happened for real, I would always stop and think before I spoke or did anything, as I knew it had been given to me for a reason. Many a time I had ignored it and many a time to my peril. I would see scenes (and still do), of cars dropping suddenly into the road, in front of me, so when I drove near this spot I would be extra cautious and lo and behold a car would pull out in front of me. I would and still do, dream of really happy occasions, where I would feel extremely loving towards David my partner, or a member of the family. Usually within a few days of this happening an argument would occur, then that happy scene would flash back into my mind and quell any feelings of anger. I would also get premonitions about family members and friends, and I visited places I had never dreamed existed.

In one dream my mother came to see me. I dreamt I was asleep and there was a knock at the door, I woke up and went to answer the door. There stood my mom. I was so excited to see her. She asked if I would like to go shopping with her and off we went. With me driving and her sitting in the passenger seat. I kept saying to her, 'I cannot believe you have come back, I never thought I would see you again until I passed over'. I remember thinking how pleased the others would be to know she wasn't dead after all, but had been allowed to come back. Quite solemnly she sat down and talked to me about what would happen if she did come back now. For one, she pointed out she didn't have a body to occupy. She then carefully explained to me that it was her time to die and when someone's time came, they had to go over, as hard as they found it, this was their chosen time to go. She went through with me all her medical problems at that time. Did I want her to stay with all the problems she had? I looked at her and shook my head, no, I didn't want her to live on with a body so racked with illness her quality of life would have been extremely low. She smiled, she was glad I could understand why she had chosen to go over. But she told me she would continue to come over and see me from time to time. That trip to the shops felt as real as if it actually happened. I know my mother has used my dream state to try and explain why she had to go to the other side. She has popped in to join me in my dreams several times since. Although I suppose as a Medium I am lucky because I can feel her around me at birthdays, Christmas and special anniversaries.

Another way my dreams have assisted me in my career: At one point I appeared to be a serial job changer. It felt as if I was moving from one job to another. It is easy to see a change of a job as resolving an issue, but it can be that you are merely side-stepping round some issue.

I had decided once again the NHS was not for me and I duly applied for another post. This time I was going to change direction again and go back to working for the Council. So I applied for a post with Sandwell Council, in their Learning and Development Department. On three consecutive evenings, as I arrived at an island in Dudley, I saw a bus coming down Castle Hill. I don't even know the number of the bus, but on the side the sign said 'all roads lead to Dudley Road', which is the former name of the hospital I worked at. In my dream a bus appeared briefly and said, 'it's not your stop this one'. I knew I wouldn't get the job and told my partner so. But this time I went along for the interview simply to learn from the whole experience. I came home from the interview and lay on the settee, trying to rest my pounding head. I suddenly felt as if something had landed on me, at the same time, as a bright light filled the room. Seconds later they rang to tell me I didn't get the job. An extremely polite, well mannered gentleman explained it was to be offered to someone else. My only regret was I wouldn't be working with this man. Otherwise I wasn't the slightest bit bothered, as I had already known the outcome, not for the other candidates, but for myself.

Six months on the feet were beginning to itch again, but for all the wrong reasons. This time it was a job within the Trust, I felt quietly confident. I filled the application form in with ease and as I set off for my holidays I felt sure I had a fighting chance. I certainly met all the points set out in the personal specification. As Gozo arrived, I quickly forgot all about it.

Half-way through our second week I had what I always describe as my dream scenes, and in it two woman were walking along together when one turns to the other and says 'so that will be two jobs you have applied for that you haven't got'. Nothing else was said, merely this conversation between two women. I got up the next morning and informed David I wasn't going to get the job. "Give it a chance, they haven't even short listed yet". "No" I replied, I was empathic. "The job isn't mine, watch this space". It didn't bother me in the slightest. I decided I obviously had more work to do where I was. I wasn't the least bit surprised when I didn't even get short-listed for the post.

Time for Me

Despite being a working Medium, I have always tried to find time for me, to continue my own spiritual development. I believe advancement is an ever evolving process that needs to be worked at and the moment we stop seeking and working towards progression, we are likely to plateau or stagnate.

I practise my own development through shared meditation. This goes back to the time when Cherry and I used to meditate together, during my many trips to Cornwall, although we continued meditating together whether we were physically in each other's company or not. Two or three times a week, we would 'link' together. 300 miles distance between us was no barrier to our shared meditations. Each meditation was carefully planned with precision. Prior to beginning we would speak on the phone and discuss what we were going to do or what we were going to ask for and achieve. We would synchronise the time, then both go off to our own meditation zones, with the view of sharing our meditation, despite being over 300 miles apart. Before we set off, we would pre-arrange for how long we would meditate. When we finished we would both make short notes, then while the information and experiences were fresh in our minds, one would ring the other to discuss our findings.

It was fascinating how we would either see or sense the same things, visit the same places, see the same beings and be given similar information, yet we were sitting miles apart. I remember on one occasion where we had both had very strenuous and arduous days at work and both felt exhausted. Rather than miss our meditation we decided not to work or set ourselves goals. We would ask to be embraced in a healing energy and we would sit back and bask in this energy. Afterwards as we discussed it, and compared notes, we were both very sure we had felt, and had experienced contact with Quan Yin. She had taken us both on a journey, to similar places and exactly the same time in the meditation. It was situations such as this that I found very difficult to grasp. Cherry was far more knowledgeable and worldly on all esoteric subjects, having read extensively on the subject since the seventies. No matter how many times she tried to explain how this could happen, how a spirit being could fragment themself and be in two places at once, I never fully grasped the situation. It is only when, through a very vivid dream, where I experienced this fragmentation of the soul and its ability to remain whole, yet communicate with several other people, in different places at once, did I fully understand what Cherry had tried umpteen times to put in a language I understood. Until this point, I knew it was happening, the two sets of notes confirmed it, yet like many experiences Cherry and I shared, the wow factor was off the scale.

When Cherry and I moved on with our lives, I sadly missed our 'joint meditations' and will always be indebted to her and the world of spirit for the wonderful experiences to which I was privileged to be a party. We were extremely fortunate and I couldn't remember an evening where we didn't see, feel, sense or hear anything.

After we both moved on I began to sit and meditate with Karen, Martin, David, Nick and Stella, although the latter two, who were also a couple, rarely sat together, it was one or the other. Alas the church commitments meant daily meditations would sadly be a thing of the past, so I settled for once a fortnight. Over the years we too have shared some wonderful experiences together and our format has changed very little. Our meditations are usually shared experiences as we tell each other what we are receiving. It is very difficult to try and explain to people the events that unfold during our meditations. But like a living story we, the participants, are consistently given a slice of the story that joins together and guides us all, through magical experiences where wisdom and knowledge is given with startling reality. For example, one person may say 'I have a pyramid, giving no description of its size, colour or shape'. Someone else will interject "so do I, it's huge" this is often followed by "yes I had one a short while ago, constructed out of crystal", and so the story will unfold. We have over the years been given some wonderful information, too vast to fully address here. But I remember on one occasional being shown how to balance my chakras on a daily basis. I was told to visualise a crystal wand with every colour of the chakras set in blocks of colour from the base chakra red, up to the crown chakra purple. I was then told to look at each colour briefly to see if there was any impurity in it. For example if the red was too pale, to visualise pulling more red energy into body, if it was too dark, to lighten it with a lighter shade of red. This would help to balance my chakras. For a long time I continued to do this and always felt better for doing so. In fact if I feel out of balance I still practice this little exercise and it never fails to work.

As part of our thirst for development Karen and I decided we wanted to spend some quality time away in order to meditate. David and Martin readily agreed so we set off to Monmouth for a three day break. During this time we decided to visit Glastonbury, which has long been a favourite place for David and I to visit and many happy time have been spent there, wandering round the shops, walking to the Tor and feeling the wonderful energies inside the grounds of the Abbey.

On this occasion I had decided to buy a crystal skull. It had only been in the last 18 months I had become aware of the vast abilities of the skulls.

At a Mind, Body and Spirit show we had organised, a wonderful woman called Magi had attended with her small assortment of crystal skulls, including a huge Citrine skull. I had stood alongside her, while she and David conversed. Exhausted by the day's events I was quite happy to stand and listen, contributing nothing to the conversation. As I stood, barely listening to their conversation, I suddenly became aware that someone was speaking to me in a rather strange voice, resembling Lesley Phillips, in a carry-on film. I distinctly heard someone say, "hello". I glanced around, turning 360 degrees; no-one was close to me, except this large Citrine skull. I was astonished; with mouth gaping open I looked closely at the skull. I swear it was smiling at me! I quickly glanced around, no there was no-one talking to me or standing close enough to make that sound, it had definitely come from the skull. I glanced at David and Magi, who showed no sign of hearing anything other than their own conversation. At this stage I decided against mentioning it. I thought about it for a moment, the conversation would have gone something like "Excuse me Magi, you have never met me before, but could you tell me, does your skull talk? Only it has just spoken to me in a rather funny voice?" No, funny farm more likely. I decided to keep quite at this moment, although I did tell David about it, at the earliest opportunity and Magi at a later date.

I had previously read about the mysterious crystal skulls and their ability to communicate information. In an effort to understand them and their functions, I began a journey which lasted months and months as I tried to understand and discover the truth about the crystal skulls.

To understand them we first have to understand the power of crystals. These have over the past few decades become more and more popular. They have long been associated with healing and have been adopted by many different types of therapists as tools to help with balancing, alignments and attunements, of the mind, bodies and souls. I was fully aware of the use of crystals in this manner and had in fact several of my own, so their power was no secret to me. I believe the use of crystals, as a means of communication, dates back to mysterious time frames on earth which we do not, as yet, understand. I believe ancient civilisations understood not only the importance of natural materials, but also the importance of adopting certain shapes to create tools of divination and this is why crystals were shaped into skulls. Some of the crystal skulls found in various locations, throughout the world have been carbon dated and are thought to be thousands of years old, which is a bit of a mystery and the more I work with my little skulls the more I am beginning to understand, along with the umpteen books I have read.

On another trip to Glastonbury Magi had held us all in amazement as she had told the story of how the huge modern Citrine had come into her possession. The crystal itself came from Brazil, it had somehow found its way to China, where it was carved in the shape of a crystal skull. It was then exported to America, where it found itself in the hands of a Dealer. A distant friend of Magi's had been in America at the time and felt compelled to contact this particular Dealer and ask if she could come and have a look around, as she was convinced he had a crystal she in which she would be interested. "By all means" came the reply from the Dealer. He then went on to tell her that for the first time in his life a crystal had spoken to him and the skull told him he needed to get to England. So shaken-up was he by this experience he agreed to this woman bringing the skull to England, on sale or return basis, and she had six months to do so.

Almost to the day the six month period had expired and the skull was due to be shipped back, Magi made contact with the keeper of skull and with the capital from the sale of her house, Magi, purchased the skull. During the rest of the afternoon, she regaled us with stories of how she had travelled round the country with the skull, with the aim of purifying the energy lines which criss-cross the planet. The scrapes and wonders of what happened to her were nearly as marvellous as the tale of how the skull had come into her possession.

I already owned a labrodite skull, but as we rode to Glastonbury I decided to use my birthday money to purchase a quartz crystal skull. I kept this to myself, so David couldn't persuade me otherwise. I decided if I found one – great - if I didn't so be it.

I really believe crystals wait for someone to purchase them, so I sent out my wish to find a skull that wanted to be with me and asked for it to be reasonably priced, to match my budget. With this in the back of my mind, we began to wander around the shops of Glastonbury. The first shop we came to had a lovely skull in the shop window. I eagerly walked into the shop. "Hello and where are you from?" greeted the smiling shop keeper. "What do you think of it here, do you like it?", the broad smile never leaving his face. I felt no sincerity in his approach, in fact I found his whole style a little condescending. The more he spoke, the more his attitude began to grate on my nerves. I rationalised for a moment and realised this was trying to tell me something. I quickly reached the conclusion this skull was not for me. For those of you who thought I was going to say 'and there was the skull waiting for me', no chance, life was not going to be that simple, at least not this time.

We continued to look around several more shops and nothing caught my eye. I was just about to call it a day and go to the Abbey, when Karen spotted a 'We have moved to the Courtyard', sign in a shop window. "Where is that?" She asked, I suddenly felt inspired, so off we went.

There was a shop of my dreams, filled with crystal skulls of every shape, size and colour. I looked at several skulls, but nothing seemed quite right for me, until I came across a rather small quartz skull. This small skull nestled snugly in the palm of my hand. As I looked at it, I instantly fell in love with him (sorry, he felt male). I looked at the price £130.00, this was slightly more than I wanted to pay. I still held onto the skull and suddenly I became aware that a small chunk was missing from his jaw, at the rear. I pointed this flaw out to the woman behind the counter. She came and inspected it, and agreeing with my findings, offered the skull for the knock down price of £80.00. Now just inside my price range. I quickly paid up. If I had any doubt about whether I had selected the correct crystal, this quickly faded. As the woman wrapped him in several layers of tissue paper, I could hear in my mind's eye, his strong objections as he bellowed 'let me out, let me out'. I decided for everyone's sanity to keep this to myself.

Later in the day as we sat admiring him over lunch, Martin said, "You are going to think I am mad, but when the woman was wrapping him up, I swear he was protesting, saying 'let me out' … honest" he added. I smiled and explained that I had heard exactly the same. Did I notice Martin was also calling the crystal him, yes I did.

Despite his protests, my skull carefully wrapped spent the remainder of the day tucked away safely in my handbag. Before we were to leave Glastonbury there were a couple more surprises waiting for us. Firstly we walked around the Abbey grounds and Martin and Karen picked up powerful

144

feelings of energy, in exactly the same spots David and I had felt this on previous visits. In fact they found a couple more for us we hadn't felt in the past. As you stood centrally in the middle of the Abbey there was a strong sensation as if something was gently washing into you, passing through and over you in gentle subtle waves. If you stood with your eyes shut, the phenomenon presented the sensation that you were in fact rocking. The longer you stood with your eyes shut, the more difficult it became to maintain your balance. We stayed in the grounds feeling and sensing energy for quite some time as the experience was extremely pleasant and peaceful. We sat basking in the energy for a while, before we strolled over to the Abbots kitchen.

With the dog in tow we couldn't all go in together. David decided to bask in the energy for a little longer, while Karen, Martin and I wandered into the cone shaped building, with its lantern style ceiling. As soon as we entered the building the most wonderful sound hit you as it resonated around the room. While hard to detect from where the sound was originating, it was, without doubt, the most wonderful sound I had heard in a long time. Without warning the sound stopped. I, and several others who had clearly been listening to the sound, stopped in their tracks and began to look and search for the source of the sound, with the sole intention of seeking more if it. Our attention was suddenly drawn to a tall blond woman in her twenties who, in broken English, asked all of us if we minded if she sang? Everyone in the room quickly shook their heads, eager to hear that wonderful sound. Nearly all of us were a little shell shocked and unsure the sound we had heard actually belonged to this woman. It didn't seem possible that a single voice, without the assistance of a studio recording system, could have made such a wonderful sound.

So memorable was this moment I can still visualise it, as if it happened yesterday. She stood centrally in the room, closed her eyes and raised her hand to her ear and as if connecting with a divine force. She then began to emit a sound that appeared to be purely angelic. We were all mesmerised, captivated by this wondrous sound. I stood and listened for a few minutes and very reluctantly pulled myself away from this beautiful experience, in order that David could also share in the magical moment. I quietly crept from the room, then sprinted over to where David was standing, imploring him to quickly go inside the kitchen and witness the experience first hand. As I left the building I noticed a woman in her late 50's came bounding across the grass, in 15th Century dress. As David walked towards the building the singer came out. Impulsively I stopped her and asked why she had stopped singing. "I am not singing" she advised me "I was praying". I apologised for my mistake and told her how much I had appreciated listening to her. She smiled warmly, thanked me and began to walk off, then she stopped and turned to me and said "Whenever the angels see a church building they always try to enter it, but they are often turned away, as they are not welcome". As I pondered her words, and before I could respond, she smiled and walked away.

Moments later Martin and Karen and all the people, one by one, left the building. "What happened?" I asked "The Cook came in and told her she couldn't do that here and stopped her" came Martin's reply, as he shook his head in total disbelief that the woman who sang so wondrously was stopped from singing, in order for the Cook to re-enact life in the Abbots kitchen! We all stood for a moment in disbelief of the 'cook's' actions, but also the beauty in this woman's voice. Her voice resonated through my soul for days to come and I truly felt I heard and experienced the voice of an angel that day. So pure was her voice, that when first heard, it was impossible to tell it was being produced by one single woman. For all intents and purposes she had developed the ability to attune herself to greater forces than can be seen by the human eye - the effect was profound.

I have seen and experienced many psychic skills applied to create connections between the two worlds. This was however the first time I encountered the singing voice as a means of bringing healing and harmony.

The Cook left shortly afterwards. Everyone had expressed their views that afternoon, with their feet. They had all walked out.

We returned back to Ross-on-Wye that night exhausted, but excited at the prospect of sitting with the crystal skull. As I drove the car, I remembered each time I had visited Glastonbury and some of the wonderful things which had happened to me.

Several years ago David and I had gone to a workshop in Glastonbury, which finished with a small ceremony on the Tor. It was a sunny day on an August bank holiday, Glastonbury and the Tor was alive with people. Neither David nor I were very keen on singing and chanting in the open on the Tor, but events seemed to overtake us and we found ourselves joining a small group, who stood together holding hands chanting 'Awens'. As the 12 of us stood together, waiting to get started, a young man in a bandanna approached the group. Without a word he gently eased himself in-between a couple and joined in the process. As he chanted and held his notes I couldn't help but be amazed at this wonderful sound which came from this man who, had I met him on a dark night in the street, I would have been felt afraid by the way he presented himself physically. This just goes to show, you cannot judge a book by its cover!

That night was the first of hundreds of meditations we had with Phlian, as I found was the crystal skull's name. I found communication with him very easy, but that's another story.

A Development Circle

Church Services are only a small part of the range of facilities and support available within a Spiritualist Church. Healing is also a vital part of the spiritual movement. Becoming a healer is an arduous path and it takes two or more years to train to become a fully fledged healer and this involves courses assessments and observations. Healing is usually available on a weekly basis and for many it is extremely effective, whether it is healing for the body or the mind.

Another valuable service available in the churches is the opportunity for church members to attend circles or classes for their own personal development, at a nominal cost. Churches are individual units and the range of personal development provided is dependant on a multitude of issues, from its size to the premises they use. Generally this can range from awareness classes, to open circles through to a closed circle. Invariably however, all churches will usually provide an 'open circle'.

Awareness classes often teach about the spiritual movement and all aspects of development, including the many tools you can use to advance your skills.

The open circle affords the opportunity to be guided by an experienced Medium through into Mediumship.

The final one, a closed circle, is where members progress onto, if they choose to see if they can advance their skills further.

The whole concept of development is without pressure for achievement. Members self-select how much effort they are going to put into the process and whether they wish to go beyond the awareness class. So for an annual fee of around £10.00 and then £2.00 to £4.00 per session members can enjoy some excellent teachings and explore pathways, rarely open outside of the spiritual movements.

For many people 'spiritual terminology' is very unclear. Many people don't realise, until they have been members at a church for quite a while, that 'the circle' is actually a development opportunity. One has to ask the question, why call it a circle? When you have attended once, the answer is obvious All who attend always sit together in a circle, the more people, the bigger the circle will be. The circle is always protected and overseen by an experienced Medium, who monitors the activity of the circle and sets the pace. The attendees sit in the confines of a protected circle, where they are taken on a guided meditation, with the hope of receiving information from the world of spirit for other members of the circle. Before the end, this information is relayed to the person it is intended for, or if the person doesn't know who it is for, it is thrown open to see if anyone can accept it. Majority of the Mediums associated with spiritualist churches will have begun their Medium careers this way and a lot will in turn become circle leaders and give back, what they received, and usually ten-fold.

On of the seven principles of the SNU is the provision of evidence that irrefutably proves the existence of life after death. In terms of the Services and any development this ethos is paramount. With this in mind, during groups Mediums will teach attendees to understand and recognise the difference between 'psychic skills' and 'spiritual connections'. Anyone attempting to work using their psychic gifts only will be frowned upon, because of this principle.

One of the first priorities is teaching members how to establish a link. I truly believe, providing someone is mentally stable, anyone who sits in development with the view of advancing their skills for the good of others, will never be disappointed. Beginners to the 'art' of Mediumship are their own worst enemies. Years of cynicism and self-doubt are blights that inhibit the use of this unique skill.

It is very difficult to actually teach someone how to receive information, as a Circle Leader all you can do is provide the opportunities, skills, knowledge and environment. The remainder is down to the individual and their helpers.

Like the unused road, you attempt to use skills you have probably not consciously taped into since you were a child, and must therefore be patient and don't expect miracles to occur overnight. It takes practice, practice and more practice, all applied with utmost patience. As stated previously in this book, meditation is a vital part of receiving information and if you don't meditate and learn how to still the mind, then the Communicator is unable to get through. Patience is essential. Cherry sat every night for six months before she began to receive information, so don't expect it to happen overnight. If it does it is a gift, if it doesn't be patient, it will.

It was difficult to remember exactly how I became involved with the Development group at Wolverhampton church, but get involved I did. There was a need for a closed development group and at that time, no-one to run it, although plenty had taken their turn in the past. Wolverhampton was my own church and I wanted to give something back to spiritualism, as it had so freely given to me. So I volunteered and was voted in by the Committee and for numerous years I held the onerous title as Leader of the closed development circle. When we hear the term Committee we often groan. They may not always get it right first time, but we need to remember they work relentlessly and sometimes for years to ensure the doors of the church stay open and without their effort many churches would fold. They are the unsung heroes of the spiritualist movement.

A natural human emotion when placed in a learning environment is to compete with fellow group members to demonstrate a superior skill. The need to compete is a basic emotion, which in the general scheme of things has, up to this point in life, always served us well, so to suggest we function without it is a quite a difficult concept for us, as humans, to grasp. But a development group needs a stimulating environment where everyone is striving to progress and maximise their own potential, but not in competition with each other. One of the underlying ethos of our group was to recognise no-one is better than anyone else, and in fact people are merely at different stages in their development. They are where they are because that is where they need to be. A further factor to recognise is people need to be at different stages of development if they are to help each other. The new members to the group can aspire to be at the stage the older members are and the older members can give something back into the pool, by offering guidance and assistance to those who are at the stage they once were. A simple agreement but an important factor. It has the potential to move the energies from one of competition to nurturing, which is conducive to a learning environment.

There are many stages on the road of 'spiritual advancement'. The first is actually open your receptors to be able to receive. As stated earlier in the book, a quiet mind is a vital component if you wish to receive information. As stated several times during this book, spirit communication can only take place if there is 'a vacant plot' in the mind to receive it! In other words, a moment in time when no thoughts are taking place. If you have doubt in understanding think of a moment when you are day dreaming and how 'odd' thoughts will often pop into your mind. This is because for a momentary second the mind has switched off, leaving a gap for external information to be able to come in.

Once we have discovered the art of receiving and are able to consciously create the stillness of the mind we are now on the road to Mediumship. The next stage is probably the most difficult; we need to learn to give it off in a manner which is meaningful to the person for whom it is intended. In the early stages information is often jumbled together, a name closely followed by a description doesn't mean they necessarily belong together. In other words, once you have begun to receive you now have to develop your own unique style of delivering that information, in a manner which the recipient is able to understand. This is very difficult and has been the downfall of many a good Medium. In the early stages once you have opened the road to communication you now need to learn to understand and control the flow of data.

In our everyday lives we are taught certain communication skills and to follow certain patterns of etiquette. For example, as a sign of good manners when introducing one person to another we will follow a certain format, exchanging names, then giving personal information. What we exchange depends upon the social setting of the meeting. When the spirit world is communicating with us they have to overcome many factors. When they first pass over they too have to learn the 'art' of communication, initially the message can be confusing.

Through the group we have often all learnt from laughter, especially when the message goes something like:

"I have a lady here, who is saying 'auntie', I believe she is your auntie. She is very tall with long brown hair and is full of laughter. She is giving me her name, Elizabeth. She is talking about a heart condition she passed with. She is also saying she had gout."

The recipient shakes their head. After several minutes it transpires Elizabeth was her mother's auntie. Mom had the long hair and her grandfather had gout and the auntie had passed with a heart condition.

So inadvertently what we have built is Frankenstein's monster. We have bulked all the information together to describe someone who doesn't exist. Had we given off the information a bit at a time and given it as it was meant to be, the message would have made perfect sense.

You can see learning Mediumship is a very difficult art and for many can be a long and arduous pathway. But there is no doubt we all have the ability to learn this skill. We may not all develop into 'platform Mediums', for many it will be a skill that can be used for personal use with close friends. For others they too will also become a platform Medium and join the circuit that ensures the doors of churches will remain open.

I'm sure my group at Wolverhampton view me in the same manner as I viewed Val: merciless. Always pushing and striving to make them go the extra mile, refusing to accept that they cannot do something and above all never allowing them to ask questions.

What I do know is I have been privileged to have worked with them and I have enjoyed every moment, watching them shift from fledgling to extremely good professional Mediums.

The Animal Kingdom

You only have to stand and watch a wild animal grazing on the side of the road or see a deer in a forest to realise the joy animals bring into our lives. There is nothing so uplifting as to listen to the gentle tap of a woodpecker or the dawn chorus. We are truly gifted by the presence of the animals that grace this land. Animals bring many qualities to this land. But the joy is usually associated with spotting these animals and birds in their own surroundings, not impounded or caged in a zoo. Experience and research over time has shown the 'value' of having animals around. Research has shown patients who were visited by dogs recovered quicker than those who weren't and the nineties saw the introduction of dogs into our homes and hospitals as a tool to aid recovery.

Dolphins have long been associated with healing powers and there has been case after case where patients have recovered from terminal illness's after swimming in the company of dolphins. As more people have searched for this experience, the greedier man has become. Dolphins have given their time and love willingly and participated in this process, but man not being content with this has imprisoned these wonderful creatures for their own gain. A close friend brought back some pictures of dolphins off the cost of Mexico. As she produced the pictures, I carefully asked, before accepting them, "are they free to roam or imprisoned?" "Free of course" came back the response. As I looked at a picture of a close shot of a single dolphin, I couldn't help but notice a tear in the corner of its eye. As it transpired, freedom was freedom to roam around a small area in the harbour, where a group of dolphins were imprisoned, to ensure people who wanted to swim with these lovely creatures were guaranteed to do so, as these beautiful creatures were no longer free to roam, they were held in captivity for the pleasure of humans.

I remembered Funghi the Irish dolphin, who single-handedly, had stimulated the economy of Dingle, a small fishing town in southern Ireland. There was no need for captivity. This dolphin had suddenly appeared 11 years ago in a town which was barely surviving. Now there exists a thriving community where seasoned fishermen discuss the virtues of swimming with the dolphin. Throughout the summer months there are a continual stream of boats out into the harbour to see the dolphin. Each trip is guaranteed to bring a sighting and the operators, so sure are they of this loyal dolphin's appearance that each trip is 'payment by results'. If the dolphin fails to appear, you get your money back. Apparently he rarely fails to appear.

The Irish dolphin is one of many such creatures that have frequented towns and become tourist attractions. The pelicans of Paphos in Cyprus were world known and people actually visited Paphos with the sole purpose of seeing the pelicans.

History is filled with stories and tales of how wild and domestic animals have helped to save the lives of humans. There was a famous story of a young American teenager on a shooting trip with his father and somehow they became separated. Lost in the American Rockies, he was forced to spend the night in sub zero temperatures, without even a top coat. When he was found alive the next day he spoke of two large Elks that had lain beside him all night, ensuring his survival. His story was authenticated by the markings of two animal bodies in the snow, where he had collapsed with cold and exhaustion. The very animals they had set out to kill that day were the saviours that night.

The same applies to domestic pets; history is peppered with stories of faithfulness and loyalty, at all costs. Dogs that have fetched assistance for injured masters, leading the rescuers for miles, to where their injured human lay. Dogs which have woken families, who would have perished in house fires if not for their fast response.

Farmers, shepherds and indigenous people have often observed the behaviour of animals as predictors of pending natural disasters or severe weather warnings. Wild animals and birds will invariably evacuate an area up to 24 hours before an earthquake or volcano erupts. What basic instinct are they using, which we, as the 'more developed' species have clearly lost the ability to use?

It has in recent years become very fashionable to try and follow the 'old ways'. Sweat lodges, chanting and drumming week-ends are readily available in most western countries. But are we truly following the 'old ways', or merely dipping into fragments that appear attractive, and completely missing the point of what the 'old ways' represented? Psychic journeys and experiences were a small part of the 'old ways'. The greater part of this existence was to encompass mother nature and live their lives with respect for her and all her habitants. Not to see themselves and 'better' or of 'greater importance' than any other animal or creature, but to try and live their lives in harmony with the planet and all other occupants. While they killed the buffalo for their meat and fur, they tried to do so without harming the 'eco system'. The civilised 'white man' on the other hand, who saw these people as savages would shoot the buffalo from trains for fun, until all the buffalo were gone.

As we look back on our history we can see that we have made many poor judgements regarding our relationships with animals, but each decade provides us with fresh opportunities. We do not need to keep looking back and seeing how badly we have failed, but to look forward to the future and make changes for the better happen. We should begin to choose pathways which allow us all to begin to live in harmony with the animal kingdom and begin to understand the importance of a balanced relationship, if we are to create a better place to live in. For our survival the balance of the eco system is vital as we are unfortunately beginning to discover.

Domestic Animals

Dogs and cats for many make wonderful companions. I believe there sole purpose of being on this plane is to offer companionship to human beings. With the role of being a dog or cat owner comes a lot of responsibility. By the very virtue of acquiring a pet we accept this responsibility to walk, feed and meet the animal's creature comforts. To seek help when they are sick and to treat them with love and respect, at all times.

For many, especially those who are on their own, animals give great comfort and joy. Both dogs and cats are remarkably different in characters and personalities and they are equally capable of helping us. For those who are alone in this world, especially older people who find getting out the house difficult, they can be your best friend. Someone to communicate with, a means of feeling loved, and something with you can also learn how to share love.

It is the many gifts they help us to access, which often makes their departure so very difficult to bear. For those who have never owned or loved a pet it is difficult to understand how someone can get so emotionally attached to a four-legged creature that cannot converse and appears quite dumb. Animals are anything but dumb, as with wild animals there are many, many stories that tell of the amazing skills and gifts of these animals. How they are able to find their way home, when stranded miles from home. How they have woken families in the face of diversity, such as fire or intruders in the home. Animals that have been able to detect cancer or other serious conditions. Pets that seem to know when you are sad and unhappy and who will try to comfort you in your hour of need, as if they are trying to soften the blows of life. They are truly wonderful spectacular creatures, who without their very existence, for many, this planet would be a sadder, more miserable place to live.

I also believe in reincarnation and that animals will return time and time again to be with you and they always seem to be able to find their way to you.

Encountered Stories of a Different Kind

I have over the years sat and listened as person after person has recalled and told the most fascinating stories. These are ordinary people from ordinary lives; some have never stepped inside a spiritual church and have no connections with anything remotely etheric. What has marvelled me more than anything is that none of them found their stories to be extraordinary. Yet I'm sure if anyone else told them, the same or a similar story, they would be fascinated by the whole event and maybe a little sceptical at the possibility that something so wonderful could happen here on earth. Here is a selection of these stories.

Beryl was a Senior Manager with a lovely bright personality, who was full of laughter. Kindness itself she would do anything for anyone. During a lunch break from a training course she told me how she had lost her husband several years ago. She told me how she knew he was going to die. She said "Because suddenly the whole room was filled with a wonderful blue colour and in this colour were thousands of silver shimmering lights and it was as if the lights lifted him and took him away". She then went on to say at that point he died. This had taken place on a bright sunny afternoon in August, as she sat in a side room at a local hospital as her husband lay dying in the bed alongside her. When I asked her what she thought was happening, she merely replied, "I don't know, I've never really thought about it until now". As she sat pondering the events she went on to say it had given her great comfort and helped her cope with the death of her husband at the tender age of 32. She also felt it was a sign. Confirmation, that someone had come and fetched Phil and had taken him to the other side. As quickly as she had begun this conversation, she ended it, almost as if there was nothing to add. This is how the afternoon unfolded, nothing more, nothing less.

On another occasion many years ago, I had been doing some work privately, training staff on how to manage a patient in his own home with a paraplegic injury. Geoff's injury was fairly recent and he had sustained it in a car accident. Geoff, Sheila and the two boys were travelling to their holiday destination, where they were meeting up with Sheila's family. She had purchased two little plastic moulded angels, as a gift for her sister. All Sheila's family were devout Catholics and Sheila felt her sister would love these angels. Travelling along a deserted dual carriageway somewhere in Wales, at 5.30am in the morning,   Sheila had a strong desire to get the little angels out and examine them. As she bent down to retrieve them from her handbag, the ford escort they were travelling in was hit from behind by a drunken driver. While Geoff had been travelling at a mere 50 miles an hour, investigators estimated the speed of the car that hit them was in excess of 100 miles an hour. The impact knocked them into the central reservation barrier. The action of reaching to her handbag saved Sheila's life and she managed to scramble out of the wreck, relatively uninjured. Her sons were not quite so lucky, but their injuries were not life threatening, unlike her husband, who broke his neck and spent 12 months in hospital recovering.

Geoff by trade was a lorry driver and ironically, they were rescued by a man of the same trade. Months later he came to see Geoff in hospital. This driver, like every one involved in this accident, was amazed that anyone had survived this horrific accident, which completely crushed the car, let along walked away unscathed.

Sitting chatting to Sheila, he said he knew there was an accident around the corner, because the whole sky was ablaze with the most amazing blue light, which appeared to encase the whole car. He told Sheila it was as if an angel was wrapping herself around the vehicle to keep the occupants safe. Sheila went on to say, amazingly for her as she was helped from the car, the two little angels were no longer in her possession, but were perched on the dashboard, directly in front of her, completely unblemished by the experience. Sheila felt this act was a sign from God, and that angels were indeed watching over her whole family that morning.

She never gave those angels to her sister, in fact she kept them, with her sisters blessing, as reminder of how lucky they all were, the day the angels watched over them.

Pauline was a senior nurse I met at work. For Pauline religion played a very important part in her life and had for all of her 34 years. Her family had always attended church several times a week and so had she. Her father was a lay preacher and her mother helped with Sunday school. She told me of an incident which the family had talked about for years, where they believed an angel had visited them and saved Pauline's life, many years ago.

Pauline and her parents lived on a very busy main road. One day when Pauline was three years old her mother had been busily doing her household chores. She had nearly finished, as her husband was due home any moment in time for the morning service. With only a few tasks left she had hurried upstairs to make the beds. She believed Pauline was in the adjacent room, where she had left her a few moments ago. A glance out of the window told her otherwise. To her horror there was Pauline outside playing on the drive. In those few minutes Pauline had gone downstairs and opened the front door and was now playing on the drive. Her mother quickly shouted out of the window to gain Pauline's attention, then beckoned her to come back into the house.

Unfortunately for the family at the same time her father was walking up the road, on the opposite side of the road. As Pauline's mother tried to get her to come back into the house, Pauline caught sight of her father on the opposite side of the road. In between Pauline and her much loved father, was an open gate and a very busy main road. Her mother's words were falling on deaf ears. In her small confused mind, what she believed she saw was her father beckoning her to come to him. What he was actually doing was shaking his arms frantically shouting "No go back" her little child ears and eyes didn't see this and she began to run towards her father. As the traffic roared either way, crossing was impossible for the father; he frantically dodged and moved on the pavement as he tried to find a way of reaching his daughter. There was nothing he could do, but to desperately beg her to stop. At the same time a huge lorry was proceeding down the road, seconds from where Pauline was fast approaching the kerb. Without any hesitation she ran directly into the pathway of the oncoming vehicle. The driver well within the speed limit, braked for all he was worth. When he finally stopped the huge lorry, he fell from the cab and dropped to knees, his hands covering his face as he sobbed, for what he had done. No-one else moved, they were paralysed, by what they had seen. As Pauline leapt from the kerb, it was as if an angel had grabbed her, because instead of stepping forward she spun around, so now, instead of facing her father, she was facing her mother who had ran for her life to try and reach Pauline before she reached the road. Her mother was a few feet away from Pauline when the miracle occurred and she had witnessed the whole event. Crying, screaming, laughing and shouting all at the same time, she held Pauline, as if she would never let her go. All the driver could do was look in absolute amazement. He was convinced the child was lying underneath his truck. In fact he swore on his life he had seen her step from the kerb. Pauline herself remembers the event with extreme clarity. She can remember the colour of cab and seeing the name of the truck which was set in the grill on the front of the lorry. Then she remembers someone physically pulling her round.

Pauline's memory of the event reflected exactly what the mother and father said. Her mother who was closest to her, with a clear view watched her daughter stride off the kerb, in full stride she suddenly spun 180 degrees, almost directly into her mother's arms. Believing herself she was running towards her family, Pauline was at the time quite confused. Her family believed an angel had truly saved their little girl that day. Through their involvement in the church, the story has been told time and time again and no doubt given joy, comfort and hope to thousands that help from the other side is possible and here is a small miracle to prove it.

At the end of a private reading Barry, who had recently lost his wife told me the following story. Both had had many discussions regarding the existence of the after life. Both husband and wife made half-hearted promises to each other that whoever would pass first, would come back as a bird, to show the other that there was life beyond life. His wife's sudden death hit him very hard. Ten days after his wife's death, Barry sat contemplating how he was going to survive life without his wonderful, beautiful wife, when he noticed a Robin on the windowsill. The bird began to tap on the window of the lounge. As he rose to get a closer look, the brave little bird refused to fly away and continued to tap on the glass. For three days the little bird returned each day, at the same time and merrily tapped on the glass, for several minutes. Then as quickly as it arrived, the bird disappeared and was never seen again. In his heart Barry knew it was his beloved wife, fulfilling her promise. It gave him great comfort to know his wife had survived death and was now occupying a space where it was possible to communicate with this world. This event saved his life. Barry hadn't coped with the death of his wife and longed to join her, the little tapping bird not only gave him evidence his wife had survived death it gave him hope and courage to continue life without her. If she can find the strength and resource to come back, I can stay and be a good dad, he said.

As he told me the story I understood he was telling me, in hope that I would ratify his theory. Before he had chance to ask me I leaned forward and said 'before you ask, she is telling me yes, it was her". A huge grin spread across his face. That is what he had come to hear.

On another occasion a member of a church down south told me her husband was forever dialling one number incorrectly. This went on for years. Because it happened with regular frequency, the old lady, Mrs Smith, who's number he always called in error, and Frank became friends and they stayed in touch. Six weeks after Frank's untimely departure from earth, Mrs Smith received a phone call from him. She hadn't spoken to him for a while and without doubt it was Frank on the phone. Mrs Smith was not a spiritualist and what happened next astounded her. Early one evening, just after Frank's death the phone rang. As Mrs Smith answered it she heard Frank on the line. In his usual tone he said the same words he had always said when he rang her: "Hello Mrs Smith, its Frank here" he said to her. The woman was speechless "Who is this?" she asked. "What's the matter with you?" she said, really taken aback by the call. "Mrs Smith it's me Frank, what's the matter?". Then the line went dead. I couldn't help but feel how resourceful this spirit person was to use the telephone as a form of communication. I have heard of long distance, but really, this was going too far. Mrs Smith was really shaken by the telephone call, but Pat was ecstatic, to her this was real evidence that Frank was desperately trying to reach her. Like many other people she had merely accepted the evidence without questioning or being overcome by wow factor of this event. In a matter of fact way she had accepted this phone call. Mrs Smith on the other hand was another story and remained quite shaken for several days.

Messages beyond the grave are not limited to evidence of survival, as I have discovered through my spiritual work. Jayne had been raised by her grandmother. Her relationship with her mother had been blighted by her mother's poor mental health. The arrival of Stanley into her mother's life appeared to help and stabilise her. So at the age of 13 she and her grandmother found themselves both back living with the mother and her new husband. Everything was turning out well and for two years they all lived in harmony together, until her grandmother suffered a mild stroke. She was taken into hospital and the prognosis was not good. For two days the family stayed at the grandmother's side. Then when she appeared to stabilise, the family went home for a much needed sleep. At 1.15am Jayne woke suddenly and found her grandmother standing at the foot of her bed. She had woken to the sound of her grandmother calling her name. As alive and well, as if she was in the flesh, she told Jayne it was her time to go, but not to worry her own mother was fine and she would take good care of her, as she whispered the words 'I love you', she faded in front of her eyes. Jayne immediately rose from her bed and went to her mother's room and told her what had happened. Jayne's mother was trying to comfort her explaining it was all a dream, when they received a call from the hospital advising them that Jayne's grandmother, without warning, had indeed passed to spirit. It later came to light she had passed over at 1.15am. Jayne knew, as a last port on her way home, she had diverted to Jayne's bedroom to pre-warn her of her death and comfort her by telling her things would be okay between her and her mother, which they were and still are, twenty years on.

These stories are just a few from the selection I have heard over the years. As I said earlier they are extraordinary tales, from ordinary people, who - had these happened to other people and been told to them - would very much have questioned their sanity. But to them, it was an event they accepted without question. Which is often the case, when we are given a life changing experience, we rarely question it. We know it happened, we don't question it, just accept as fact and event that happened to us.

Miracles in Disguise

We are often given help from the other side and, for many of us, we may never know that help was given. How many times have you had the urge to contact someone only to discover they were in need of a real friend at that moment you happened to call? How do we deal with it? We put it down to coincidence. We will tell the story to many people and never fail to be amazed by the turn of events. Neither will we question why we took the action we did and most times if we did, we would never reach the conclusion that somehow, someone from the other side managed to influence our thoughts. The concept is quite frightening, because if we believed this, we would then have to face the prospect that our mind can be influenced and not all our thoughts are original. This then takes us down a pathway where all our beliefs and the status quo is questioned. So for most of us, it is far easier to remain amazed by the event and not analyse it.

A similar event happened to me. On the spur of the moment I decided to book a day off work. For me this was completely out of character. Two of my five weeks leave are annually spent serving churches in and out of the country. So I tend to be very frugal with my leave. I had no reason to book that day off in December. I had purchased all the Christmas presents I needed to, in fact for the first year in my entire life I was prepared for Christmas, like I had never been. I had begun my purchases in October, not the week before Christmas day which was my normal practice.

So here I was wasting a day's leave for no rhyme or reason. On the morning of my day off, I decided to go to my daughter's house. My son has said the night before she wasn't well. I had sent a text the night before suggesting I take Liam to school, but had received no response. So again on a whim, I decided just to turn up on the doorstep. I couldn't believe my eyes when I saw her. She looked dreadful. She could hardly talk, as she couldn't breathe. I quickly took Liam to school, called at the doctor's for an urgent appointment and against my better judgement agreed to leave her to go to the doctor's while I dashed over to Birmingham to pay an urgent debt that couldn't wait.

Beverley was admitted to hospital directly from the doctor's surgery, in an ambulance with its blue lights ablaze. She was immediately diagnosed with pneumonia. For seven days her life held in the balance as she lay in the Intensive Care Unit unconscious attached to a machine, which was breathing for her. It took a further week in hospital to recover.

Unable to talk Beverley had turned her phone off. Had I gone to work that day, or had ignored that urge to visit that morning there is no doubt in my mind, or that of the medical profession who treated her, she would have died. I gave thanks to God that I followed that inner voice that told me booking a day off would be a really good idea. I also gave thanks that I got up early on that fateful day and followed my instincts to visit so early.

The period of time my daughter was in hospital was probably one of the most tragic times in my life. As a mother I never expected to see my daughter on the brink of death. As I sat beside her I called upon Jesus, one of the greatest healers ever to walk this planet and asked for him to heal her. I sat and watched as he hovered by her bed-head and gently told me she would be healed but her body had to heal itself. The very force of a one-shot healing process would itself kill her. I called upon Quan Yin, as the mother energy to give us both the strength to conquer this demon which raged through her body. I prayed and prayed she would live, but not at any cost. When they told us her kidneys were not working too well, which is a sign that there maybe brain damage, I changed my prayer. I stated I only wanted her to survive, if she was without significant brain damage. If the brain was severely damaged, then I asked that she be released and return home to the world of spirit. Beverley would not want to live with severe brain damage. As a mother I desperately wanted her to live at any cost; but this would have been a selfish prayer. So with a dry mouth and a thumping heart I changed my prayer, to what I believe Beverley would have wanted.

When we are in crisis it is difficult to follow a spiritual pathway. It is the greatest test of faith, when we are presented with a life threatening situation. All our beliefs temporarily disappear as we struggle to survive. Because of this it is very difficult for guides and helpers from the world of spirit to be able to reach and offer the assistance we are seeking. As we shut down and operate in survival mode, so do our psychic receptors. Hence, this feeling of being alone and deserted in our hour of need. Despite being a Medium I was no different. It took great effort and concentration when calling for healing or saying prayers, something I could normally do with little effort. Our helpers will use any means they can to reach us. For me during this crisis I didn't receive my answers through the normal channels, which is to either appear spontaneously in my head or to feel which is the right and wrong pathway, but through my dreams.

When in a calm state I felt in my heart my daughter would live, as it didn't feel her time to go. Unfortunately this feeling of calm only came and went momentarily, it is the remainder of the time I sat with a feeling of dread. On that fateful Friday in a quiet moment spent by the ladies' toilet I prayed and asked for the truth. Was this her time to go home?

As I woke the next morning, I lay momentarily to search my mind for any dreams. This is part of my daily routine, for I know once I get out of bed and begin my daily routines, any dreams will be gone out of the window. I began to recall a very short dream. Two bags of shopping had been delivered to a property when the owner was out. When they came back and were presented with the bags the owner of the house was complaining. They were not for them and the time of the delivery was most inconvenient. "Who are they for asked the owner?" Before anyone could answer she said, "It's not convenient and they are not for me". As soon as I woke and recalled the dream I knew they were telling me, 'its not her time to go, the timing is all wrong". During the week, as she stayed on the ventilator I still had my moments of despair, but from the dream held the knowledge she wouldn't pass over.

The next hurdle to overcome was this theory that there may be brain damage. As the doctor warned us of this possibility I tried to hold the positive thought that she was in several healing books in spiritualist churches scattered across the Midlands. David gave daily healing, better than I did and Wolverhampton Spiritualist Church had held a healing circle for her the day before. While I had cancelled all my bookings, I did to everyone's amazement one last closing service. As the service finished I told everyone about Beverley's condition and asked that they spend one minute sending healing thoughts to her. In my heart of hearts I knew this minute would create a powerful healing moment for Beverley that would help her on her way to recovery. Is it any wonder her kidneys were functioning better than could have ever been expected?

By the end of the day she was still slowly recovering from the effects of the powerful sedatives. Having changed my prayers for her only to survive if she was free of life changing brain damage I went to bed with another burning question. Would Beverley suffer from brain damage? Again as I woke the next morning, I recalled a dream where someone had been hit with a football. This had knocked the person unconscious; as they lay on the ground a crowd gathered looking down over them. After a little while they began to come round and smiled at the crowd. A voice in the crowd said "There's nothing wrong with them, come on". With that comment the crowd began to disperse. I felt this was telling me she had suffered a serious set back, and it may take a little while to come fully round. This is precisely what did happen.

During this terrible time, it would have been so easy to have missed this vital information. So for anyone out there next time you are faced with a crisis, take the time to ask for assistance and have the belief to know, once you have asked, help is always given; but this requires some effort on your behalf. You must make space in your mind to receive this information. Sit quietly as you send out the thought and try to still your mind. If you are unable to do this, as you awaken in the morning, no matter how pressing resist the temptation to jump out of bed as soon as you awake, take the time to recall any dreams you have had to see if the answer is given hidden in a dream.

During Beverley's time in hospital I received many more dreams and knowledge which helped to guide me and give me hope, at times when there appeared to be no hope. But we also receive assistance in other ways. The day before Beverley was taken into hospital there was a very strange noise coming from underneath the bonnet of the car, which stayed with us all the way to and from Oswestry. Strangely enough when we discovered what was wrong with her the next day, the sound went. At possibly the worst moment during the episode we lost the recently purchased weekly pass into the car park. David used it to get in through the barrier, then, within minutes he couldn't find it. We both emptied his pockets searching each one meticulously, even turning the pockets inside out. The pass could not be found. We were both really fed up by this and at a loss to know where it had gone. It had been quite a difficult process to obtain the pass and now it was lost. It seemed to be another burden at a time we could do without it. We decided to cut our losses and forget about the ticket.

Several hours later David put on his jacket as we began to get ready to go home, having spent another tiring day at the hospital. As he checked his inside pocket of his jacket, he immediately came into contact with the missing ticket. He pulled the ticket from his pocket and as we sat in amazement looking at the ticket, I knew the event was telling us, when everything appears lost and you have given up hope, then hope will be found. Just as this ticket had re-appeared.

As Beverley began to recover and all the signs were indicating a full recovery, yet it felt almost wrong to feel the elation that was rising inside as you saw other families where we had been several days ago, when there appeared no hope. As I walked past a mother and daughter, I could feel their pain and despair. As we had sat by Beverley they sat diagonally opposite, with what appeared to be the husband of the older lady and father to the younger one. This man was attached to machines the same as my daughter was. All the families with loved ones on this unit appeared to sit in isolation. All were at different stages, on a similar pathway, some had passed the crucial stage and were on the road to recovery, some were held in abeyance while the machines did all the vital functions, so that the body itself could rest and begin the recovery process, while others were just beginning the journey. Yet no-one reached out to anyone else.

As I looked at mom and daughter I decided in a split second to try and change all of that. I stopped and explained that Beverley had been at the same stage as their relative was and we had also been without hope, but she had pulled through. I apologised if I sounded like I was gloating but went on to explain this was not the case. I just wanted to give them hope, that when everything appeared lost and there was no hope, little miracles did happen and if it could happen to us, then it could happen to them. As I looked into their eyes I know my words had given them some comfort and a glimmer of hope, that people did leave this Unit, by other means than a covered trolley. Both mom and daughter thanked me and we chatted together for a little while about how it felt as relatives to sit and watch our loved ones lie motionless attached to all these machines. They wished me well for my daughter and you could feel the sincerity in their voices and I also wished them well. As I walked away, for a moment I was the calm Medium, who could see this man would survive. I merely wanted to help them and ease their pain.

Four days later on Christmas morning, as we walked past the open plan café the wife of the gentleman was sitting close to the main thoroughfare. I knew as soon as I saw her, without her speaking, that things had improved. As we exchanged pleasantries she told me he had a long way to go, but he was awake and sitting out of bed. She thanked me (and you could feel her sincerity) for giving her hope at a moment when there appeared to be no hope.

As I walked away from her and towards the ward I felt an inner satisfaction that is very hard to describe, a kind of triumph, that in my own hour of need I had the self-resource, that when the balance of the scales had tipped into our favour, I had been able to share this with others as a guiding light of hope. My only wish now was that this woman would do the same and in turn others would also help those find hope, when there appeared to be no hope. In other words create a chain of ever-growing hope.

Lightning Source UK Ltd.
Milton Keynes UK
16 June 2010

155662UK00002B/17/P

9 780956 159038